PRAISE FOR LAU
BITTER SPRINGS

"Highly recommended... *Bitter Springs* is a wonderful depiction of a lost period of gay life and history in the rural West of the 1800s."

—*American Library Association, GLBT Roundtable*

"Stone deftly mixes yearning and hot passion with sweet tenderness and a love of nature in this engrossing and deep coming-of-age love story."

—*ALA Booklist*

"Readers will savor this sweet, loving historical."

—*Publishers Weekly*

"Compelling and deeply satisfying...the representation of ethnic, racial, cultural and sexual diversity in an Old West setting is both refreshing and historically accurate."

—*RT Book Reviews Magazine*

THE BONES OF YOU

"By the time the book ended I was in love with the characters to the point I couldn't let them go."

—*USA Today*

"Stone's sensitive debut... plays the relationship with restraint, letting it unfold slowly and organically."

—*Publishers Weekly*

"Their beautiful love story will bring plenty of laughter, and even a few tears, as these men grab hold of their rare second chance. It was appreciated that neither man was willing to give up his dreams because that wouldn't have felt true to the love they have shared since boarding school."

—*RT Book Reviews Magazine*

AND IT CAME TO PASS

A NOVEL
LAURA STONE

interlude **press** • new york

interlude press • new york

To T.J. and B.F. I'm sorry you can't come out yet,
but I understand. To Laura B: thanks for setting the
example and for being hilarious while doing it.

AUTHOR'S NOTE

MY GREAT-GREAT GRANDFATHER, THOMAS FEATHERSTONE, was converted by the second wave of LDS missionaries to England in the mid-1840s. He kept a journal detailing his conversion and oceanic trip to the United States to join the Saints leaving Missouri for Salt Lake City. Sections of his journals are now stored online at BYU's Mormon Migration domain. Thomas was one of the first people publicly called to polygamy in Salt Lake and had twelve wives sealed to him—only three were living at the time of their sealing. The other nine were sealed to him after their deaths. His tombstone—which he shares with two of his wives—is in American Fork, Utah.

His family multiplied and spread all over Salt Lake and Utah Valley, with most of them concentrated in Lehi, American Fork, and Santaquin. My father, the thirteenth of fifteen children on their sprawling Lehi farm, moved away after marrying my mother, a native of Dallas. The vast majority of my family still lives in Utah near Salt Lake City. It's a large family, as those old Mormon families tend to be. My cousin, Vaughn J. Featherstone, is one of the General Authorities (second-tier leaders of the Mormon Church) and was president of the San Antonio mission for years and years. My uncle gave seed money to start Day-Timer Day Planners®, the pet project of FranklinCovey®. Less prestigious cousins opened (and then closed) the 49th Street Galleria, a family-fun center in Murray, Utah. Other uncles and aunts work for the Church in official capacities at their ranches, tune their pianos, paint their churches and stake centers, write their hymns, and volunteer in their temples and genealogy efforts, actions many other Mormons do, as well. And all of us, at some point, sold both Melaleuca and Nu Skin.

I was "born in the covenant," as it's called when parents are sealed in the temple for time and all eternity. I grew up extremely devout. I loved being Mormon. Growing up, I usually held a leadership position in Young Women's, and when I went "back home" to Utah for college, was called as a Gospel Doctrine teacher for years. I served in the Young Women's Presidency, was co-director for YW Camp, taught in the Primary, and am well-trained in the arts of canning, quilting, and managing food storage and can make four different kinds of sparkling punch on the fly. I know that the missing 5th can from the ingredient list of 5 Can Casserole is my attitude. "I 'Can' Do It."

My three children were all blessed in the Church, but none ultimately were baptized. I began backing away from the Church before they were old enough. My family—all 130+ first cousins, 70+ second cousins, etc.—are all still actively Mormon. (And a handful are quietly polygamist, too, but we only have them out once a year for the big family BBQ and try not to comment too much about it, as it's not seen as polite party talk.) Now that all three of my children have come out as LGBT, I'm grateful I did not saddle them with a faith that does not want them. The Proclamation of the Family as well as the Handbook all LDS priesthood leaders receive upon their calling makes this very clear.

No religion can claim a monolithic adherence to its tenets and beliefs, and Mormons are not exempt from that. Utah Mormons aren't the same as Californian Mormons or other Mission-Field members. There are, of course, similarities among all of us, but some Mormons refuse any soda with caffeine, while others shrug and drink the Barq's. (Most Mormons can tell you how much caffeine is in any beverage, however. We're all quite adept at knowing this.)

This novel reflects either direct experiences from my life or from the life of loved ones. There are some quirks of behavior that are idiosynchratic. The doctrine, however, is all straight from the source. Mormon culture and Mormonism are a closely looped Venn diagram of thought, in other words.

CHAPTER ONE

"[SACRIFICE] HELPS US BECOME WORTHY to live in the presence of God [...] We must also believe that we will receive the promised reward." (Fifth Missionary Discussion, 1986 Missionary Discourses, The Church of Jesus Christ of Latter-day Saints)

"THOU WAST CHOSEN BEFORE THOU wast born." (Abraham 3:23, Pearl of Great Price)

BARCELONA, SPAIN: LDS MISSION FIELD

Adam Young sat quietly in the car's backseat as his finger absentmindedly traced over the embossed gold outline of his name in the lower corner of his worn, leather-bound quadruple set of scriptures. He'd been traveling for just over fourteen hours, from the Church of Jesus Christ of Latter-day Saints Missionary Training Center in Provo, Utah to the Salt Lake City airport to his final stop, Barcelona, Spain.

He was rumpled and achy from sitting in a cramped space. His stomach had been in knots for the past few hours, and it wasn't from the lack of food on the flight. He *should* be halfway to passed out. Jet-lagged or not, there was no way he would fall asleep in the car. He was too energized by being somewhere new, seeing a new country, new people, heck, even new plants and trees—anything that wasn't the oppressively familiar look of his hometown, Provo.

There were palm trees. Actual palm trees like in Las Vegas, but these weren't the thin, reedy palm trees of the desert. One stood tall and wide in a grassy circle near the entrance to the airport, surrounded by a group of trees he'd never seen. As they pulled out of the airport proper, he couldn't see much of the city beyond the distant skyscrapers, but it already felt huge. Even the air was different: brighter, livelier. Probably because they were close to the ocean…

In Provo most of the greenery was confined to the mountains that backed the town, leaving the populated areas filled with not much more than cement and power lines, though some trees and plantings crept out of their sidewalk planters here and there. To make it worse, Provo was usually hit by an inversion in the winter that created a pocket of polluted air over the whole of the Utah Valley, leaving the already bland urban areas grey and dank for weeks. Here, though, buildings were bright and colorful; a breeze had blown through the car window when he'd momentarily opened it. A pollution haze hung over the skyscrapers, but the city—what he could see from the car at least—still seemed different to him, wilder, somehow. Provo was so orderly, so typical with its strip malls and chain businesses on every street.

He sat back, mouth gaping, awestruck by the strange beauty of this new city he would be calling home for the next two years. One tall building looked as if it had plants growing all down the side. He flashed to the drawings of the Hanging Gardens of Babylon in his LDS Church-issued Bible study guide from his childhood. He rolled the window back up and felt guilty as the Mission President glanced at him in the rearview mirror. He hadn't been told he could roll the window down, after all. He folded his hands neatly over his scriptures and turned his body to gain the best view.

The strangeness of this city coupled with the excitement of travel went a long way to calm his anxiety about serving a mission. It had slowly built up over the past month and a half of mission and Spanish language training back home at the MTC, as those in the Church of Jesus Christ of Latter-day Saints, or LDS Church, called the Missionary Training Center. His anxiety about serving—about being a complete success as a missionary—had been building for most of his life.

"All right back there, Elder Young?" the President asked, chuckling at the name as Adam nodded.

"Elder" was the official title of his new priesthood office, and it mingled ironically with his last name. He knew he'd take flak for that unfortunate title for the entire two years of service, service that started in earnest today. His stomach twisted again as if he was going to be sick. He was just nervous. Serving a mission was a big deal. His family and the Church had put a lot of expectations on his shoulders. There were souls in the world whose eternal salvation depended on him finding them and baptizing them, saving them from eternal damnation. He wished he'd kept the window rolled down.

His Mission President, engrossed in conversation with the driver, another Church member, didn't pay him much attention, but Adam didn't mind. The view just beginning to present itself was fascinating and beautiful and unlike anything he'd ever seen, and he'd barely seen more than the airport's entrance, for crying out loud. As they moved into the city, he wanted to press his face against the glass; he wanted to get out and walk around.

Barcelona was a long way away from the cinderblock retaining walls and bland, square houses of Provo. Everything so far looked vibrant, color-drenched and visually busy. Tiny scooters, oblivious to traffic or safety it seemed, zipped among the cars on the main road. Horns honked constantly. The sidewalks were packed with people, bicycles and scooter drivers taking any opportunity to keep moving. Even skateboards weren't allowed on most city sidewalks back in Provo. He tried to picture the guy, clad in only board shorts and a helmet for Pete's sake, who was passing them so closely on a turquoise scooter that his shoulder almost hit the side-view mirror, zipping up State Street to weave between all the monster SUVs and the moms pushing triple strollers on the sidewalks. He laughed to himself.

"Whoa," Adam murmured, smiling as he caught sight of the ocean. The water was an almost-unimaginable blue, so different from the often-smelly grey-green-brown of the Great Salt Lake, the only major body of water close to where he'd grown up. He could see long piers reaching out into the choppy water and wished it wasn't a mission rule that they weren't allowed to swim.

Adam, or Elder Young as he should now refer to himself, was officially a missionary for the Church of Jesus Christ of Latter-day Saints. He'd grown up singing the Mormon indoctrination hymns "I Hope They Call Me on a Mission" and "Called to Serve." On more Sundays than he could count, he'd listened to the tearful, emotional services for older boys and a few girls in his home ward, what the LDS Church called the geographically-bound congregation similar to a Catholic parish, as they left their families and friends to serve the Lord on their missions. In his Priesthood meetings, he'd nodded along, as was expected when he and all the other boys in church were told of the vast importance of mission work, of how the Church and their fellow man's eternal salvation depended on it, of how he was expected to choose to serve. The Church itself proudly stated that their number one priority on Earth was mission work. He could also remember the judgmental tone in his parents' voices when they discussed those members who didn't choose rightly, who didn't serve. "Selfish," his father had always said.

"You're quiet back there," the Mission President said, catching Adam's gaze in the rearview mirror. "Tired?"

"A little," Adam answered. "Mostly it's just…" He nodded out the window. "Overwhelmed by it, I guess?"

"It's a beautiful country. Beautiful people, too. Family-oriented, like we are. These should be two of the best years of your life, son."

Adam smiled weakly and sank back into his seat as the two men up front continued their discussion about all the transfers happening in various districts. He pushed his fist into his churning belly and strained to see the ocean as they wove through traffic.

All of his life, his friends, family, and church leaders had spoken of how amazing this moment would be, how life-changing this experience was for those who answered the call to serve. His friends had been laser-focused on how much they were looking forward to becoming missionaries; Adam had always smiled and nodded, but never with the same zeal. Over and over returned missionaries spoke with passion about how they were overcome with emotion the first time they heard the thousands of missionaries at the MTC singing "I Hope They Call Me on a Mission" in unison. For Adam, that experience had just been a reminder that there was something wrong with him, because instead of feeling overwhelmed with the Spirit, he'd felt like a failure for *not*.

Serving a mission was something he was expected to do, so he would do it. He'd never felt all fired-up as he'd been told he would. It was more like a chore, something he had to cross off his "True Blue Mormon" list like attending Sunday School as well as Seminary—Mormon religious training at his local high school—becoming a Boy Scout and getting his Eagle rank. It was going to be a huge disruption to his college years, not to mention potentially jeopardizing his athletic scholarship if he became sick on his mission.

Why wasn't he excited? After all, he'd grown up watching his three older brothers and sister serve, had seen their glowing, happy faces when they'd come home, had heard all the stories about how changed they were, had watched his parents seem proud and satisfied as each of Adam's older siblings followed the practically pre-ordained course for all Mormon youth, particularly the boys.

"Elder, you're what, nineteen?"

Adam blinked himself out of his thoughts and nodded. "Turned nineteen a few months back. I, um, I didn't feel ready to put in my call at eighteen."

"Nothing wrong with that," the Mission President said, pointing out a sign to their driver. "I know Heavenly Father guided the leaders into lowering the age, but I'd rather have you kids out here when you feel ready. Then again," he laughed, "You don't want to push it off too much! Some of those guys might get too cozy at home not serving if we didn't crack the whip, eh?"

Adam gave him an answering smile and hoped it didn't reveal how close that had been to Adam's pre-mission life.

"Were you in school, son?"

"Yes," Adam answered. "University of Utah." He'd put the second half of his sophomore year at the U on hold to devote two years to the Church, and that meant his athletic scholarship for football, as well.

"Uh oh," the Mission President chuckled. "Cougar here. Proud graduate of Brigham Young University."

"That's okay," Adam said, grinning. "I'm the only Ute in my family. They all went to BYU, too."

"Turncoat, huh?"

"Scholarship."

"Oh, is that right? Academic? Wait, those shoulders…" The Mission President twisted in his seat and smirked. "Young, right. I think I've seen you play. Didn't we kick your butt last season?"

Adam grinned. This he could do. Talking sports wasn't personal. "No, sir. We beat the Y forty-three to twenty-one."

"Hmm. I think we had to play our second string quarterback that game. Lots of injuries on our side." He scowled at Adam, then winked. "Well, out here, 'football' means something completely different."

The driver spoke, his lisping accent indicating his Castilian heritage. "You need to decide if you're Real Madrid or Barcelona." He pronounced the 'c' in Barcelona with a 'th' sound. "Everyone has a team, and there are enough Real Madrid fans here that it's not as easy to assume."

"Good point, Rodrigo. Elder, you think people back home get excited about BYU versus the U games, you haven't seen anything like *fútbol* games in Europe. The whole city tuned into the World Cup. An entire family could be divided by someone defecting to support the other team. You're lucky your family didn't disown you not going to the Lord's University."

He laughed, but Adam's insides twisted unpleasantly. The only reason he'd been allowed to go to the U in Salt Lake City instead of Provo's BYU was his athletic scholarship. His mother, Janet, hadn't liked that, but Adam's overbearing father, Gerald, had decided Adam would take it. And when Gerald Young decided something, Janet never argued. Gerald was very clear that the scholarship would help offset the cost of Adam's mission and wondered just how long was Adam going to dillydally before he put in his call?

Adam had kept putting off the inevitable. His father had had Adam's visa papers filled out on the breakfast table a month before his nineteenth birthday. "You don't know where you'll be called, so it's best to prepare for any and all."

Gerald's tone had made it clear that there would be no more putting off the inevitable.

The car turned off the main road that ran parallel to the beach and looped back through the city. There were more "Hanging Gardens" buildings with what looked like overgrown forests growing down the side of them; a veritable jungle crept around the odd-shaped windows. Nestled next to a standard-looking high-rise was a building that might have been built by hobbits, its thatched roof was so rounded and oddly wonderful. Everywhere Adam looked bright colors and strangeness confronted him. He knew traveling to another country would require an adjustment, but this was like being dropped into a fanciful Renaissance painting of a circus that had come to life.

The President turned in the front seat and pointed out the left-side windows. "Different, huh?"

Adam nodded with his hand on the glass as they passed what looked like a construction site, though people were swarming all over it.

"That building right there," the President continued, "the one you'd think was half-built, is actually finished. It's part of a university. Great place for you boys to proselytize. They have a lot of crazy-looking buildings here. It's where the team 'gaudy' comes from, the guy who started building the church that still isn't finished, Gaudi. Picasso has some stuff here, too. You'll either love it or hate it," he chuckled, turning to face forward.

Adam wondered if that was true as he ducked to see the top of the round building the President had pointed out through the car's window. It did look half-finished, open as if a piece of pie had been cut out of it, exposing the interior stairs and rooms. It, well, it was indecent, as if someone failed to zip up their pants. What happened when it rained? That was a college? Adam shook his head, and the car rolled on. This place was foreign in every sense of the word.

"Many beautiful girls here," the driver Rodrigo said, nodding as a group of college-aged women crossed the street in front of them. "You remember your covenants, eh?"

"Football player, uh oh," the President said. "You must have the cheerleaders lined up for you back home."

Adam forced a smile on his face. "No, uh, didn't want to have any distractions."

"Smart. You're here to work. I like that. You and your trainer will get along just fine, you know. He's like you: here to work."

Adam would be delivered to his new companion, who would also act as his missionary trainer, showing him the ropes of the city and how the mission operated. Missionaries for the Church of Jesus Christ of Latter-day Saints were required to follow a long and specific set of rules, one of which was to always be in the company of their companion. Missionaries didn't date, drink coffee, listen to music not approved by the Church or watch television or movies. They couldn't join local intramural teams or swim. They were allowed to call home on Mother's Day and write letters—chaste and devoid of anything salacious, negative or unbecoming of a representative of the Church—once a week. They were not to use the Internet, be alone with female peers or be out of their dress pants, white shirt and ties unless they were in bed or on Monday, when they were allowed to do laundry.

They were on their missions to bring souls to the Gospel, period. A girlfriend back home "waiting" for the missionary was common, but Adam didn't have a girlfriend. He had female friends who tagged along with the group of guys he ran with, mostly his teammates, but Adam didn't date. He went to school, he played football, and he studied his scriptures.

"We had some boys get themselves in a little trouble last year," the President said.

"Oh?"

The man shifted in his seat and fixed Adam with an intense gaze. "I know it's hard being your age and having to put, well, the whole world aside for two years. I remember being young myself."

"Fifty years ago?" Rodrigo joked.

"Hey, now... It was only twenty. But, Elder, to my point. If it was easy, anyone would do it. And the Lord has called you to do something extraordinary, hasn't he?"

Adam stammered, "Y-yes?"

"Yes," the President agreed. "He has. I know it's difficult out here with all these young folks everywhere you turn partying and what not. Well, it's not quite this busy out west and north in the smaller villages, but it's hard here. Temptation seems to be everywhere you turn. But don't you forget that Heavenly Father has a plan for you. He meant for you to be here right now at this very point in your life."

He seemed to expect it, so Adam nodded.

"Last year a couple of missionaries started 'proselytizing' at college parties." His tone made it clear there was nothing spiritual about the situation. "Now, I didn't see anything in your file about any trouble you may have repented for before getting your mission call, so I hope that means I won't have to worry about any... football player antics out here with any ladies."

"N-no, sir."

"Good." he turned forward and began fiddling with the air conditioner.

Adam didn't care for parties. They were too noisy, and, since he didn't go to BYU, there tended to be alcohol at most of the ones his teammates attended. On a weekend night right before he got his mission call, he'd been talked out of going to a scheduled youth activity at the Institute, a Church group for college-aged youth.

"Don't you get enough religion?" Thompson, the team's center, had asked. He was a guy from Oregon, not Mormon, and he thought all the Church stuff was weird. He was usually cool about Adam and a few others being devout, but as he'd said that night, "You have to live in the world, too, man."

Adam had agreed to ride along with the caveat that he would bail if "things got crazy." He'd had a good time at first listening to some guys from cross-country talk about a crazy fifty-mile marathon in Bryce Canyon National Park that they wanted to do when he'd noticed a guy standing with a girl in the corner. The guy had really broad shoulders and looked as if he played a team sport. Lacrosse, maybe? He was fit. Healthy. Bit of a tan still, which, this deep into winter, meant he must ski or maybe snowboard. He looked to be around six feet, just shy of Adam's six-foot-two. The girl with him was tiny, tucked in at his side with her cheek pressed into the round swell of the guy's shoulder.

Adam had imagined that would feel nice, having someone bigger with their arm around you, especially in a big, noisy crowd like this. It would be a buffer; you could block out any commotion with the ease of pressing your face into the warm cotton of a T-shirt. The hard muscle underneath would be a steadying presence. Or, well, that would be comforting for a girl, he supposed. The girl in question certainly seemed happy right where she was. But Adam's gaze kept dropping to the guy's big arm around the girl's shoulder, how his hand dangled loosely, how thick and long his fingers were. It was one of those hands with ropey tendons visible, indicating a real strong grip, and his hand was right at the girl's ample breast, close enough that the slightest twitch of his fingers would stroke her silky shirt. He'd feel her breast, no question.

Adam had grown hot all over, agitated, as though he wanted to do something, help the girl. But that was stupid. He was being prudish. He'd been teased enough for not joining in the typical locker room talk to know most non-LDS guys weren't so closed-off about sex stuff. It had been hammered into him from childhood that women's bodies were sacred. He never even *thought* about girls in a sexual way. He wasn't supposed to, so he didn't.

He'd looked again and saw the guy's index finger lightly tracing the top curve of her breast. The girl had shivered, but didn't move. In fact, she'd clutched his T-shirt over his abs. Then the guy had his fingers sort of curled up and was brushing the backs of his knuckles over her shirt, down the side, then back up to rub his middle finger right over where Adam assumed her nipple was.

It had been indecent, obscene. It was disrespectful, that's what it was. He was disrespecting this poor girl and he needed to cut it the heck out. Adam looked up from the almost hypnotic motions the guy's fingers made over the rising bud of her nipple, shaking himself as he did. The guy stared right at Adam, smirking. Adam's mouth dropped open. It was so… so blatant. Cocky. The guy licked his bottom lip and winked, and all the blood in Adam's body rushed to his groin.

He'd gone hot all over before his stomach flipped. Had he been implicit in this… indecent act? He should've said something. He should've gone over and pulled that poor girl out from that guy's grip. He could have done it. Adam was strong. Coach had praised him for how well he always worked the weighted sled in strength-conditioning sessions. He'd get his hands around that guy's shoulders and push him back, shove him up against the wall, get in the guy's face about it.

Guys like that… They just shouldn't treat girls as if they were objects. It really got his blood boiling. He'd excused himself and went outside where the crisp February mountain air cooled his face. That had been his one and only college party. He'd seen enough.

It was about *respect*, that was what'd had Adam so hot under the collar. It absolutely wasn't anything else, because what on earth could there be? Adam… well, he didn't know what it could be. He didn't like to think about that, any of that stuff.

No. College parties weren't going to be a problem for Elder Adam Young, that he knew for certain.

The car turned again and continued down the ocean-side highway, where it passed buildings that were more typical to what Adam was used to seeing back in the States, a few storeys-high and dotted with cafes and modern-looking store fronts. He shifted, stretching in an attempt to catch sight of the massive and bizarre uppermost spires of La Sagrada Família, out of the back window. The church, with its echoes of the Salt Lake City temple, eased some of the unfamiliarity of this new world.

"You doing okay back there?" Rodrigo asked, catching Adam's gaze in the rearview mirror.

"*Sí, Señor*. Uh, *gracias*," Adam replied, remembering belatedly to speak in nothing but Spanish now that he was active.

"*Bien*," the President said. "*Ya casi estamos*. We're almost there."

"So, Elder," the Mission President said, now speaking completely in Spanish, "we only have one companion exchange today. We're shipping Elder Watson back stateside for his last few weeks. Picked up a bacterial infection the doctors here couldn't help. Antibiotic resistant, apparently."

"Really?" Adam startled. He'd heard of missionaries contracting diseases. That was common in the South American missions—Adam's oldest brother Seth's companion had contracted a flesh-eating bacteria in Guatemala, in fact—but it wasn't as common in Europe. "Gosh! Is he going to be okay?"

"Oh, sure," the President said with a dismissive hand wave. "We haven't lost anyone out here yet! And really, he only had two weeks left, so letting him recuperate near his family seemed best."

Adam sank back against the seat, wondering how that would have gone down in his house: two weeks left in his mission only to be prematurely discharged for bodily weakness. He had no doubt his father, Gerald, would see it as a weakness and not as an indulgent Mission President letting a good kid be with his family sooner rather than later. Gerald Young was the sort of man who tested another man's mettle by their handshake and their list of honorably completed Church callings.

Adam tried to picture his mom and dad visiting him in the hospital if he got sick. They probably wouldn't be able to visit if he was in the big one in Salt Lake or up in Ogden instead of the closer one in Provo. Driving over the Point of the Mountain in all of that traffic always made his dad cranky. Crankier. He was a busy man, and his time was important. He'd told Adam that often enough over the years.

Adam seemed to be expected to say something about this Watson guy, so continuing in Spanish, Adam responded with, "I bet that'll be nice for him to be close to his family, then."

"Well, you know how mothers can be," the President said with a knowing smile. "She would have flown out here if we hadn't let him come home! I'm sure your mom is outdoing herself with all the letters and care packages already."

Adam pasted on another smile and made a noncommittal sound. It had only been six weeks since he'd left home, and he'd gotten one letter for every Monday he'd been gone: an impersonal replay of all the activities in his family's life. He did like the "Love, your Mother" at the end of each one, though. And now he had ninety-eight weeks left. Ninety-eight weeks before he could stand up in his congregation back home and tell them how this had been the best two years of his life, just as all missionaries were expected to do, just as his brothers and sister had done, just as his parents expected him to do.

Maybe he'd be lucky and get an antibiotic-resistant bacteria, too.

He chastised himself for entertaining the idea of going home, even in a fantasy about being sick. He'd just need to stop focusing on being selfish, only thinking about what he wanted, or rather, what he didn't want, and stick to obeying the rules. That would make it easier. After all, when you don't have to think for yourself, you don't have to think at all.

"I remember being a greenie just like you," the President said, smiling up into the rearview mirror for Adam's benefit. "Best time of my life. Some of the best friends I've ever had are guys from my mission. We get together with a sort of reunion every year, too."

Adam's smile was a flat, forced line. Of course it was the best time of this man's life. Adam didn't know what was wrong with him, why he just couldn't let himself be consumed with joy about serving the way everyone else seemed to be. Well, he didn't know what it could be other than the constant worry about disappointing his parents, about not baptizing anyone and going home with a zero for the entire congregation to see, about failing to serve the Lord and his spiritual brothers and sisters fully.

"But, hey," the President continued. "We're putting you with a great group of missionaries, good guys. Strong spirits, each and every one of them. So don't worry. They won't razz you too hard for being green."

Adam wasn't worried about that. He never had problems getting along with other guys; he had preferred the comfortable camaraderie of his football and baseball teammates and of the guys he'd grown up with in his home ward. He'd spent his high school free-time on Boy Scout camping trips, weekends with friends in the mountains to hike, eat beef jerky and generally horse around, or in weekend-long video game battles with the guys on his block. He'd always been more comfortable with them, happier, even if he was never really close to any one of them. He'd been friendly, helpful, but he tended to keep himself at an emotional distance, especially from the girls he'd grown up with.

Most girls made him nervous. Well, perhaps it wasn't the girls themselves but rather the expectation that soon after his mission he would have to pick one to marry in the temple, whether he was finished with school or not. Just thinking of all that was required of him had his hands sweating and his stomach in knots.

Again, he seemed to be expected to say something, so Adam cleared his throat and replied, "I guess my mission'll keep me too busy to worry about anything but doing my best."

The President nodded, seeming satisfied by the canned, pat response. But it was true. Adam wasn't worried about being accepted socially; a mission wasn't about being social, after all. It was about being dedicated to the Lord. They were to be up at six-thirty every morning, have their scheduled prayer and appointments and wrap up every day with required lights-out by ten-thirty. The well-ingrained routine made it easy to follow along, to do what was expected and to get through the next two years. And maybe, somewhere along the way, he'd figure out how to actually love being on a mission, love spreading the Gospel instead of just enduring it.

He felt sick just thinking that. He wasn't *enduring* the Gospel. He just... he just didn't have all the pieces yet, hadn't felt that spiritual fire burning in his heart as proof it was all worth it.

"Your new companion is quite the missionary. Heck of a guy." The President riffled through a leather-bound organizer, talking over his shoulder. "So I hope you take note of how he works. This is a tough mission, son. We talk about Spain being a 'Second Harvest' but there aren't a lot of baptisms in the city. You'll get a lot of takers from the refugees and immigrants out in the sticks, though. It's not like those guys who have it easy down in South America. The European missions are what make the real leaders of the Church, Young, and Christensen is a born leader. A real go-getter. If Elder Christensen says jump, you ask how high, understood?"

"Yes, sir." If there was one thing Elder Young was good at, it was following orders without question.

Before leaving for Spain, he'd had his first companion at the MTC during his foreign language immersion. His comp, a narrow, short guy from Boston named Hagel, had a perpetual sniff and a sarcastic sense of humor that bordered on cruel. Adam didn't think the kid made much of a missionary, let alone a good guy, but that wasn't up to him. He hoped this Christensen wouldn't be as abrasive as Hagel. Come to think of it, he hoped Christensen wasn't a task-master like Adam's father, a Peter Priesthood for whom Adam could never measure up. Knowing Adam's luck, that's just what he'd end up being.

"Your *piso* is right up here," the President said, using the local terminology for apartments. "You're going to do fine, kid. Your comp will make sure of it."

They pulled up to a low-slung, nondescript building in what appeared to be the business district. The Mormon Church usually bought apartment buildings in lower-rent areas for their missionaries to live in, so it was about what Adam had expected. It was nicer than some of the run-down apartment buildings in the older part of Provo, for sure. He climbed out with his backpack and duffel bag and blinked up at the bright blue sky; the spring sun was warm on his face. The driver grabbed Adam's rolling suitcase from the trunk, handed it off and gave him a nod and a *"buena suerte"* before climbing back in the vehicle.

He'd always envisioned traveling his mission city on a bike—the stereotypical Mormon Missionary image—but they didn't ride bikes in the Barcelona mission. A bicycle was too dangerous and cumbersome. He and his companion would walk almost everywhere, and he'd been told to be prepared to walk up to twelve miles a day, all in their suits and dress shoes.

The Mission President shook his hand curbside. "Well, welcome to Barcelona. Christensen will fill you in. We'll touch base tonight, Elder. Do your best."

"Yes, sir."

Adam watched as the car pulled away, then jostled his gear in his arms just as the front door swung open, revealing a large, well-formed young man. He was about the same muscular build as Adam's six-foot-two inches, except instead of Adam's baby-fine blond hair and skin so fair his cheeks were perpetually ruddy, the new guy had inky black hair and deeply tanned skin. He almost looked Spanish himself. He was visually arresting and had an aura of confidence; his resting face radiated joy and optimism instead of the sanctimonious authoritarianism Adam had anticipated.

"*¡Hola!*" the young man said with a bright grin on his face that made Adam's stomach twist in a completely new way. It was all so unexpected to find... this waiting for him. Adam had imagined a younger version of his father, a ham-fisted tyrant with the aura of perfect obedience pouring off him in waves—a far cry from this young man's happy, relaxed charm.

"So, I'm Elder Christensen. Eh, but you can call me Brandon when it's just us." Christensen took Adam's duffel, hoisting it with ease, and they shook hands. "You're Young, right?"

Adam found himself tongue-tied, then managed to blurt, "Um, yeah. Yes." When their hands met, an electric shock ran up his arm and straight to his fast-beating heart. He dropped Christensen's hand and fumbled for his other bag. Christensen jerked his head toward the building and led the way through the interior courtyard to their apartment.

Blinking away the after-image of his new companion's smile, Adam snapped his eyes to just over Christensen's shoulder. This had happened once before, this intense reaction to another person. Adam, after careful and fearful prayer, had attributed it to a prompting from the Spirit, to the strength of the other man's faith making itself manifest. His prayer and scripture study led him to understand that it was how God helped His followers find each other. Church history was full of stories like that. In fact, it was how people described their first meeting with Joseph Smith, the Church's founder and prophet.

Adam had reacted to an older boy at church: one who was fairly tall, who had a commanding presence and a voice that was soft but strong. The older boy had been one of those guys who you couldn't help but want to hang out with, talk to, be like. He'd been a natural leader Young had been willing to follow anywhere. Adam had come to understand that this was how God made sure you fell in with the right people: giving you that feeling, that sucker punch of rightness that made your entire body shake and be filled with want... want as in wanting to be surrounded by the right kind of people, of course.

And now it seemed that Adam's new companion was that same kind of guy—the kind of person who could draw both men and women—the kind of man Joseph Smith had been.

Elder Christensen was tall and broad shouldered, obviously very fit, with a handsome face framed by glossy black hair. He, too, was in his dress pants, white shirt and tie with his shiny black name tag affixed to his front shirt pocket. He was every inch a dutiful young man serving a mission for the Lord, and, given the praise Adam had heard on the drive, was well-respected by everyone. Christensen was the perfect Mormon man, the perfect Mormon missionary, and someone to whom he'd no doubt never measure up. He shook himself, overwhelmed by the chattering Spanish as they passed open doors. He noticed how some of the older people came out to wave and smile at Elder Christensen, and his stomach sank when he thought about all that lay before him, all that he had to accomplish or face his father's continued disappointment.

A surge of frustration raced through him. No. He hadn't even set foot in his first apartment on his mission and already he was assuming his parents would be disappointed. If this Christensen was the perfect Mormon missionary, a natural leader, then Adam would follow his lead. That's what this was: someone to stand as a role model for Adam to ensure he had the best mission.

Well, good. That was… that was good. This would be good for Adam, great even. This could be just what he needed to wake up, to get that fire, that burning in his bosom about mission work.

Christensen held the door just long enough for Adam to get a foot at the base, then dropped the duffel near another door off the open, tiled entryway and walked through the efficiently furnished apartment.

"Here comes the big tour, so pay attention because I'm going to test you later," Christensen said with a grin as his hand swept to take in the small space.

Something fluttered in Adam's chest at the sight of that grin. He exhaled sharply, and quickly shut the front door behind himself.

"Here on the left, the micro-kitchen and dining area. And to the right we have the living room and study, or, as I like to call it, *la biblioteca*, which are thoughtfully provided by the gently-used table, two rickety chairs that will most likely collapse under one of us as some point and the busted, grandma's-rec-room-looking sofa in a very fashionable avocado green tweed. Warning," Christensen said, his eyebrows shooting high. "That left cushion will trap you. It's claimed the lives of three guys already."

The furniture did look well-used, but it seemed to be clean.

"Uh, okay?"

Christensen crossed in front of him. The room was so small Adam would have stepped back, but he'd stumble into one of the rickety chairs. His guide opened one of two doors on the opposite wall to the entrance. Inside was a small bedroom with two narrow singles on opposite walls. A large dresser wedged between them left barely enough space between the two beds for two adults to stand in conversation.

"And here's the bedroom," Christensen said. "Quarters are cramped, but I guess the Spaniards don't grow 'em as big as we do out west. You don't see a whole bunch of guys over six feet here, for some reason. Must be all the hormones in American milk, huh?"

They'd be right on top of each other. Young forced a laugh past the lump in his throat. It was just nerves, most likely. He remembered the stories from his older brothers about being stuck with horrible mission companions: lazy, messy, guys who constantly broke the rules. And it wasn't as though you could get any space from them. The rule in their handbook and at the MTC about proximity to your missionary companion was very clear: "Stay together. Never be alone. It is extremely important that you stay with your companion at all times. Staying together means staying within sight and hearing of each other. The only times you should be separated from your assigned companion are when you are in an interview with the Mission President, on a companion exchange, or in the bathroom."

Maybe Christensen seemed too jovial, as if he wasn't taking this seriously? Adam shook his head; that didn't go with anything their Mission President had said. Adam couldn't determine what sort of companion Christensen would be.

Christensen nodded at the ceiling. "Hope you grew up with brothers, because the guys upstairs are super frickin' loud, like, all the time." He reached up and held the bedroom door's frame using a move that showed off his muscled arms and slim waist. Adam shook his hands out at his side to get his brain back into focus.

"Well," Adam said, "it's not like we're going to be here a lot of the time, right? Just to sleep and eat?"

"You hear about Watson? My former comp?" Christensen asked, tilting his head. It made him look approachable. Looking kind and handsome as Christensen did was probably good for tracting, what Mormon missionaries called proselytizing. "That guy took things a bit too far. He got sick because he was a little *too* into it. I mean, don't get me wrong," Christensen said, laughing softly as Adam blinked and tried to make the pieces all fit. "I think we should be into our missions. But Watson fasted at least once a week. It was insane."

Mormons fasted the first Sunday of every month and on some special days. That was hard enough, so, every week?

Christensen continued. "People around here, they take long lunches, too. There's no reason to go tracting for investigators during lunch, but he insisted. We had a lot of doors slammed in our face and cafes that won't let us in during lunchtime because it's disrespectful of the culture. He didn't care. He was, you know, fanatical."

Young thought it was disloyal to talk about someone who wasn't there to defend himself, someone who had to go home sick, someone who seemed to have tried anything they could to have a successful mission. Adam's dad would expect *him* to knock on doors at lunch, cultural disrespect or not. "Aw, maybe he was all right. A little over-zealous, but isn't that what we're here for?"

Christensen looked him dead in the eye. "No. We're here to learn more, ourselves. But mostly we're here to try and spread some joy to the local people. We're not here to freak them out and make them hate Mormons more than the rest of the world already does. If we bring some of them to the Gospel, that's gravy."

That shocking statement that seemed to go against everything he'd been taught sent another thrill through Adam. His father and brothers spoke about their responsibility, their duty as priesthood holders to make nonbelievers Mormon.

He was nineteen for Pete's sake. He didn't know enough about the Gospel to be teaching it, so how was he supposed to baptize scores of people? But this… *This* was what he wanted to do on his mission, not just get numbers added to the rolls. The idea struck him, stunning him momentarily like an offensive-line block. He wanted to first find happiness, then share it. *That* was what he wanted.

"Find yourself in the service of others," Adam murmured, repeating the oft-quoted mantra of church leaders as it finally clicked. He'd never shared with anyone his hope of gaining a stronger belief in the Church while on his mission; he hadn't even looked straight at his own thoughts about it. This just might be the companion to light a fire in him, might be the leader who could get his mind where it needed to be. He could find his faith and maybe figure himself out, too.

"That's it exactly," Christensen said, rabbit-punching Adam's shoulder.

Adam let out a sigh of relief as he backed out of the claustrophobic bedroom. "I'd always figured guys were already set with their beliefs before they left, you know? And… I've been a little freaked by not being a zealot like Watson, I guess, or like some of the guys back at the MTC. I thought… I thought it meant I'm not really worthy to be here." He blushed. That also wasn't anything he had ever admitted to anyone, not even himself.

Christensen sprawled on the modest couch that came with the apartment; his bulk didn't leave much space for Adam to avoid the "man-eating" cushion. "Hey, you and me both. One of my comps when I first got here only came because his dad threatened to stop paying for his college if he didn't go."

Adam forced a laugh. That hit a little too close to his own situation.

"Dude. That guy was the laziest thing I've ever seen, too. He didn't know half of what he was supposed to teach, wouldn't bother following the *Preach My Gospel* manual or anything. That guy never frickin' washed his clothes, didn't believe in deodorant and stank to all get out." He stretched out with a groan. "I got sick of his cooking fast." He sniffed. "Probably what he wanted, me to take over all the food. He cooked nothing but ramen noodles because all you had to do was heat water. Complete bum."

Young carefully lowered himself into one of the rickety arm chairs. It creaked, but held his weight. "I'm not like that. I'm not lazy, I mean." He laughed. "And I'm *not* a fan of ramen, so no worries there. I, uh, I make a pretty decent grilled cheese, though." Janet Young didn't like her sons to be in "her" kitchen. One of Adam's teammates in high school had taught him how to make grilled cheese with an iron. They were ridiculously good, if unconventional.

"Nice." Christensen held out a fist for Adam to bump; Adam barely grazed it.

"It's just… well, there are some things, some doctrines that I haven't gotten that… that fire for yet, I guess. I'm a little nervous."

Christensen laughed. "Well, that's okay. We all feel like that. I mean, you can't know everything! How boring would that be, being a know-it-all by twenty? Not to mention how many times you'd get your butt kicked by people sick of you preaching to them." Smiling, Christensen threw a pillow at Young's head. "I figure there's loads out there left to learn. I'm all about being open to new ideas and people. There's a whole world of ideas out there we don't know anything about, Elder."

CHAPTER TWO

"Before I formed you in the womb I knew you, before you were born I set you apart." Jeremiah 1:5

"I find that when I get casual with my relationship with divinity and when it seems no divine ear is listening and no divine voice is speaking, that I am far, far away. If I immerse myself in the scriptures, the distance narrows and the spirituality returns. I find myself loving more intimately those I should love with all my heart, mind, and strength." LDS President Spencer W. Kimball

Transfers happened on Preparation Day, or P-Day as the Church called it. This was the one day of the week when the missionaries were excused from a full day of tracting. They were allowed to log into their email accounts, which were owned and routinely monitored by the Church, to touch base with their families; they could do their laundry, stock up on groceries and spend leisure time with other missionaries as long as that leisure time fit in with the strict rules of the mission field, and even better, they could dress in casual clothes as long as they weren't connecting with investigators or active members of the Church outside the mission field. Adam and Christensen decided to finish Christensen's laundry, then meet with the rest of the elders in the district for some half-court basketball; missionaries weren't allowed to play full-court basketball.

"Gotta keep you awake for a few more hours and used to the time zone so you're not totally dragging tomorrow," Christensen said, tossing Adam's duffle onto one of the beds.

They dressed in their "civies," normal every-day attire without their name tags pinned to their chest as when they wore their dress clothes. Adam was careful to avoid seeming to watch Christensen change into his loose, nylon basketball shorts. Playing sports all his life had trained him well for how to behave around other guys. Locker room rules were easy to follow, and Adam was excellent at following rules.

They headed off to the basketball court in a city park. Christensen seemed to realize that Adam needed to adjust to how different the city looked. He quietly walked alongside him while Adam gaped as they passed buildings with stacked glass striping their fronts, giant grey pods with rounded domes that appeared to be what the city used for dumpsters and delicate-limbed trees that were so far removed from the heavy, snow-sturdy cedars and junipers of Provo.

Christensen nudged him to cross the street from where he'd come to a standstill. Adam had been confused by the different cars, some brands Adam had never heard of. Even the vans and trucks looked different, smaller, more rounded. It was as though Barcelona couldn't make its mind up on whether to have straight lines or wavy; where one expected one kind, the other turned up. Adam thought he'd been dropped into a Dr. Seuss book.

Instead of poured cement, large sections of the sidewalk were paved in tiles, decorative and beautiful. They made Adam think of the pressed-tin ceiling in his grandma's old Victorian farmhouse in Santaquin, a small farm town located up the mountain from Provo. Everything in Barcelona was designed to be beautiful, it seemed, and was meant to be admired and appreciated. It was as if the idea behind the Mormon temples—no dollar spared to make the House of the Lord as beautiful as possible—had been applied to the entire city. He wondered if he'd get a chance to visit other major cities, like Madrid, and see if they, too, were as oddly beautiful.

By the time they got to the park, which, with its sandy floor and surrounded by the delicate-looking trees in orderly lines, was unlike the familiar chain-link-fenced blacktop Adam was used to, six other missionaries were already there. Christensen shook hands with several of them and pulled two into bear-like hugs.

"Dudes, let me introduce you to my new companion, Elder Young."

As expected, several of the guys made cracks about the title, and the two guys Christensen had hugged stepped forward and shook his hand with firm grips. Their expressions were friendly and open.

One of those guys, who was built like a linebacker and sported a crooked grin, called out, "You better watch out, Young. Your comp's a legend. He's the only one of us who's baptized anyone in the city this whole mission."

Adam was astounded. Only one person? "How long have you guys been here?"

A tall boy with a strong Caribbean accent twisting his Spanish into something almost lyrical said, "Long enough. I've only got eight weeks left."

The linebacker-type popped the basketball off his own chest and caught it. "You're getting trunky, LaSalle. Me?" he said to Adam. "I'm Sorenson. I've been here fifteen months and thinking about extending. I can't go home with a zero, no way. My little brother is in Colombia, and he says they're like lemmings off a cliff. He's baptized almost fifty, only been there nine weeks."

The group gasped.

"I know," he sighed. "But then, we all know the real men go European."

A few of them high-fived as Christensen smacked the ball out of Sorensen's grip and took control of it. He rolled the ball down one arm, behind his head and down the other until it spun on his finger. "What are we playing, teams? Three-a-side and tap-in?"

The Caribbean boy, Elder LaSalle asked, "Yo, Young. You any good?"

"I guess."

LaSalle laughed to Christensen, "Greenie's on your team, then, Brandon."

Christensen slung his arm around Young's shoulders and gave him a squeeze. Somehow Adam's chest constricted from the contact instead of his shoulders.

"Don't let it get to you. They're good guys," Christensen said, and his breath was warm and intimate on the side of Adam's face. "And hey. You're on my team because I want you there. But, uh, really. *Are* you any good?"

Adam shrugged off the arm. His nerves jangled from the close contact and his cheeks flamed hot, probably bright red. He tried to hide his reaction by grabbing the ball and dribbling it between his legs. He kept his gaze down, concentrating on the ball while trying to force his face into something neutral. Really close contact made him nervous, that was all. And Christensen's breath had been on his *ear*. Who did that?

"Yeah, I'm all right," Adam replied. "Don't put me post, though. I'm a better guard."

Christensen proved to be a great shot and an innovative passer—no surprise that he was an excellent team player. The other team had a ringer in Elder Guymon, a ridiculous six foot eight guy who couldn't have weighed more than a buck thirty and hailed from a small town in Idaho. His strategy: stand under the net, hope not to fumble a pass and just drop it in.

"Whoa. Greenie's got a wicked hook." LaSalle bounced the ball between his legs while tossing Young a chin nod. He passed behind his back to Sorensen, who caught it easily.

"You play back home?" Sorensen asked Young.

"Not basketball, not since junior varsity in tenth grade. I, um, played football for the U."

All the guys made an appreciative "ooh" noise.

"Probably the water boy. Couldn't get into the Y, huh?" Guymon sneered.

"Neither could you, Ketchup. Heck, neither could I. Family couldn't afford it," Sorensen said to Young. "But hey, Dixie's cheap and an hour outside of Vegas, so I can still live at home." He laughed, faking a pass to Guymon and bouncing it to Christensen as they lined up.

"Ketchup?" Adam asked Christensen quietly.

Christensen shuddered. "He puts it on everything." He nodded at Guymon. "His mom sends him a care package once a month. So frickin' nasty."

"Okay, gentlemen!" Sorensen posted up. "We have a professional in our midst now."

Adam blushed, but no one seemed to be bothered or looked as if they thought he was bragging about playing at university level.

"Finally got ourselves a real game, huh? Had to go bring in the big guns to beat me?" Sorensen laughed.

Christensen grinned. "I can't wait to watch you cry when we crush you."

"Oh, big talk from the big man. Let's see what your greenie's got, bro."

Normally Adam would have taken that on as a burden, a responsibility not to fail. Looking around at the guys—LaSalle's easy grin as he hip-checked Guymon, the Romney kid's serious face as he dropped into his stance, the other guys' laughter and camaraderie as they jostled each other on the court and sidelines—settled some of his unease. It was important to get along with all the other missionaries. Having each other's backs could only help them in their goals. If they believed in each other, they could do anything.

"That's four to zip, us. Gosh, if only we were allowed to make bets." Christensen passed the ball back to Sorensen.

"You wish!"

As they played, the guys grilled Adam.

"How many kids?" Romney asked. "Me, we have four. I'm second-oldest. We have three out on missions right now, too. Crazy. My mom's going nuts. Gardener's family has six, kids that is, not out on missions, and he's square in the middle. You can tell he's a middle kid by how shifty he is. So?" He raised his eyebrows.

"Uh, five of us," Adam answered.

"Look at motormouth here." Gardener laughed. "And? Well? Which are you?"

"Oh, right. Sorry. I'm the youngest."

Sorensen whistled. "Tough. Me, too, youngest of six. So are you the screwup or the perfect child because you're the baby?"

"Um." Adam hesitated. He didn't really *know* these guys yet. Christensen caught his eye and seemed to sense that Adam was uncomfortable.

"I think we know which one *you* are." Christensen made a chest-pass to Sorensen, who held it and grinned.

"Depends on who you ask," Sorensen replied. "I would say, and my wonderful mother would agree, that I'm the perfect child."

Guymon snorted. "Pretty sure that means the majority of your family sees you as the screwup." He failed to block the pass Sorensen sent back to Christensen.

Adam blocked LaSalle, a lanky guy but quick-footed, and asked, "Where are you from?"

LaSalle grinned; his smile lit his dark face. "Trinidad born, my parents moved to Toronto when I was four. That's when we converted. Just me, no brothers and sisters."

"Spoiled brat." Sorensen knocked his shoulder into his companion. "You should see the care packages his mother sends."

"You're just jealous."

"Well, yeah! With six kids in my family? My mom's lucky to remember my name half the time," Sorensen said. Gardener laughed and fist-bumped him.

"Got any girls waiting for you?" LaSalle asked, as he slapped the ball out of Christensen's hand and did some fancy dribbling between his legs.

"Big stud like you, Young?" Sorensen said, rolling his neck and letting out a wolf-whistle. "Playing ball at the U? Probably got them lined up."

"N-no," Adam answered, hiding his embarrassment by easily blocking Sorensen's layup.

"What the heck?" Sorensen said. "Even this hideous string bean has a girl." He jerked his head toward Guymon, who sniffed.

"Here we go," Sorensen said, rolling his eyes. "Any chance Ketchup gets to talk about Ronda Jean…"

"It's *Randilyn.*"

The guys all sing-songed, "*Randilyn.*"

LaSalle leaned close to Adam. "She's apparently the prettiest girl in his little town, whatever that means."

"Mind you, she might be the *only* girl in town," Gardener added, laughing.

"Nah. Guymon has sisters," a thin, bespectacled blond named Larsen called from the sidelines.

Sorensen turned with his hand pressed to his mouth. "Ketchup, are you dating your *sister?*"

"You shut your mouth, Sorensen!"

The guys made an "ooh!" sound, all but Christensen, who shook his head. "Hey. Ease up."

"Thank you, Elder," Guymon said, grabbing the ball between his spidery fingers and frowning.

"When you live in a farm town," Christensen said to the group, his tone chastening, "I've heard it's perfectly normal to date your siblings." He laughed and ducked as Guymon swung a fist at his shoulder.

"Um, Elders? I don't find all this talk of girls to be spiritually uplifting," LaSalle said, his hand over his chest and eyes closed in mock solemnity. "Unless it turns out that Greenie has a hot sister."

Adam must have looked horrified, given the laughter among the other guys.

"Tough break," Romney said. "Ugly sister?"

"No? She's all right, I guess. She's just, you know, my sister."

"What's her name?" Gardener asked, waggling his eyebrows.

"Ruth."

Everyone hissed.

"Bro," Sorensen replied, dropping a hand heavily on Adam's shoulder. "That's an ugly-girl name."

Adam shook off the hand, pivoted into dribbling around Sorensen, jumped and almost dunked the ball in a modified layup. "Not as ugly as your blocking," he said, relaxing a bit at the familiarity of horsing around with a team.

"Beast!" Gardener bumped his fist against Adam's.

"Aw, man," LaSalle groaned. "He's going to kick our butts."

"I had no clue he could play." Christensen ducked so Sorensen could ruffle his hair.

Larsen began counting on his fingers. "So, no girls waiting for their Elder Kestler to return." Adam snorted at the Mormon musical reference to the missionary with the girlfriend pining for him to return and marry her. "You're the baby of the family. Now, whether you're precious and can do no wrong or are the tail end and why your folks didn't have a sixth is yet to be determined. You played football for the U, have an ugly sister… Fellas? What are we missing?"

"The fact he's fighting jet-lag, and you're all being a bunch of dinks?" Christensen asked.

"Yeah, come on, let's just play. Greenie's all right. White boy who can almost dunk?" LaSalle held out a fist for Adam to bump again.

Everyone eased off him, laughing and getting set up for another game, chirping and razzing each other genially. Something settled in Adam, as if his lungs hadn't properly drawn breath until just then. This wasn't what he'd expected. He'd thought his mission would be full of strict, sour looks from the other elders if it wasn't all gospel doctrine and accomplishing goals. But so far this was just like hanging out with the guys on his team back home. One of his older brothers, Jacob, had talked about how great P-Day had been, a chance for all the elders to unwind, but he'd never expected it to be… fun.

Adam could hear his father's disapproving voice responding to that thought: "Missions aren't meant to be fun. They're your duty." Well, at least Jacob had been right about this much. Besides, it was just his first day. The other guys all seemed pretty chill, and that was the complete antithesis of what was expected of him by his father, Adam knew. He still had to figure out what the heck his companion was like apart from this break in routine and order and whether or not he would ever be able to let his guard down.

They played four more half-court games, all of which Young and Christensen's team won, though the Missionary Guidebook clearly stated that scores weren't to be kept when missionaries were engaged in casual P-Day sporting events. They quit when Sorensen begged off, complaining about being hungry as he filled his water bottle from the park's ornate bronze and stone water fountain.

"Never took you for a sore loser," Romney said, high-fiving Christensen.

"As if." Sorensen toweled off his face. "We have a dinner appointment tonight, and you know how rare that is. Usually you just get invited around for lunch. Oh, the wife said she's making us *chuletillas*." He rubbed his belly, then grabbed his bag.

Christensen hollered after him, "Elder Sorensen! Remember: Cava is *not* a fancy type of grape juice!"

Sorensen turned, walked backward toward the bike racks and grinned, "Hey, we're supposed to respect the cultures of the locals. The Native Americans get to smoke peyote, you know."

Christensen turned to Adam and must have seen Adam's worry.

"He's just joking," Christensen said, bumping their shoulders. "He knows it's wine and won't drink it. Cava is Spanish champagne. There's no mistaking what it is."

"Hey, Young, easy," Sorensen said. "You think I'd do anything to upset the big guy?" He pointed at Christensen, then laughed and pointed at the sky with a wink. "Aww, B, did they send you another greenie with no sense of humor?"

Adam rolled his eyes.

"Just messing with you, dude. Lighten up! You're all right, Young."

"For a Ute," Guymon said.

"Ugh, give it a rest, Lurch," Christensen sighed. "You don't get brownie points for sucking up to the Y. Like, you're not going to come home and find an acceptance letter waiting for you."

"You'll learn to ignore Ketchup," Elder Gardener said, grabbing up his bag. Young thought he heard Gardener mention earlier that he was from California, the same as Christensen. "We all do. But yeah, it's getting late, Rom."

The rest of the group decided it was time to get back; they all wanted to have a quick bite, hit some neighborhoods for potential members, and be back home in time for the required 9:30 p.m. curfew. There were high-fives, fist bumps and firm handshakes all around as the pairs left, leaving Young and Christensen on the court. They wouldn't be canvassing that night, not until Adam got settled in. The sun began to set, casting a pretty orange glow over everything. A couple wandered nearby arm-in-arm, giggling and poking each other before sitting on a park bench. Adam looked away when he saw them kissing.

"Wanna play a little one-on-one?" Christensen asked. "Show me what you got, Elder."

Adam caught the ball bounced to him and tossed it back. He was nervous without the group of guys to help carry the conversation. "Yeah, sure."

"Don't go easy on me, U." Christensen bounced it back and moved in, arms wide, attempting to block Adam's shot. Adam pivoted on his right foot trying to find an opening, but Christensen shifted and blocked his jump shot. Their bodies collided. The force knocked Adam backward onto the court.

"Here. Sorry, man. That's probably enough, huh? Hey, you've had a long day. Let's get you back home and get you to bed. Bet you could use the sleep."

Christensen held his hand out to pull him up on his feet. Feeling wrong-footed, Adam ignored the heat building in his face. Most likely it was just because he was tired; the jet-lag was finally hitting him as

Christensen said. He couldn't help but focus on the rough strength in Christensen's hand, on the tendons twisting and flexing under Christensen's smooth, tan skin, on the ease and strength in Christensen's hold as he tugged Adam to standing. It brought to mind the image of Christensen standing in a baptismal font with his white temple clothing stark against his dark skin and with whomever he'd baptized holding onto his forearm that was raised to the square, steady and sure as they became sanctified, cleansed, born again into the Gospel. Renewed.

The wrought-iron street lights turned on with a loud pop, and Adam jerked, stepping back from his companion. As Christensen loped to the side of the court to retrieve their gear, Adam turned away from the lithe manner in which Christensen seemed to do everything. He watched moths as they swarmed, attracted to the glow of the lights. They circled feverishly, unaware of the danger of dying from touching the light they couldn't help but be drawn to.

The men started the mile-long walk back to their *piso*. Adam wobbled as the pressed-tin-looking grey cement tiles of the sidewalk changed into tiles that were crisply white with an art deco flower design pressed into them. It didn't feel decent to step on them, but others were, so he lengthened his stride to catch up to his companion, who was patiently waiting a few yards ahead. He listened to Christensen talk about various basketball players he liked as they walked back to their apartment. His companion's appealing voice was both soothing and heady; the background symphony of car horns, traffic, and people moving all around them combined until it became a white noise that in his jet-lagged state lulled him into a stupor.

Adam tried not to get too close to Christensen on the narrow streets, but it was a challenge. A lot of people were walking home, hurrying to their own suppers but flashing smiles and calling out friendly "¡Holas!" to them and to others on the streets and in doorways. He was nearing exhaustion, which explained how he kept getting distracted by talk about mundane basketball facts and losing his footing as the foundation of the sidewalk changed from one intricate design to another. He flashed again and again to the moths attracted to the halogen lights, unable to help themselves.

CHAPTER THREE

"Your goal is to help investigators become converted by the Spirit. . . To do this you must help them feel and recognize the influence of the Spirit. As they feel the Spirit, you will be able to help them make and keep the commitments that lead to conversion." ~ (Missionary Discussion Handbook, First Discussion)

"Remember the worth of souls is great in the sight of God." Doctrine & Covenants, Section 18:10

Two weeks in, and Adam Young still didn't know how to define Christensen or if Adam liked him. It wasn't that he *didn't* like Christensen, but he couldn't get a bead on whether Christensen liked *him* or if he was just affable by nature. It was unsettling to think of investing himself in connecting with Christensen if Christensen was simply making do with Adam because of circumstances. His companion wasn't sending signals that he was *enduring* Adam's presence, but Adam couldn't tell if Christensen's pleasantness toward him was genuine or a by-product of his religious station. Since the rule for missionaries was never to leave one another's side except when using the bathroom, he'd had plenty of opportunities to study Christensen and make up his mind.

Adam just, well, he *couldn't.*

Christensen behaved like no other guy Adam knew. Christensen was clearly a man's man and had grown up that way. He was tough, physically strong, but there was a gentleness to him as well, a softness toward others. In Adam's family, the men didn't do anything their father considered a "woman's sacred responsibility," which meant things that revolved around comfort and support.

Janet and Ruth had always found it odd that Adam had wanted to play with his toddler-aged nieces and nephews, for example.

"But your brothers are watching the game with your father," Janet had said once. Her voice dripped with suspicion as she buttered the Sunday rolls.

"Yeah, but...." Adam hadn't wanted to spend the next hour listening to his father's pointed commentary on men of age not serving their missions, like the U's current point guard. "I can go hang out with the kids, maybe pull out the old ping-pong table?" Adam offered.

"No. It's buried behind my quilting rack. Just leave the grandkids alone," Janet said. "You get them all riled up with the rough housing and Claudia—" That was Adam's brother Seth's wife. "—needs them to go down for naps soon."

"Yeah, leave them alone," Seth said as he grabbed an apple, then settled in on the giant sectional in the front TV room. "You don't know what to do with kids, anyway. Come watch our team kick the U's butts."

"What kind of eighteen-year-old boy wants to play with little girls and their dolls, anyway?" Gerald had asked.

But Christensen... Christensen had little sisters: Brenda, sixteen, and Mary, nine. He talked about them as if it was normal to do stuff with them, as if his *family* thought it was normal for him to do stuff with them.

"Oh, man, Mary got a manicure kit before I left: all these weird little stickers and polishes in every color you could think of. Some of them had glitter, so those were her favorites, of course. She loved painting my nails," Christensen said. "It had these little pens? You ever see those? She made ladybugs once, little spots and antennae. Cute as frick. She showed me off to everyone," he laughed.

Adam stared at him.

"What?" Christensen asked. "It's really hard to do your own left hand, so I let her practice on me. What's the big deal? They're just fingernails, dude."

The most important parts of whom Christensen saw himself to be and what he saw as his duty as a servant of the Lord seemed to be those very ideals Gerald Young had tried to beat out of Adam. For example, Christensen didn't think anything of talking about his feelings.

"Cried like a baby when we had to put our dog down," Christensen said as they walked toward the city center to pass out pamphlets during Adam's first week. "My sister Sarah still makes fun of me for it, but she was a good girl, Sally Dog," he said about his former German shepherd. His voice broke. "Ha, sorry about that. It's only been two years. And Sarah can laugh all she wants. I know all about her crying over some boy-band dude getting married. So, how about you? Any pets?"

"Oh, no. My mom doesn't like the mess they make."

"Uh oh. Your mom would probably hate our house, then." Christensen laughed. "Eight kids, a big dog… My little brother Bill once had to bring home silk worms. Class pet sort of thing. They broke out of the Tupperware thingy they were kept in. We found them the next morning, webs spun all over the place and fat, squishy cocoons wedged in every crack and crevice you can imagine. Frickin' nasty as all get out, dude."

Adam shuddered at the thought of his mother's reaction had that happened in their house. Janet Young considered herself a failure as a homemaker if there weren't vacuum tracks on the carpet before they all turned in at night. The Young children were required to make their beds before they were allowed breakfast. A chore chart had been mounted on the wall of the laundry room with the title, "Have I Done Any Good In The World Today?"

"My mom made everyone check their phones for any pictures of the worms' box before they'd made a break for it. She even sent out a text message to all Bill's classmates asking them, too."

"Why?" Adam asked, hopping onto a low wall to allow a group of school kids to pass, smiling shyly and waving as the kids stared at their black, shiny name tags and chattered in Spanish about the "*misioneros.*"

"The pictures? Oh, to see how many worms there were so we could try to find them all," Christensen answered. He adopted a high falsetto Adam assumed was meant to be his mother and spoke in English. "'John, if I catch you trying to bait that dog with a cocoon one more time, I am going to tan your hide!' He was trying to teach Sally Dog what they smelled like so she could find them."

Adam laughed. "Did it work?"

"Of course not! Sally was a champion butt-sniffer, but she wasn't like, you know, a *forensics* dog. We found squished cocoons in bookshelves and in cupboards for weeks. So gross."

Instead of talking *at* people, the way Gerald Young did, Christensen encouraged others to talk so he could listen. The more Adam realized that Christensen really listened when people talked, made them feel as if every word they said was important, the more Adam clammed up. He squirmed at the realization that someone was really paying attention to him, especially someone with such laser-focus as Elder Christensen. The more they talked—or tried to talk—to the locals, the more Adam understood that the Spanish people had this in common with Christensen. The locals stood very close when in conversation and gave their full attention. Some older people would cup the nape of the person speaking to them to keep them close.

It was unnerving and seemed to be inescapable. The locals, his companion.... Adam didn't know if it was a by-product of the mission, or if Christensen was that laser-focused all the time. He always seemed to know what was happening in the other missionaries' lives, too, things about their families and personal struggles, and was always ready to offer words of encouragement or at least lend a willing ear.

It became clear that the other missionaries tolerated Guymon's negative attitude, but Christensen seemed best equipped to look past that and create a space where Guymon could be productive in the group. Guymon and his companion Gardener stopped by one evening. Christensen, who clearly didn't want to be overheard by the others, pulled Guymon aside in the kitchen. That left Young and Gardener to chat.

"'Sup," Gardener said, bro-clapping Adam's back and tugging him into a brief one-sided hug. "So what's your story, man?" he then asked, dropping his Doc Martens onto the dilapidated coffee table. "Town, family, girls writing you letters… There has to be one or two who snuck in there. Come on, let's have it. We're brothers out here. Plus, Guymon's boring, and I've heard all of his stories at least nine times. I want fresh meat."

Young glanced toward the kitchen. Christensen's face was the picture of concern. Guymon had his back to the living room and was hunched over with his arms tightly wrapped around his waist.

"Don't sweat it," Gardener said. "Ketchup does this every few weeks or so. Needs to just run his mouth." He leaned forward and rabbit-punched Young's shoulder. "So? Speak."

"Oh, um, like I said, I'm the youngest of five." At Gardener's irritated expression, he added, "Four brothers, one sister. Dad works in contracting for the Air Force out at the OO-ALC in Orem."

"Military guy, huh? No wonder your place looks like this."

Young looked around the clean apartment.

"Ketchup's a total pig. Leaves his dishes and laundry everywhere," Gardener said, picking at his slacks. "But then, so do I." He laughed. "Works out pretty great. And hey, that's what P-Day is for, right?"

"Dude, don't get your bad habits all over my comp, Dave," Christensen called out, pushing to his feet.

"Got him potty-trained already, Christensen?" Guymon asked, slouching into one of the rickety chairs.

Young looked over at Christensen, who rolled his eyes and mouthed, "Sorry." Young watched as Guymon gnawed on the edge of his thumb. The rest of his fingernails looked pretty raw, too. Clearly the guy had poor coping skills. Adam chose to ignore any further comments, since Guymon was clearly a bit of a mess. Young had enough on his mind, anyway, like marveling at Christensen breaking off to fill glasses of water for everyone and passing them out.

"*Gracias, Madre,*" Gardener said.

"*De nada, Puerco.*" Christensen settled right next to Adam's side. Adam stiffened at the warm, solid line of his companion's body pressed right up against his. He glanced at the others, who were frogging each other's thighs in a flinching competition. Neither of them commented on his and Christensen's sitting arrangement, so he guessed it was okay. They were in close quarters and all. And there was that bad cushion Gardener perched over, apparently aware of its hidden dangers.

"So tell me about tracting yesterday, Elders," Christensen asked, leaving Adam alone with his unwelcome thoughts as Gardener and sometimes Guymon talked about their afternoon at one of the universities. As their District Leader, Christensen was all ears, making appreciative or consolatory noises at various points, offering fist bumps, shoulder squeezes and back-pounding hugs as the others gathered their things to leave.

"Proud of you guys," Christensen said, reaching up to wrap a hand around the back of Guymon's neck and shaking him a little. "Keep at it. If it is to be…"

"It's up to me," Gardener said, grinning.

"Uh, thanks, B," Guymon muttered, nodding his chin at Adam as they headed out and grinning shyly when Christensen fake-punched him to make him duck so that Christensen could ruffle his hair.

For a big, strong guy like Christensen, the gentleness, the touches he passed out to the other missionaries and the way the other guys ate that up, how it made them relax or smile… It was absolutely foreign. Christensen behaved in a way no male in Adam's family behaved, and Adam didn't know what to make of it.

Publicly, Adam's father gave his mother a kiss on the cheek on anniversaries, offered one-armed hugs to Ruth when she came visiting, laid a stern hand on a grandchild's head when asking about their behavior that day and shook the boys' hands, sometimes going to far as to clap a hand on their back when they attained some milestone. Gerald Young simply wasn't a demonstrative man and had always said that growing up on a farm and enlisting in the military meant there wasn't time for any of that "soft stuff."

Janet was taciturn and aloof at best, displeased with those around her at worst. She often told Ruth that affectionately touching her children too much would "spoil" them. Adam thought that if she hadn't been an alcohol-abstaining Mormon, his mother would have fit the stereotypical 1950s role of the housewife stealing sips of sherry to make it through the day. She was an unhappy woman, Adam had always thought, and didn't want others' happiness within her perimeter. She took the Church's commandment to be perfect—not to strive for perfection but to *be perfect*—to heart, and to her children's detriment, Adam had started to realize.

Beyond the Young brothers razzing each other, the normal wrestling and manhandling when they were younger, there hadn't been a lot of physical contact in the Young house. And Adam was six years younger than his closest-in-age brother, Jacob. The older boys, Seth and Paul, had been too big to play with Adam. If it hadn't been for sports, he wouldn't have had much physical contact with other people.

Christensen, however, always hugged people—the kind of hug that made you feel better instantly. Christensen routinely pounded the side of his fist on the other missionaries' shoulders, looped an arm around Adam's neck, squeezed people's arms and hands. It was constant contact, as if Christensen *needed* to connect with people that way; a smile and handshake just wouldn't suffice.

Evidently everyone in his family was the same.

"Well, I didn't grow up in a big house," Christensen said, shrugging. "I shared a full-sized bed with my little brother John, and my older brother Jack got the top bunk, lucky jerk. Brenda and Mary got my older sister Joanna's room when she moved out. It's freakin' huge, but it's also right next to my folk's bedroom upstairs, so that sucks for them.

All the boys are down in the basement. You just, you know, adjust. And my mom can't keep her hands off us, always fixing our hair, wiping our faces, makes us kiss her cheek before we leave... You know. That handsy-mom kind of thing."

No, Adam didn't know. An ache for something he'd never experienced began to build. Could a person be homesick for a family to which they didn't belong?

Later that same week, Sorensen and LaSalle dropped by.

"Oh, District Leader," Sorensen said with a bow. "We come bearing cookies."

Christensen took the offered Tupperware container and opened it. "Oh, whoa. *Dude.* Are these those fig things?"

LaSalle grinned and rubbed his stomach. "There is nothing like a woman who knows how to cook."

"Unless it's a woman who knows how to cook, *loves* cooking and, more importantly, takes it upon herself to fatten up some poor foreign missionaries," Sorensen said stealing a cookie before Christensen could twist them out of his grip.

"How many of these have you had already?"

"One? Two dozen?" Sorensen answered, looking to LaSalle.

"Yeah, seems about right. Hey, don't hate us for finding a family who wants to feed us," LaSalle said, settling into the sofa. He sank into the bad cushion. "Man, why can't they get us better furniture? I never remember which one is the janked cushion over here."

Young laughed, then thanked Christensen when he held the cookies out for him.

"I'm going to hide them over the hood vent," Christensen said. "Sorensen can't reach that high." He laughed, easily brushing his fingertips along the ceiling of the apartment after stashing the container.

"Bro, please. Those four inches you got on me are just a waste. It's all about a low center of gravity," Sorensen said before lunging toward him, wrapping his beefy arms around Christensen's waist and lifting him up easily.

"Here we go," LaSalle said, wriggling to get comfortable. His knees were up near his shoulders.

"They do this often?" Young asked. Rough-housing while playing a sport was one thing, but this was their missionary apartment. They were still in their dress shirts. They all still had their name tags on. What if Christensen's got ripped off his dress shirt and tore a hole?

"They do this all the time. Sorensen's always looking for a chance to get his hands on that boy," LaSalle laughed.

"Can you blame me?" Sorensen said, grunting as he hoisted Christensen over his shoulder in a fireman-carry, twirling back and forth. "Look at his fine booty," he added, wriggling Christensen around, who cracked up. "This is some Grade A, prime-time American meat, boys."

"Okay, okay," Young said, getting to his feet. The guys' shoes were a mess at the front door. Also, Sorensen was pretty close to knocking over one of the lamps with Christensen's head. "You guys? Come on."

"I'm just honoring God's creation," Sorensen said, putting Christensen back on his feet and catching his breath.

Christensen began whistling the chorus to "Put a Ring on It" as LaSalle did the dance's distinctive arm moves from where he was trapped by the bad cushion. Christensen winked at Young, then plopped onto the sofa. "Sorensen, you wish you had something this good looking. Now tell me how we get some of those leftover *chuletillas...*"

Yeah. Adam was having a hard time figuring out his companion. More importantly, he was having a hard time figuring out his reactions to Christensen, why he was making him so prone to anger. Anger was *not* an emotion he should be experiencing on his mission.

They were active servants of the Lord. It seemed to Adam that doing anything as indulgent as being so casual—especially all the touching—with a fellow missionary made light of the seriousness of their tasks, of their duty.

If he allowed himself to think about how he found himself reacting, he might have admitted that Christensen's familiarity made him feel lonely, hungry for something he'd never had but wanted all the same. That seemed disloyal to his family to say or even think, so he quickly squashed it when it popped up in his thoughts, and was left with residual anger that he couldn't understand.

Every day had the same routine. The two woke up at the required time of 6:30 a.m., made their beds, showered, dressed, prayed over their meal, ate then sat at their small table and studied their lesson ideas for the day. Christensen would hum hymns under his breath as they walked through the streets of Barcelona canvassing for potential converts. It was a Catholic city, so they most often got polite smiles with a head shake. "*No. Gracias, no.*"

For long stretches of time they walked back and forth offering smiles and conversation, yet were routinely avoided by people on their way to work or the beach. Christensen used these moments to try to pry personal information from Adam.

"So, you're a jock," he asked, smirking when Adam rolled his eyes. "Hey, you played at the U. You're officially a jock."

"Did you play anything?" Adam asked, eyeing Christensen's athletic body. He was lean, so he could have been a running back. Slightly too bulky for soccer, Adam thought.

"Wanted to play football, but it was too expensive to play multiple sports," he replied. "Baseball, mostly."

"Yeah? Me, too. High school, varsity league."

Christensen shook his head. "Is there anything you're not good at?"

"What?" Adam spluttered. "Just, like, everything."

Christensen stopped and put a hand on Adam's chest to get him to halt as well. Adam jumped back a step; his face heated in his embarrassment.

"Uh, are you for real? You played varsity. You were good enough to get a frickin' scholarship. We played basketball the other day. You're a freaking natural, dude."

Adam stared at the toes of his shoes and made an X on one of the sidewalk tiles. They were perfect squares with circles pressed into the center of every other one and spread out in front of him like an endless one-player tic-tac-toe board. "I... don't know about that."

Christensen fell silent. Adam glanced over, and at that Christensen smiled, laughing softly to himself. Adam looked straight ahead.

"Modest, huh? I respect that. Hey. I didn't mean to make you uncomfortable. Come on, let's go around the corner. There's a chocolate shop you *have* to see. Might be a good place to meet people, too, huh?"

On Sunday they made a point of arriving early at the church in order to help families with many young children settle in and be reverent for Sacrament service. For all that *that* was normal, it took several minutes for Adam to realize that he was in a church. The design and the entrance were all wrong. Back in the States, all stand-alone LDS meeting houses followed a common blueprint. The familiarity of the location of Sunday school classes, bathrooms, gymnasium, breezeway and the chapel served as a touchstone for Mormons when they traveled. But in Barcelona, the church sat in the middle of a glass and red-brick skyscraper that covered almost an entire city block. It had a nondescript doorway in the middle of a long line of parking garages and office fronts on the skyscraper's first floor. The only way Adam recognized it as being associated with the Mormons was from the standard grey-granite sign bearing the copyright-protected font the LDS Church used on all buildings, temples and printed materials.

At least the service was the same, even if it was held in Spanish. Adam was adding colloquial fluency to his textbook Spanish; he could now participate in the little in-jokes among members. The preteen boys called Adam "*chaval,*" and now when he and Christensen arrived, their calls of, "*Oye, chaval!*" made him laugh at being called "Greenie" by a group of cocky twelve-year-olds. The little ones were trained by Christensen to call Adam "*gigante blanco*" or "white giant," much to Adam's consternation and Christensen's glee.

All missionaries were trained to be very cautious around small children, especially when it came to physical contact. Well, male missionaries were trained to be cautious; sister missionaries were often expected to hold and console crying children during service. Christensen, however, didn't seem to worry too much about his behavior with the kids, not that Adam could see a reason for worry. He assumed Christensen was so comfortable around them because he was one of the oldest in a huge family of eight children.

Christensen would whisk babies from a harried mother's hands and coo and make faces at them before passing them back once the mothers seemed to have pulled themselves together. Toddlers would get tucked against his side and a crayon and coloring book would appear before they could fuss.

"You know," Adam said quietly, as everyone pulled out their hymnals. "My folks wouldn't let me color during Sacrament service."

"What?" Christensen looked scandalized. He plucked a purple crayon from the box and passed it to the three-year-old sitting next to him. "Never? Not even before you were baptized?"

"Nope. It wasn't reverent."

Christensen shook his head before joining in with the congregation, singing tenor alongside Adam's baritone.

Adam's heart stuttered when Christensen calmly took the crayons from the little girl's hands and showed her how to fold her arms and bow her head for the prayer and she solemnly blinked up at him and nodded before copying him.

Christensen seemed to make everyone want to be their best. Funny how he leads by example and not by coercion, Adam thought. Christensen apparently loved to be in the thick of things and seemed to delight in forcing Adam into the middle of the action as well. Sister Lupe twisted around in the pew in front of them and passed Adam her baby, who looked ready to cry.

Adam tucked the little blanket-wrapped parcel against his chest and gently rocked from side-to-side, marveling at how something so small carried so much weight in his arms. Sister Lupe smiled at him, turned to listen to their speaker and left Adam with the now-sleeping baby.

"See?" Christensen said, bumping his shoulder against Adam's with a soft smile curling the edges of his mouth. Adam couldn't help but return it. "We're here to help the locals. And doing an excellent job, if I say so myself."

That wasn't quite what Adam had been raised to believe a mission call would be, but he was, well, he was dealing with it. Surely his mission companion—the District Leader, no less—wasn't doing anything the Lord wouldn't approve of, right? It was okay to be so... happy? So engaged? Sitting here with someone so good, so well-liked, while singing hymns that he loved about families being forever, bouncing a baby on his shoulder... There was no worry that any fidgeting on his part was proof to his parents that he wasn't listening to the lesson, proof that he wasn't a worthy vessel for the Holy Ghost and the Light of Christ. There were no niggling thoughts that he could be doing more, praying more fervently, getting better callings, living up to the righteousness of his brothers and sister. Instead, he felt only a sense of peace and calmness of spirit, something he'd never really experienced before.

It was almost perfect. A part of him longed for this to be every Sunday, forever. A cold chill raced down his back at the thought of that. He didn't mean... Not with his *missionary companion*, but the feeling, the goodness of being with people who were singing about joy, the simple pleasure of a warm, sleeping baby on his shoulder, the lilting voice of the speaker talking about how sacred temple marriage was and—

He sighed, adjusting the baby in his arm. He wasn't thinking about *marriage*.

Okay, so maybe Adam was a bit of a nervous wreck. Though he could see that being forced into these social situations with the locals was turning out to be good for him, tapping into a part of himself he had never been allowed to access before his mission, and though he could see how Christensen's inherent kindness set a wonderful example for him to follow instead of the ham-fisted authoritarianism of his father, it was the *other* part of his companion's personality that was throwing him for a loop.

It was all the questions. Where Hagel back at the MTC had been a sarcastic layabout with no interest in intellectual conversation about the Church's doctrines—*Rule number four: Do not get into debates or arguments*—Christensen was nothing *but* questions. Adam had never spent a lot of time dissecting what his religion taught aside from following along with the Church-sanctioned study questions shared in Sunday School and during Family Home Evenings on Monday nights. Seminary and the college-age version, Institute, were Sunday School classes guided and controlled by the Church's educational program, as well. Teachers posed the questions and provided the answers.

He'd been well-trained to parrot back what he'd learned in these various classes, as was expected of him. To question anything—to ask things not listed in his study guides—led to confusing thoughts, and confusing thoughts, as his parents and priesthood leaders had always explained, were a sign that Adam wasn't letting in the spirit of God, wasn't setting himself up to *believe.*

"Elder," Christensen said one morning, "I've been thinking about something the prophet Alma said, and I could really use your thoughts."

"Oh?" Adam stopped shoving pamphlets into his messenger bag. Christensen perched on the edge of one of their rickety chairs with his head bowed and his hands worrying themselves in his lap.

"You know how Alma, in chapter thirty-two, talks about how knowing something isn't believing something, because you know it?"

Adam nodded. Every missionary knew Alma: 32 in the Book of Mormon. It was all about his missionary work among the ancient Americans.

"I read that this morning during our personal study time, and that got me to thinking about having a testimony."

"Okay?"

"Well," Christensen paused, chewing his lip. Adam sat across from him, narrowly avoiding the busted cushion. "A testimony is about our faith. It's when we express our faith out loud, for others to bear witness, right?"

"Yeah?"

"And what do we all say?" His face was twisted into a wry grin. "We know the Church is true. We *know*."

"Right." Adam nodded. It was pretty typical to say that and how you knew Joseph Smith was a true prophet of God and that the Book of Mormon was true.

"But don't you see the problem?" He pushed to his feet and began pacing. "You can't believe something if you know it."

"That doesn't make any sense." Adam sat back to watch his companion pacing more and more agitatedly in their tiny apartment. "Of course you can."

"But the prophet said you *can't*!" He turned, his face stricken with worry to the point where Adam wanted to put his hand on his companion's shoulder. Adam forced himself to stay where he was.

"Verse eighteen." Christensen pointed toward his open scriptures on the kitchen table and quoted from memory, "'Now I ask, is this faith? Behold, I say unto you, Nay; for if a man knoweth a thing he hath no cause to believe, for he knoweth it.'"

"Elder," Adam said rubbing a hand over his face. "I don't follow where you're going here."

Christensen dropped his forearm against the wall and pressed his face against it. "I'm supposed to have a perfect faith. *We're* supposed to have faith in all things."

"I know, but—"

"But I want to *know*." His back heaved from the force of his breathing. "Am I… Isn't it wicked to want to know? To want proof? Isn't that… wrong?"

Adam's mouth dropped open. He'd always felt guilty for wanting proof of anything related to the spiritual. He remembered asking his father something along this same line when he was twelve or so.

"You're setting yourself up to sin, to stray off the path of righteousness, by questioning our leaders," his father had replied. "I think you need to remind yourself of 2 Nephi. If you don't have a perfect faith, you cannot be saved in the kingdom of God. Don't you want to go to the Celestial Kingdom?"

"Y-yes, sir."

"These questions… Do you need to talk about things with the Bishop?"

"No, sir." Adam had fled to his room to reread his scriptures.

That following Sunday had been his father's chance to talk to the congregation after the sacrament had been passed, and he'd chosen to speak on a perfect faith.

"Faith," Gerald Young began, his tone stentorian and his gaze upon the congregation stern, "is an active choice to believe in the word of God. It is an active choice we undertake to know the truthfulness of the Gospel. We don't need to *see* things to have faith that they are real. I've never seen Australia, for example." The audience laughed softly. "But I know it's there. We don't even need to fully understand these things to believe. We simply need to hold onto the hope that one day we will understand. Our Heavenly Father will reveal truthfulness to us when we're ready for it and not a moment sooner.

"I'd like to tell you about a conversation I had with my youngest son this past week."

Adam sank low in the pew, feeling everyone's eyes on him.

"He began to question the truthfulness of the Gospel. He began to question why he would even question it, as if to say isn't *that* a sign of some dark portent, some sign of treachery or duplicity on the part of our leaders. And there is one answer for that." Gerald looked briefly at Adam before turning back to scanning the congregation. "It is only proof of a considerable and troubling lack of faith. So how can we increase our faith? The same way we can improve our health, our worldly knowledge, our physical strength: we work at it. We accept that we won't have all the answers, and that it's greed motivating us to *have* all the answers right away. We accept that the Word of God is just that, His Word."

Remembering that intense feeling of shame, the fear that he'd be left behind, ostracized from his family for all eternity because of his lack of faith, Adam's heart was heavy at the thought of his good and seemingly righteous companion experiencing anything resembling that. He worried the shiny fabric over his knees, trying to put into words an answer that could help Christensen get past this. He didn't believe he was up to the task to help anyone in a faith crisis. But hang on, what was he on his mission for, if not to help others?

"Well…" Adam started, allowing his thoughts to settle on just the right answer. "But if you have faith, doesn't Heavenly Father promise to reveal truths to us? So we don't have to have faith in those things any longer, because God Himself answered us?"

Christensen sighed and sat back down.

"And the chapter goes on about the seed, remember? That if a seed grows, it's good." Adam frowned, calling the scriptures to mind. "Our faith is a seed meant to grow."

"Perfect faith to perfect knowledge," Christensen added, the deep lines in his forehead smoothing out. "I just… I worry that there's something wrong in wanting to know more, I guess. Heck, Joseph Smith said that 'The glory of God is intelligence,' but we're not supposed to ask questions that might contradict the Church. Maybe the answers would *build* our faith, instead of us just being blind and accepting. But how will we know if we don't, you know, seek it out?"

Up until this moment, Adam would have said there was something wrong in asking those sort of questions. His father had made it clear that a good Mormon didn't question the Church, its leaders or the Doctrine. They were to have hope that Heavenly Father would reveal truth to them. Gerald Young expected his children to exercise their faith by being patient, by waiting for the truth to reveal itself.

"You know," Adam said with a strangled sort of laugh, "that's what I thought my mission would do for me." Christensen seemed confused, so Adam pressed on. "My blind and accepting self would suddenly know, right? The things that didn't make sense to me... I sort of hoped being here, teaching the Gospel to strangers, that it would just...click. I'd finally understand the things I didn't."

Christensen nodded solemnly. "I guess I've been thinking that, too."

Adam didn't know what to say. For the few weeks he'd been here, he'd assumed Christensen already knew everything, had a perfect testimony of the Church and its teachings, but Christensen continued to obliterate that image with every new question he now posed. It was as if after he'd asked Adam for help that one time, Christensen could no longer hold back the flood of questions he'd evidently walled behind his perfect Mission Leader exterior.

Some of Christensen's questions were ones Adam hadn't considered, particularly those about deep Mormon Doctrine that were usually off-limits in discussions with any investigators they met on the street. Christensen apparently had no issue bringing them up.

"Why do we teach that nothing is more important than the family, yet everyone's father is gone from sunup to sundown for meetings on the Sabbath?"

And, "We're taught that we have free agency, that it's imperative that we have free agency to fulfill God's Plan, but then if we exercise it, we're disappointing Heavenly Father. What the heck did He give it to us for?"

Or the doozy, "If God will never lead our prophets to do anything contradictory to His will, then how do you explain polygamy, or the Laws of Consecration and Adoption that were basically men sealing other men to themselves for time and all eternity?" Christensen paced in a tight circle in their apartment with his hand roughly scrubbing over his head, messing up his thick hair. "Brigham Young loved that one, you know. He wanted a special room in the temple for men to be sealed to other men and said it should be above the Celestial room where men and women are sealed. Well, hmm. That one is out there, I know, but that's true."

Adam hadn't known that, but he also knew that Christensen had a complete set of the Journal of Discourses, the books of lectures and speeches from the early leaders of the Church. Adam hadn't been allowed to read them. There were a lot of books Adam hadn't been allowed to read that dealt with early LDS Church history, he'd discovered.

"Or what about black men having the priesthood when Joseph Smith was in charge, then Brigham Young took it away and called them all fence-sitters and unworthy because their skin was the 'Mark of Cain'? Then they gave them back the priesthood in the '70s and… Why the heck does God change his mind so much?"

Adam should have been outraged, or at least very concerned for his companion's eternal salvation. It was a criticism of the Church, of its leaders and of their divine inspiration from Jesus Christ Himself. His father had been outraged with *him* after all whenever Adam came to his father with doctrinal concerns. Questioning the Church was as bad as questioning the Lord. Questioning the Lord meant… Adam's heart began to race when he thought about what that could mean. He could only picture darkness, loneliness, no family, no Church, no eternal peace.

But Adam knew Christensen was a good man. Heck, he was the only missionary who had baptized anyone in the city. He knew Christensen was a person of deep love for God, for his family, who wanted to know everything about the Gospel he could. Maybe if his companion could make sense of it all, it would all make sense to Adam, too.

Christensen shook his head and smiled. "Sorry. Thanks for letting me blow off a little steam. Sometimes I just struggle to make all the pieces fit, you know?"

Yeah. He did.

CHAPTER FOUR

"And if you have not faith, hope, and charity, you can do nothing." D&C 18:19

It was the middle of the week. The lengthy two-hour lunch that locals insisted on drew to an end, and people trudged to work or home. Christensen and Young hoped to catch folks in their post-meal stupor along the palm-tree-lined promenade that ran parallel to the beach. This was the time of the week when it was safe to be near the beaches; Adam had been horrified to learn they were bathing-top optional.

Adam nodded at an older gentleman who was leaning against one of the rough, peeling trunks as he shuffled a few cloth bags and a well-worn cane in his arms.

"*Hola,*" Christensen said. "Sir, a word? Have you ever wondered where you came from? Where you're going?"

The man's grin was crooked as he said with a Basque accent, "I came from my mother and I'm going to the market."

Adam laughed, then clamped that down. Christensen didn't have a problem laughing, though.

"Fair point. I'm Elder Christensen, by the way, and this is Elder Young."

The man raised an eyebrow and shook his head. "My name is Iñigo Duarte," he added, shaking their hands.

"I wonder if we could walk with you and maybe talk to you about Jesus Christ?"

"You let me ask questions first," Iñigo said to them with a finger raised, "and if you answer well, I will listen to you, too."

"Absolutely," Christensen said. "And if I can't answer it, then my companion here surely will."

Adam's stomach fell. Christensen knew way more than he did, so certainly it wouldn't come to that.

"I want to know this thing," Iñigo said. "Why do you Mormons turn your back on the Virgin Mother?"

Christensen shoved his hands deep into his pockets and rocked on his heels. He sucked his teeth and said, "I don't believe we do."

"Yes! You do! You ignore her and her sacrifices, her importance. She, the Blessed Mother, is the Mediatrix of All Graces."

Adam didn't know what that *meant* and glanced sideways at Christensen, who looked into Iñigo's eyes and nodded along.

"She is Immaculate," Iñigo said. "She is free of sin."

Christensen continued to nod.

"So I ask." Inigo tapped Christensen's shin with his cane. "If she is free of sin, of course, then in your church must she be baptized?"

"Well," Christensen replied and smiled. "Even Jesus had to be baptized."

Iñigo laughed and tapped Christensen's shins once again. "That is true, that is true. So! Did you take holy orders of silence?" he asked, turning to Adam with a speed Adam wouldn't have thought the old man capable of.

"N-no?"

"I don't trust a man who won't speak for himself," he said, clucking his tongue. "And what do *you* think about our Holy Mother?"

"That… she… is the mother of the Son of God?" Adam said, casting nervous glances at Christensen. "That she had to have been a valiant spirit to have been chosen to *be* the mother of the Son of God?"

He wanted to steer the conversation back to the *Preach My Gospel* manual where the Church had already outlined discussion topics and how to handle questions about that material. Veering so widely off topic made him incredibly nervous. And, though Adam wouldn't admit this to a potential investigator, Mormons didn't pay much attention to Mary other than the knowledge that she was Jesus's literal mother after being visited by a physical, flesh-and-blood Heavenly Father, who impregnated her. These were topics he didn't like to think on because the answers were so at odd with Biblical scripture and general Christian belief.

Christensen, however, had no problem with these topics.

"Tell you what. We'll help you get your groceries back to your *piso*, and you can tell us what Dia de la Santa Eulalia is about."

Adam had no idea what that was, but Señor Duarte was happy to educate them, tsk-tsking them for their woeful lack of religious and cultural education as they loaded his cloth bag with fresh produce at the open market before he begged off to his dinner.

Christensen's method of engaging with people involved trading details of his faith for others. Adam had to admit that it at least kept them talking to people longer.

"It gives us insight into them," Christensen said as they headed back to their own apartment. "Gives us time to maybe even be impressed by the Spirit, to know just what they need to hear."

Christensen stopped in his tracks. Adam walked on a few paces before he realized his companion was no longer at his side.

"That sounds… wrong. Doesn't it?" Christensen asked, looking up.

"How do you mean?"

"That sounds like… manipulation."

A cold trickle ran down Adam's spine. "It's not manipulation; it's the Holy Ghost. Isn't it?"

Oblivious to the buses and cars as they passed, Christensen stared out at the street before he spoke. "Knowing what they need to hear," he repeated. "Shouldn't all of it, *any* of it, be what they need to hear?"

The thing was, that made sense. Any part of the gospel should be something a person was willing to hear, what they *needed* to hear. Adam could hear his father's voice saying, "Heavenly Father gives people what they need to know when they need to know it."

But… what if a person didn't know the question to ask in order to learn?

"Elder… Adam. I'm sorry if this is making you uncomfortable. I don't mean to."

"No, I—"

"It's just that I trust you. There's no way I could have asked Watson any of this. I feel like you'll actually take me seriously."

"I… I do." It was heady, knowing someone like Christensen trusted him. His own parents hadn't trusted him to do the simplest of things.

"Thanks. Really. Tell you what," he said, grabbing the cloth bag Iñigo Duarte had sent them home with, stuffed with cheeses and olives and a small bottle of olive oil about which the old man had sworn that, if they took a spoonful of it every night, they would be as healthy as he was. "I'll make dinner tonight *and* wash dishes."

"You don't have to," Adam said, feeling both proud to have put a smile on his companion's face and uncomfortable to be rewarded for not doing much other than listening.

"I kind of feel like I do." Christensen grinned and shoulder checked him.

———◆———

P-DAY CAME AROUND AGAIN, AND Guymon and Gardener brought the sister missionaries with them. Or rather, the sister missionaries, who were allowed a car, brought them. They'd apparently seen the guys walking toward the park and, as they were heading there themselves, picked them up to spare their feet a few blocks.

"¡*Hola!*," one of the sisters said, waving at the group as they approached. She had a long, thick blonde braid down her back, a homely yet friendly face—and an incredibly strong grip, Adam realized, shaking out his hand.

"Sister Peterson. Gunlock. This is—"

"Uh, Sister Cook," the other girl said, pointing to her name tag and smiling at the group. She had a prettier face, wore a little makeup, and dressed fashionably yet modestly in casual pants and a nice top, instead of a below-the-knee skirt like all sisters had to wear except on P-Day. "I'm from Arizona."

"Oh, yeah?" Guymon asked, smoothing down his hair. "Where about? I have family in—"

"Queen Creek," she said, blushing.

Christensen caught Adam's eye, bit his lip and looked away to hide his smirk.

"Hey," Adam said, nodding his chin at Guymon. "What about playing on the big chessboard since the girls can't play basketball?"

"Oh, we can," Sister Peterson said with a forced smile on her face. "We're just not allowed."

"You play?" Adam asked.

"Not on my mission, if that's what you're asking."

Adam bristled at her snippy tone. He was trying to be friendly.

"Uh, Sister Peterson," Christensen said, redirecting the conversation, "please tell me you know how to play chess. Like strategy stuff. I'm terrible at it."

Sorensen's mouth hung open. He mouthed to Adam, "What's her deal?"

Adam shrugged. The cute one was making eyes at Ketchup, the mean one looked ready to get them all in a headlock. Gardener walked past Adam with his hands in his pockets. "Hey. Dude. They have a car. I'll put up with a lot to spare my feet walking a few miles in shoes that pinch."

"So, I totally call Sister Peterson for my team," Christensen said as the rest of the group gathered alongside the chessboard etched into the park's pavement, which was dotted with three-foot-high chess pieces. "She's totally a female Bobby Fischer."

"Who?" Guymon asked.

Sister Cook laughed at that but no one paid any attention, which was good, as Adam didn't know who the heck Bobby Fischer was, either. Ketchup nodded along to whatever Sister Cook was saying—clearly forgetting about his beloved Randilyn back home. Sorensen and LaSalle were having a fake sword fight around the large plastic rook. Gardener, his hands folded at his chest, was stretched out on the grass several yards away near a row of fragrant orange trees. The others divided into teams with Romney and Larsen. Christensen whistled at Adam and nodded at the space next to him.

Adam tried to ignore the warm pleasure that suffused him when Christensen slung his arm around Adam's shoulder as soon as he was by Christensen's side.

"Okay, Peterson," Christensen said, "We move the king first, right?" He elbowed Adam in the side as Sister Peterson tore into him for not knowing the basics of chess.

———◆———

"You know, I remember asking my father once, *how* will I know something is true?" Adam said to Christensen one morning at breakfast.

"Finally! He speaks of his elusive family!" Christensen laughed, nudging Adam's dress shoe under the table. "No, I'm just teasing," he said when Adam shook his head and pushed his food around his plate. "Go on, please. What did he say?"

After a deep breath, Adam put his fork on the table and said in a measured tone, "He kept reading his paper and said that I'll know, and that I'll know it's from the Spirit of God because I'll have learned something."

"Oh." Christensen nodded while shoveling some scrambled eggs into his mouth. "So a useless non-answer, then."

Adam made a noncommittal noise.

After a sip of juice, Christensen asked coolly, "What about your mom? What does she say about all of this when you bring it up?"

Adam shrugged. "First off, I didn't really bring this stuff up back home. But when I did, she always told me to ask my father. They, uh, didn't like all the questions. Mom especially. It was always, 'Go ask your father.'"

"Well," Christensen said, frowning down at his plate, "you can ask me any question you want. I may not have the answer, but we can just try and find it together, okay?"

Adam's mouth hung open. He closed it and nodded his head. "Yeah. Okay. That would be nice for a change."

Christensen winked at him and pushed off from the table. "We're in this together, right? All the way, bro. Except it's your turn to wash up while I get the plans settled for the day."

Adam laughed and chucked his napkin at Christensen. He realized this sensation, this easy friendship and lack of judgment, heck, this level of support and real companionship must be what his brothers and other guys he'd known had imagined for their missions. Finally, things were starting to make sense.

———•———

THE MORE TIME HE SPENT with Christensen, though, the more it was confirmed that his companion was simply a good man. A sort of light seemed to follow Christensen around, and because of this Adam began to understand that he'd pushed down his own darkness: a constant thread of panic for not being perfect, for not knowing all there was to know about his own religion, for daring to teach it when he was such a neophyte himself.

"Hey, Elder," Adam asked, swallowing down his anxiety, "what do you think about the early days of the Church when they all lived in each other's pockets? Everybody shared everything like... like communism."

"Dude."

Adam's stomach lurched, but then Christensen nodded his head.

"Totally. Or, hmm. Maybe that's more like socialism? I don't know enough about that stuff. Let's ask my mom." He grabbed the notepad they kept on the kitchen table to scribble something down. "Um, the old fashioned way. I don't think that's a question for Church email."

That was another way they were different: Christensen never hesitated to put questions to his parents. Clearly they didn't have the same idea of how "perfect obedience will lead you to perfect knowledge" as Adam's parents did.

"Sandra Christensen was a sociology major before she was a mom," Christensen said. "She will tell you that straight up. Still substitutes at the high school. She'll eat this up."

They did this sometimes, posed questions to Christensen's parents when they didn't feel comfortable asking the Mission President or other members, or when they couldn't find it on their own in their growing library of Church-sanctioned books.

Just yesterday a new care package had come for Christensen and, in addition to some coloring books and crayon packs to pass out to kids, it was loaded with homemade cookies protected by colorful bubblewrap, funky dress socks with the Golden Plates embroidered on them and a Skor chocolate and toffee bar for Adam. Adam's face had gone hot as he'd stammered out a thanks, suddenly bashful at the thought of his companion telling his parents back home what sort of treats he missed.

It also contained a long letter, most of which Christensen read out loud.

"Okay, here's where she gets to our question," Christensen said, tucking the first page into his pocket. "'Buddy, I get what you're trying to say about manipulation, but it's only manipulative if you don't believe it or if you're just making things up to get people to believe what you want for your own gain.

"'That's something to think about, though. I'll be honest when I tell you I hadn't considered that, either,'" the letter continued. "'I guess it makes sense to move forward with that in mind, that you and Elder Young—and your father and I, too—are always cautious from this point forward to listen to the promptings of the Spirit so you know who needs help, but that you listen to them, too. Listen to what people tell you with their lives, not just their words. Are they tired? Help them carry their load. Are they struggling with personal demons? Offer to take them to the clinic, give them a hug, walk with them and let them know you're listening, something like that. Being good and kind and helpful is every bit as much a part of the Gospel of Jesus Christ as knowing which scripture to quote. Maybe even more so.'"

Well, it was clear where Adam's companion got his good nature and loving spirit from. Adam had never considered that being kind and helpful was as important to living the Gospel as was knowing the scriptures.

"Dude," Christensen said, grinning over the letter. "My mom is so awesome."

Adam nodded. In addition to the idea that the Gospel was more than words on a page, that it was how you treated others, he'd also never heard a parent talk so candidly to their child before. Christensen read on.

"'I love the fact that you care so profoundly about being your best for our Heavenly Father. Always remember how proud of you your dad and I are. Let Elder Young know we're keeping him in our prayers, too. We want you both to be successful—and a big part of that means knowing you're loved by us and Heavenly Father!'"

Adam blinked when he heard about his companion's parents adding him to their prayers.

"Then she goes on with stuff about Bill's baseball championship game and stuff like that, but…" Christensen trailed off, taking great care with folding the letter. "Well, what do you think?"

Adam didn't know how to answer. People didn't usually ask him for his *thoughts*. He was usually just asked to participate or lift heavy stuff. "Me?"

"Well, yeah, ya dink," Christensen said, laughing and slapping at Adam's shoulder with the envelope. "The whole 'it's not manipulative if you're not trying to gain something' thing?"

Put that bluntly, he could see why Christensen had originally thought proselytizing *was* manipulative. But weren't they trying to get something from these people?

"Uh oh," Christensen said, face sober and concerned. "What is it?"

"It's just... maybe there's something to that. I don't really know, though," he added in a rush. "I hadn't considered us trying to get people into the Church as anything but helping them with their salvation."

"Maybe it is that simple?"

Adam didn't know. Two months ago he would have been sure of his answer. But the longer he was away from his father and his father's persistent preaching, the less sure he was about anything. Now it seemed that the answers of which he'd been so certain were nothing more than catch phrases to toss out at the slightest sign of weakness, phrases meant to quell any real thought into the deep theological questions nagging him. Now a sparking interest grew, encouraging him to learn as much as he could about this gospel he was attempting to preach.

It was all thanks to his companion, Christensen, and his seeming lack of judgment, a completely new experience for Adam. It was both exhilarating and terrifying to realize that someone else—someone for whom Adam was coming to have a great deal of respect—also shared these nagging doubts, especially when it was someone like Christensen, someone good and kind, someone everyone liked and respected and would be willing to follow anywhere.

Adam was now wondering about those same issues. Before they'd only been seeds of doubt that he tried to pray away, or simply ignore. But now, now he and Christensen used their scant bit of free time to engage each other in thoughtful discourse. And, as was becoming more common, Christensen had more questions.

"You know," Christensen said one night at dinner, "at the start of it, the Church was so totally different than it is now. I mean, everyone lived together and had communal livestock and food. They were totally communists," he grinned, "well, socialists we decided, right? Law of Consecration and all that. But also, there was so much more debate and study, I think, than there is now. It's all been done for us," he said, carrying his empty dishes to the sink. "The work of understanding has all been done. Now we just have to memorize things."

Adam stood still, dirty plate in hand and heart racing. In Adam's house, there was no question that this would be considered outright blasphemy. His heart raced at the thought of them edging toward something dangerous. But as he'd heard in countless Firesides and Young Men classes, just because he experienced excitement didn't mean that it was founded in something righteous. "Spiritual things were emotional, but not all emotional things were spiritual." He had to remember that. He just couldn't tell what this was.

"I don't know," Christensen said, oblivious to the turmoil inside Adam as he reached for the plate that was forgotten in Adam's hand. "I just… I wonder if the old way was better, that's all. Feels like I'm being spoon-fed, you know?"

Adam slowly approached where Christensen began filling the sink. His voice thick, he said, "Sometimes… sometimes I worry that we're offending Heavenly Father by not wholly accepting everything we've been taught, though." He took his place at Christensen's left to start soaping up dishes.

"Hey. If our religion's own founder hadn't asked questions, we wouldn't even be here," Christensen replied, took a wet plate from Adam to rinse it and bumped their shoulders together.

That didn't mesh with any of the doctrinal precepts his father had hammered into his head from birth, but the heck of it was, it sounded… true. And as questioning his beliefs had always been considered to be an act that was unfounded in righteousness. The inconsistency of this made it harder to ignore and certainly harder to go along with blithely, as his father would expect of him.

"My mom said once that her job was to prepare me to be an adult, right?"

Adam nodded and began scrubbing the silverware.

"A parent's job is to teach their child so they can become independent."

"Well, yeah," Adam said.

Chewing his lip, Christensen turned to rest against the sink. "But… if Heavenly Father is just that, our parent, then doesn't He want us to become independent? We're supposed to become Gods ourselves, after all. So wouldn't that follow? The growing up and past-being-children bit?"

"I... I don't know," Adam replied. He'd never considered that.

"I guess I just wonder if God is tired of having to spoon-feed us."

Adam dropped his hands back into the water and scrambled for missing silverware.

"Hey, um..." Christensen laid his hand on Adam's shoulder. Adam couldn't breathe. "I want to thank you for letting me be open about this stuff with you. I can't really talk to a lot of people about this stuff except my parents, and that takes too long out here. And as much as I love the guy," he laughed, squeezing Adam's shoulder. "Sorensen's too much of a goofball for this sort of thing. I just want you to know that I appreciate you. Thanks."

"I... yeah. Sure." Adam pulled the drain plug and watched the soapy water swirl away. "I'm surprised you do talk to me about this stuff, though."

"Why's that?"

Adam carefully dried his hands and said quietly, "No one ever talks to me about this sort of thing."

Christensen regarded him, then said, "My grandma had a saying: Still waters run deep. I know you don't talk much, but you're always thinking. And it's clear you're smart. For a jock." He ducked away from Adam's wide swing, laughing. "Honestly, I thought I might explode if I didn't have someone to talk to about all of this and not be scared you were going to turn me in to the Mission President. So really, thanks."

"Yeah. Yeah, no it's fine," he answered, thrilled that someone found what *he* thought to be of importance.

Later, while lying in bed, he thought back on their conversation. What if Elder Sorensen, or heck, what if *Ketchup* had asked him any of these questions? He'd be put out, no question. He'd think they were apostates, probably, or on the road to becoming one. So why not with his companion?

The thing was, Christensen was so sincere when he brought up these sticky topics that it made Adam pay close attention, made him wonder about these things, too, instead of dismissing them offhand as he would have before his mission. This wasn't some disgruntled member trying to kick a hornet's nest, or a lonely missionary wanting to go home so he could go to the movies, date and get back to being an irresponsible teenager. Christensen wasn't trying to shirk his duty or rush home to friends and a social life. He was a great guy, one everyone in the mission field admired and one who thought deeply about his actions and beliefs. Something about his earnestness let those questions sink in, instead of Adam automatically bristling and dismissing them as anti-Mormon stuff. Adam's parents had drilled in his head since childhood not to doubt but to trust, not to question but to have faith, that if his faith was strong enough, he would know.

So far that hadn't really worked. Maybe… maybe his companion had a better way to get answers. Maybe asking questions and continuing to ask questions until they got *real* answers was the way to go. Thank goodness Christensen's parents weren't like Adam's.

Adam added Sister Christensen to his prayers of thankfulness.

———◆———

AFTER THAT CONVERSATION, IT WAS easy to bring up concerns during their downtime. Christensen's regular response became, "Let's look it up." He loved that Christensen didn't dismiss him or make him feel stupid or ashamed for not knowing or fully understanding some complex principle. He was still pretty shocked with himself for daring to pose philosophical questions out loud.

"So don't get weird," Christensen said as they packed up their laundry on another P-Day, "but I asked my mom about some of the questions we've had about the Book of Mormon and history and stuff."

Adam's skin prickled all over as if he was suddenly cold. "You asked your mom about that?" General philosophical questions were one thing, but questioning what they'd been told about the Church and its founders seemed disloyal and dangerous.

"Yeah, dude. She's the smartest person I know." Christensen set down the laundry basket and laid a hand high on Adam's shoulder, almost covering his neck. "Don't worry. My mom is super cool. She's the least judgmental person there is. Oh, she got you more Skor candy bars, too." He jogged to the kitchen and grabbed a small box.

Dumbfounded, Adam opened the lid to find it filled with bubble-wrapped Skor candy bars, his favorite. "What… *more?*"

"Eh," Christensen said, dismissing Adam's concern with his hand. "She knows they're your favorite. I may have mentioned that I assumed your family kept forgetting to put some in your care packages."

Adam hadn't gotten any care packages beyond extra socks and a new tie two weeks ago.

"But anyway, back to the doctrine stuff. Hang on, let me get it." He grabbed an opened letter from his dresser drawer and skimmed it for a minute, before reading out loud. "'Mistakes are to be expected, I'm afraid. Remember that the scriptures were written by humans, and we all mess up. We all make mistakes. There isn't a book published without typos and errors, after all.

"'I want you boys to think about how you feel when you read and study certain things. I want you to ask yourselves how you feel when we live the principles of the gospel. *That's* what's more important than all the editorial corrections in scriptures. Ask yourself if you feel good? Do you feel righteous? Do you feel selfless? If so, then you're following something good and worthy. You believe in something good and worthy. I hope that makes sense.'"

Christensen folded the letter and snagged a candy bar from the box in Adam's hand. "Let's pray about that tonight, what do you think?"

Adam held the gift in his hands and stared at his companion. Light appeared to be emanating from Christensen, just as the Church leaders had always said would happen around righteous, good men of God.

He was just… so noble and thoughtful, and so was his kind mother. And everything seemed to make sense when he said it. It didn't feel scary, trying to understand these tricky doctrinal… flubs, these knots in the doctrine that tangled up Adam's heart and thoughts.

"See? Told you she was awesome," Christensen said. "Come on, man. We better get these clothes in the wash before they grow legs."

They decided to go tracting after regular P-Day chores and after Adam wrote a thank you letter to Sister Christensen while still sucking toffee from his back teeth. They'd gone old-style door-to-door for a solid week. They weren't having any luck. No long chats, no discussions, certainly no baptisms. Most people saw them coming and went the other way or refused to open the door and yelled at them to keep walking. One woman had crawled under her dining table—she was completely visible from the front glass door—and waited them out as they pounded. Adam had considered shouting, "I can see you!" but had refrained, knowing that wouldn't help them. It hadn't occurred to him until much later that his father would have expected just that.

Why wasn't he forcing the issue with these lost children of God?

That question began to weigh heavily on him.

"I think we're not making any headway with anyone because… well, because we're questioning the Church ourselves." Adam worried at his tie and squinted at it as the sun shone on the mirror, reflected from the cement sidewalk. "If we could just have a perfect faith, we'd be able to find the people who need us." What he didn't say out loud was: If *he* would only stop questioning, he could finally believe it all. He could get a baptism just as Christensen had and prove to his father that he was worthy of his priesthood, worthy to, well, exist.

Christensen attempted to placate him. "Dude, we're sowing seeds. Don't let it get you down, man. 'Success is the progressive realization of a worthy goal.'"

Adam laughed. "Was that the daily quote in your Franklin Planner today?"

"Nope." Christensen threw an arm over Adam's shoulder, chuckling as he playfully ruffled Adam's hair, then smoothed it back to rights. "That was yesterday's. Thanks for giving me the chance to actually use it."

"Well, then. What's today's?" Adam asked.

Christensen glanced at the open organizational-planner on the dilapidated coffee table and read, "'Happiness is measured by the spirit of which you meet the problems of life.' Someone needs to send that to Ketchup. Glass half full right there."

"Practically empty," Adam agreed, warming at the sound of Christensen's laughter and flushing all over when he slung an arm around Adam's neck.

"Man, I'm so glad they sent you to me instead of pairing me up with Guymon again. Three weeks last year was enough. Well, ready to get a move on?" He grabbed both of their bags. "I thought we might try down by Güell Park. If we don't get any bites, at least we can check it out. There's this water fountain with a big dragon covered in tile, these cool built-in terrace thingies, it's awesome. I love that place. It's like Tim Burton reimagined Saint Basil's Cathedral."

"Was that supposed to mean something to me?" Adam asked, taking his bag and locking their door.

"You'll see. I'll educate you yet, Provo."

"Oh, okay, California," Adam laughed. "I forgot how urbane and sophisticated the 'burbs of Sacramento' are."

"Whatever, dude. My folks took us to museums and let us watch cable television," he said, gently punching Adam's upper arm.

They continued to tease each other as they made their way to meet investigators. They were comforting, if disconcerting, these random moments of affection and camaraderie. Adam almost couldn't believe how wary he'd been at the start, how he'd questioned letting Christensen past his barriers. He'd never really allowed himself to have a close friend. He'd hung with his team, socialized with the local guys, and that was about it. Christensen was more than just his missionary trainer and companion, however. He was Adam's friend.

And friends did things like touch each other with joke punches, shoves, stuff like that. Christensen had been a demonstrative guy from the start, and some of that demonstrativeness was rubbing off on Adam. He didn't balk at the head rubs and close contact the way he had in the beginning. It was… nice. He supposed he'd been touch-starved, and now lit up at the simplest of contacts.

Adam told himself that he wasn't doing anything to encourage the contacts. That was how a lot of guys were with each other; that certainly was true among the other missionaries here, Sorensen especially. He would sit in any available lap if no chair was free.

"I don't do floors, man," Sorensen said, wriggling his tush more comfortably into LaSalle's lap. All the missionaries were gathered at the apartment to give a quick evening report to Christensen.

"Man, get your big butt up," LaSalle groaned. "You're going to break my legs in half."

"Nah. You're comfy as heck, bro. Now, if you were a stick like Ketchup here," Sorensen said, ducking when Guymon threw a book at his head.

"LaSalle isn't *that* sturdy," Christensen said.

"*Thank you.*" LaSalle shoved Sorensen's solid mass off his lap.

"Look, you can squeeze in over here. Stop throwing my things, Guymon." Christensen shifted over and tugged Adam closer to make room on the sofa for Sorensen to shove himself in. It was for everyone's comfort that Christensen had his arm on the back of the sofa and that was why Adam ended up angled under his arm, pressed against Christensen's side.

"Don't worry," Sorensen said, perching on the edge of the cushion. "We won't be here long. We have a dinner appointment—"

"Another one?" Gardener cried. "How the heck are you scoring so many meals?"

Sorensen looked at his nails, huffed on them, the buffed them on his shirt. "Guess we're the new stars of the mission field, huh?"

"Man, don't even front," LaSalle said. To the rest of them, he said, "It's like this. Sorensen here is the champion of looking starved. He works the sympathy angle with the older types. Plus, they like that I speak Basque—"

Everyone laughed and fake applauded.

"Thank you. That's a Canadian education for you. And we get some good food out of it. Now be nice about it, and maybe we'll bring y'all's sorry butts some leftovers."

Christensen leaned close to Adam and whispered, "We have *got* to get the hookup on some home-cooked meals. No offense to your mad grilled cheese skills, of course."

Adam flushed from head to toe, worried that the others would misunderstand what they'd seen. If they'd seen anything. He forced out a laugh, because who would be watching him? Also, there was no reason to be uncomfortable. What, just because he could almost feel his companion's lips graze his ear? They were wedged in like sardines, of *course* weird touching would happen.

Okay, so maybe he was uncomfortable because it was new for him to allow that sort of contact. Maybe because Christensen was in a position of power over him, maybe that made it inappropriate. In the army, captains and majors weren't supposed to fraternize with the grunts. He understood the principle. But part of him thought that fraternizing was what made Christensen such a good leader. And part of his thoughts twisted ugly and bitter later that night when he saw Christensen hug and wrestle the other guys as they went off to their own apartments.

So, fine. He now had a habit of hanging on Christensen's every word, and he had a pattern of becoming upset with himself for being so worshipful of his senior companion.

God wasn't a respecter of men and all that. And Adam shouldn't be, either.

It was confusing, all that there was to learn. There was figuring out how to navigate this huge city, the people and their customs, and how to live in such close quarters with another person, especially one with as big a personality as Christensen, let alone his physical size. And those close quarters were another problem of their own. Adam's family had a big house in Provo, big enough that Adam never had to share a room with his brothers. And they just weren't close, not the way he'd seen other brothers behave, always hanging off each other, frogging the other's arms, jumping on each other's backs. Okay, that last one was mostly Sorensen, who was a big goofy puppy, and usually pretended to crack a whip, demanding horseback rides from everyone.

One morning, thrown off balance when he and Christensen headed for the same narrow path in their tiny living room, Adam planted his hand on his companion's broad chest to keep from falling over. He quickly pulled his hand back.

Christensen said, "Hey, man, it's okay. No big. We're going to ding-dong each other on occasion." He laughed. "With eight of us in a four-bedroom home, you either learn to get comfortable around other people in tight quarters or you go bananas. Plus, we were the hangout house. Nonstop crowds at Casa de Christensen."

Adam nodded, trying to avoid watching Christensen tuck his dress shirt into his suit pants.

"I loved it, though. We had a big screen TV down in the basement," Christensen said, looping his belt and heading to the kitchen. "Everyone in the neighborhood was always coming over. We had a huge backyard, too. Half the neighborhood had sleepovers all summer long, like, twenty kids in sleeping bags playing Graveyard or Truth or Dare until a neighbor would yell at us to shut up. Mom won't know what to do with herself when we're all moved out and on our own. She still has four of us kids living there, not counting me, so she's making do." Christensen poured two glasses of juice and handed one over. "Honestly, this is the most space I've ever had to myself." He smiled brightly. "You're better company than my older brother, that's for sure. Easier to get along with, too."

"Heh, yeah. Um, same thing. The easier to get along with part, I mean."

Christensen squeezed Adam's arm and shot him another of those infectious grins and went off in search of his scriptures.

Adam understood that it should seem like brothers between them in their apartment; it should seem familiar and familial when they would kneel together in their living room, their knees and thighs almost touching as they prayed together morning and night. It didn't. It seemed like something bigger, something that stuck in Adam's throat, that threatened to choke him with how much he didn't want to feel any of it because of how desperate it left him, how much more he wanted, especially when every night before turning off the lights, Christensen would put his hand on Adam's forearm, warm and sure and intimate, and say softly, "Goodnight."

Christensen was only being his typical, demonstrative self. He was everybody's friend, even though it seemed like something different to Adam, something private and just for him. Or maybe he simply wanted it to be more?

This whole mission was becoming an experience much larger than converting people, an experience that had the very real potential to swallow him whole. Under the euphoria from building what was swiftly becoming the most significant friendship of his life coupled with having the mental space to learn what he actually believed, was a mounting terror about something he had never, not once, allowed himself to explore. What scared him was that, with every passing day in Christensen's company, free to become himself for the first time, he began to notice the cracks in his own armor—armor meant to protect him from unknown and sinister forces in the world.

The hints of what may lie deep within himself terrified him. The thoughts he'd carefully kept locked away, thoughts he never entertained except in frustrating dreams that left him cold and horror-stricken upon waking; those thoughts could lead to his eternal damnation.

"The Family: A Proclamation to the World," the Church's official stance on who men were to be and what was expected of them, made it clear: Adam would marry a woman in the temple. He would have children with her. And he would touch no other person with love nor lust than this mystery woman. He wanted to hit something when he thought about it. He wanted to cry, thinking about forcing a woman into becoming his wife for time and all eternity, when he didn't want her. He imagined her becoming as bitter and sullen as his own mother.

While Christensen took his shower, he stared at the wall and envisioned making a fist and punching its pure whiteness, cracking and splitting it open to reveal the structure underneath. He imagined himself in the armor of the ancient warriors of the Book of Mormon, the brass chest plates and red capes hanging from their shoulders, their feet and ankles wrapped in sandals, powerful with their swords in hand, and saw the armor crack open, fall away, leave him vulnerable and unhidden—and unashamed of who he really was.

He wanted it to do just that. Wanted his companion—the man by his side in every sense of the word on this spiritual journey of his—to be the person who finally cracked him wide open and helped him discover himself, the real him. He *trusted* Christensen, trusted him with the secret places in his heart he'd never shared with anyone, with his doubts, his hopes, his fervent wishes.

Adam would be lying to himself, however, if he didn't acknowledge how afraid it made him, this need to connect with his mission companion in ways he didn't fully understand.

As he listened to Christensen settling into his bed one night, the thoughts that he'd never let himself look at head-on were growing more and more persistent. He was desperate for Christensen to look at him in a new way, to somehow communicate that his affection for Adam was more than it was for Gardener and LaSalle, even more than his obvious deep friendship with Sorensen. Adam wanted *more*. These thoughts kept him up late that night, long after he should have fallen asleep.

And that was how he learned about Christensen's penchant for touching himself. He probably thought Adam would be sound asleep since Adam would lay so quietly in bed. Adam knew guys did that; they didn't all have strict fathers like Adam's. He just never in a million years expected a guy to do *that* in the same room with him, and he *never* thought it would happen while serving the Lord on a mission.

"Chastity is sexual purity," his father and various Church leaders had stated time and again.

"We have been commanded by our Heavenly Father to obey the Law of Chastity. The law," his father had emphasized. "Not suggestion, not a do-you-think-you-can. We have been commanded to obey a *law*. And if you sully yourself both in body and spirit with sexual transgressions like masturbation, you close the door on letting the Holy Spirit enter you and guide you in your life. You are sinning, and Heavenly Father cannot dwell within a house of sin."

The first time it happened, Christensen doing… that, Adam lay perfectly still with this eyes screwed shut and his mind replaying hymns to block out any sounds. He was certain that he was complicit in the act, because he was supposed to report that sort of thing to their Mission President. It was a rule. He couldn't bring himself to do it. He struggled between seeing his companion as the guy whom the Mission President praised as one of their best—*knowing* how good a man Christensen was from being constantly by his side—and seeing him as a sinner who abused himself almost nightly. Adam had to think of it as a sin, because it had been pounded into him that a man did *not* do that. It was self-abuse. It was a waste and an affront to God.

At the ten-week mark, Adam had a meeting with the Mission President. Christensen was in the kitchen being fattened up by the President's wife, Sister Jensen, while the President interviewed Adam in his study.

President Jensen shut the door and motioned for Adam to sit. "Good to see you, Elder Young! How are you getting along, son?"

"Fine?"

"You don't sound too sure of that." President Jensen laughed. "Don't be nervous. This is just a formality. You know how it goes, dotting the i's, crossing the t's. That is," he said, sobering quickly and leaning forward, "unless you have something you need to get off your chest?"

Adam could do it. He could tell the President about Christensen's nightly activities. He was supposed to. He flashed back to an incident that happened when he was about thirteen. The family had just finished dinner, and, instead of Adam being left to gather up the dishes for his mother, Gerald had instead grabbed him by the upper arm and led him out of the room.

"Come with me, son."

Adam had instantly become nervous, but he wasn't sure why. His father marched them to Adam's room, then used Adam's arm to shove him onto the mattress. He pulled something from his back pocket.

"I think you need to spend a little extra time with your personal scripture studies tonight, and this should tell you what to focus on."

He handed Adam a beige pamphlet with what looked like a pencil drawing of a young man, titled "For Young Men Only." Adam's hands began to shake. How did his dad... How did he know what Adam had done last night? Everyone had been asleep. He'd *checked*.

"If a person doesn't know something is a *sin*," his father said, in a tone that meant he didn't include Adam as unaware of what constituted a sin, "then they can only be held accountable if they do it again, once they learn how grievous that thing actually is."

Adam nodded.

"Your Heavenly Father is watching you. His angels are always watching you. Do you doubt He loves you?"

"No, sir."

"Then you're telling me that you, you what? You do that... *that* knowing He's watching you?"

Adam felt trapped, frozen by the look on his father's face, by the calm tones that Adam knew meant Gerald was exercising extreme control. "No, sir?"

"No, sir? You don't know?"

"No! No, sir," Adam answered in a more sure tone, his face aflame with mortification.

"What are you, some kind of pervert, then?"

"No!"

His father looked at him, and shook his head with mild disgust. "You get some damn control. If that... happens while you're asleep, then that's one thing. You don't go turning on that factory, you got it? Cleaning only."

"Yes, sir."

His father stood and walked to the door. "You remember: God is watching you. His angels are always watching you, recording your trespasses. You do what's right, and there won't be any problems."

Adam didn't think touching himself would ever be a problem again after that embarrassing encounter when Gerald had given a shaking, terrified thirteen-year-old the Church's infamous "masturbation" pamphlet. He'd had no idea how his father had known Adam had given into the impulse the night before. It had been the first and last time he'd ever touched himself, with the exception of cleaning. Any time he started to think about maybe giving in and doing it, he had the horrifying notion that his father would be watching, not just that *God* would be watching.

He'd been raised to believe, as all Mormons had, that angels kept a "book of life" about their sins and accomplishments, something to aid Christ in determining one's worthiness to enter the kingdoms of heaven. He imagined everyone he'd ever known listening to an angel reading out loud for all to hear that he'd abused himself, had broken the law of chastity. Eventually, he felt sick to his stomach if the thought of doing it entered his head, which happened often, since he was a healthy young man.

There in his quiet mission apartment, his breath had caught the very first time he heard movement from the other bed. At first he worried that his companion had gotten sick. Christensen's back was to him and he was ever so gently rocking, making quiet, but desperate, gasps. Before Adam made up his mind to check to see if he was okay, Christensen moaned softly. His back spasmed, then Christensen went still. When he turned to grab a tissue from his bedside table, Adam feigned sleep once again as his heart raced.

"Well? Elder?" President Jensen's face was full of concern. "I assure you that anything you tell me is confidential. If one of the other guys has—"

"Oh! No, sorry. It's just been a long day," Adam said, forcing his face into calm neutrality. "Lots of walking. We met up with Señor Duarte today."

"Did you? Any luck there?"

"No, he's still very Catholic," Adam chuckled. He diverted the conversation from anything uncomfortable and talked about some of the service projects they'd proposed to the local branch to involve more of the community.

When it was Christensen's turn to talk privately, he clapped a hand on Adam's chest and winked as he passed into the office.

"Brandon, did you hear who made the Final Four?" President Jensen asked, smiling briefly at Adam before shutting the door.

No. Adam wasn't going to rat out his companion. He'd understood that his dad was a little more strict than other guys' fathers, but he'd always chalked it up to Gerald Young being a military man as well as a high-ranking leader in the Church. Gerald had always told the Young family that, because of their heritage, people expected them to be worthy of it. And that they would be.

Sister Jensen took a phone call, leaving him to his thoughts (as well as a huge dish of paella). He spilled a little on his chest and, as he wiped it off, recalled the sensation of Christensen's hand there moments before. And unbidden, he imagined Christensen's strong hand down... there on himself. Adam could recall being thirteen with perfect clarity, could feel again the visceral shock at watching his fist work over his own body in that new and intimate way, and as suddenly as that image was conjured, he pictured Christensen's hand there instead of his own.

He almost knocked the bowl of paella to the floor, he shook so badly.

The shame and guilt he'd been infected with from adolescence came flooding back from just thinking about masturbation. And worse, he was thinking about it while on his *mission*. In his Mission President's home just after being interviewed for personal worthiness. Every Mormon was taught that thinking about something was the same as doing it, so did *that* mean he had done it to himself, too? Or... or to his companion because Christensen had been the one touching Adam in his thoughts?

He fell silent for the rest of the evening, ignoring the looks Christensen kept shooting his way.

"Still Waters?" Christensen asked.

"Running deep is all," Adam said with a weary sort of grin.

"You want to talk about anything?"

Adam sighed, running a hand over his face. "Nah, it's okay."

"Are you sure?" Christensen asked. "Do... do you want to talk to someone else?"

Adam couldn't stand the look of worry on his companion's face. This wasn't *his* fault, after all. It was Adam's. He knocked the side of his fist into Christensen's strong shoulder and said, "Nah. Just worn out."

The stiff line of Christensen's shoulders relaxed at that. "If you're sure. I'm here for you, man."

"Yeah." Adam said. "I know. Thanks."

He spent extra time that night with his own personal prayers and scripture study, trying to replace the memory of the enticing sound of Christensen's choked off gasps with the voice of God.

CHAPTER FIVE

"A NEW COMMANDMENT I GIVE unto you, That ye love one another; as I have loved you, that ye also love one another." John 13:4

"CUT YOUR HAIR REGULARLY. KEEP your hair clean and neatly combed at all times in the approved style." LDS mission rules 7 and 8

AFTER A FEW MONTHS, THE two settled into a routine. They had no success in making appointments to teach in people's homes, but they were meeting a lot of people in the city. Señor Duarte enjoyed meeting them in the park for chess, mostly as a way to chivvy them for their lack of education on Catholicism.

"You come to a Catholic country and can't even tell me who the Pope is!" he chided them, shaking his head in disgust as he knocked bird droppings from the park's chess table before setting up the game pieces he'd brought.

"Can you tell me who the Mormon prophet is?" Christensen grinned as he lined up his black pawns, moving one to counter Duarte's opening pawn move.

Señor Duarte scoffed, waved his hand dismissively and moved his bishop.

"Did you get your medicine this week?" Christensen asked as he shifted a pawn two spaces.

Right. Iñigo had mentioned something about that when they'd met him two weeks ago. Adam was astounded once again at the care Christensen paid to everyone they met.

"Oh, *sí, sí,*" the old man replied, clearly pleased by the attention— either that, or by the ease in which he scooped up Christensen's pieces.

"Is it helping your knee?" Adam asked as he elbowed Christensen and pointed at one of his rooks.

"That is cheating!" Duarte said. "Don't help him. And he can't move that piece, anyway. Hopeless, the both of you." He settled back in the folding chair, arranging his cane between his bandy legs.

They stayed for three more games. Some of Duarte's friends joined them to laugh at the boys' dismal chess playing and to discuss the merits of the Catholic faith versus Mormonism. Adam glanced at his companion as the older men laughed at some of the tenets of the LDS Church, but he didn't argue.

"Why aren't handsome boys like you taking out girls?" asked one of the men Adam knew only as Hugo.

Another, Señor Vidal, a clever-eyed but stooped older man, sighed at Adam, "Ah, if I was built like you, every father would hate me."

"Why is that?" Adam asked.

"Because of what he would be doing with their daughters!" Hugo said, shouting with laughter. The other men joined in. Christensen, Adam noticed, did not.

"Ah, but you are both men of God," Duarte said, "and are maybe not so interested in that sort of thing?"

"Shame," Señor Vidal said, shaking his head. "If only I had hair like yours," he added, patting a worn hand onto Christensen's forearm. "My wife once told me that she didn't mind my eyesight going or my back stooping, but she did regret the hair loss." He tugged off his cap and grinned toothily as his bald and liver-spotted head was exposed.

Christensen did have a good head of hair, Adam thought. Thick and shiny and beginning to curl over his ears. Adam thought it was just long enough to wrap around the tip of his finger. Christensen glanced over, caught Adam's gaze on him and tried to comb the sides back. Adam flushed at being caught staring and worried about what his companion must think of him.

"Are your uncles bald?" Hugo asked.

"Oh. Uh, one of them is," Christensen answered.

"If it's your mother's brother, then you'll go bald, too. That's how it goes, you know," Señor Vidal added. "Find a wife with a bald father. She might not mind you losing your hair so much, then."

"I'm not… That's not a worry," Christensen added, sounding flustered for the first time since Adam met him.

Señor Duarte chided his cackling friends. "Now, now, these are good boys who made a promise not to get into trouble with girls. They're servants of God, even if their God isn't quite like ours."

"Well, I wouldn't say that…" Christensen said, trying to steer the conversation back under control.

"Well, I do," said Hugo, a little snappish with his tone. "I know you mean well and that your heart is in the right place, but come, now. You are boys, the both of you. Here, move aside and let me show you how to challenge that opening that Iñigo keeps using to trap you."

Since not one of the men was interested in listening to a proper lesson from their missionary manual, they made their exit. The older men were gracious, but firm. They did not want to hear about the Mormon Church. Adam was frustrated and had no problem saying as much as they left the park and walked aimlessly down a narrow street.

"We're not *getting* anywhere."

Christensen clapped a hand to Young's shoulder and gave him a firm squeeze; his hand lingered. "We're setting an example, Elder. We're showing them we're not pushy, that we respect their rights. Spaniards respect each other's boundaries and get offended when not offered the same courtesy. They're not afraid to tell you to shove off, either. They'll respect us for not pushing. Maybe that will come to something. Sowing seeds, man."

"Right." It felt useless to Adam.

They headed to Las Ramblas, a combination park and open market where the old Roman parts of Barcelona blended with the new, so they could meet with some of the other elders at the Font de Canaletes, a wrought-iron drinking fountain built in the nineteenth century. They cut down a side street in the Ramblas to avoid walking past a stretch of bars and passed a sunken garden that had lush plantings encircling it.

His hands in his pockets, Christensen stopped and whistled, looking around at the old, ornate buildings with a few modern structures here and there.

"You okay?" Adam asked.

"Yeah." He shot Adam a bewildered grin. "Sometimes I just get reminded that freaking Romans walked here. Like, right here," he said, hopping a little.

Adam couldn't help but laugh.

"Dude. It's just… History, you know? My town in California is a hundred years old, if that. This place is like, thousands."

"Yeah." Adam jerked his head toward the area they were headed. "One time, my family went camping in the Arizona strip down west of Kanab and there were T-Rex footprints in the ground. The Navajo guide on our hike said they used to have one with a claw still in the ground, but some people sneaked out there at night and stole it."

Christensen stopped. "Whoa. That sucks. But a T-Rex? Okay, that's way cooler than Roman soldiers."

They merged onto a raised walkway. Below them, rounded terra-cotta tombs dotted the gravel bed with a few plants dotted here and there. A sign stated it was a Roman necropolis from the second and third centuries. "I don't know. This is pretty amazing."

They met with the others a few minutes later and took the all-important drink of water from the Font de Canaletes, water that tourists were told that, when drunk, would ensure they would return to Barcelona.

One of the missionaries was in town from Huesca on splits—where missionary companions are "split" up to ensure no one was alone—teamed for the day with Sorensen and LaSalle while his companion took care of some business with the Mission President. The new guy was an eighteen-year-old kid from Nephi, Utah named Eli Smith.

"No relation," Elder Smith said after introductions. "Well, not direct, at least. They're all down in St. George and Gunlock," he added when shaking Adam's hand. "So I heard that one of the city guys took a faceful of chewing tobacco? I'd say this was a heck of a lot better," he said, nodding at some college girls in tank tops. The girls noticed them and tossed their dark hair over their bare shoulders, smiling and laughing as they walked past the group. One even waved and giggled at Sorensen, who flushed deep red before turning away.

"Well, I don't know about it being tobacco," Christensen said, lowering his voice, "but one of our guys did get spit at. And that would be Guymon."

LaSalle groaned, "Of course it was Ketchup."

Smith made a disgusted face.

"That reaction is about right," LaSalle said.

Christensen let out a frustrated noise. "He's kind of a jackhole, Guymon. Sorensen here had him as a greenie. I got stuck with him for a few weeks. Every time I try to give the dude a chance, he'll just bork it up. I try, but…"

Sorensen rolled his eyes. "Dudes, you don't even know. Ketchup told me once he felt his 'heritage and strength of spirit' would bring the flock to him. Total moron."

Smith nodded and laughed, but was approached by an elderly couple with a request to take their photograph in front of the Font de Canaletes. The couple pulled in some of the boys, treating them like a landmark or tourist attraction. Sorensen mugged for the camera and dragged Christensen to pose the way he was, taking a huge gulp of the water that sprayed from the brass nozzle mounted on the side of the giant iron fountain.

Adam watched, thinking about what Guymon had told Sorensen. The thing was, Adam had been taught that his was *also* a noble heritage as a descendant of the Prophet Brigham Young, the Mormon Church's second prophet and President, and that the righteous would feel *his* presence.

At least he'd never been spat on, he thought, as the older man kindly shook his head no at the pamphlet Adam held out.

———•———

P-DAY ROLLED AROUND AGAIN, AND instead of meeting up in the park or traveling out of the city to hike, all the missionaries were coming to their apartment to get much-needed haircuts. Christensen apparently was the designated barber for their district. Adam busied himself straightening their books when a buzz suddenly twanged. He turned to see Christensen testing a set of clippers.

"My mom sent me a new pair just before you got here," he said, switching it off. "She knows I like to keep it neat. Since then, everyone bugs me to cut their hair when we have the chance," he shrugged. "Saves on bucks."

LaSalle brought over the new companion for Elder Smith, a greenie fresh from the MTC.

"Fellas, this here is Elder May in town from the Vic." That was what they all called the outskirts of the Mission's territory, a place rich with refugees and immigrants from Ghana, Morocco and Nigeria. "Let's show him the Spanish love, okay?"

A round of handshakes, ¿Como estas?, and the typical discussion of family trees revealed that May, who hailed from a central Utah town, Richfield, and Sorensen were third cousins. Sorensen proclaimed his new-found cousin to be his "protégé" and said no one should mess with him.

"Oh, wait! Did your mom send you jars of peanut butter, B?" Sorensen asked.

Christensen laughed and laid out a towel on the counter. "Yeah, and she told me not to touch one of them because it was for you. Man, quit working your mojo on my mom. She can't help but want to feed you jerks."

Young flushed thinking about the package of deodorant—the same kind Christensen used—several Skor candy bars, and a personalized and very motherly note from Sister Christensen's monthly care package that she'd sent to him that week.

Dear Adam,

We feel so blessed to have you in our lives as Brandon's companion. You've been such a source of comfort for him. He talks about your strength of spirit to us all the time. It's so important that you boys and girls out there have mission companions who you can trust with your thoughts and feelings. Make sure you boys lean on each other so you can have the strength to get the job done out there. We're so proud of you and keep you in our prayers and hearts.

Keep up the good work!
Sister Sandra, aka, Mission Mom

Somehow knowing Sorensen also got packages from Sister Christensen made his feel less special. But then, she hadn't sent it to him with a note, thought the jealous, mother-starved part of him. He immediately felt ashamed. Sandra Christensen was obviously a mother hen who liked to tuck strays under her wings. She was being generous. Young shouldn't feel *jealous*. That was ridiculous.

"Whatever, man," Sorensen said. "I can't help it if your mom enjoys getting letters from your friends, especially when it ends up with me getting stuff."

"Dude, you're writing letters to my *mother?*"

"Uh, she loves it? Chill? I sent her a thank you note for the peanut butter cookies you shared with us. Ease up." Sorensen threw open the cabinet doors rooting around for his jar. "And I may have mentioned how hard it was to find my favorite kind out here. Ah, yes! Crunchy..."

He found the plastic jar, ripped the lid off and jammed his finger in, swiped out a blob and plugged his mouth with it. "Ohhhhh," he moaned around his finger. "If your mom wasn't married, bro..."

"Okay, that's definitely crossing a line." Christensen crossed his arms and frowned. "Dude, you're so nasty! Get a frickin' spoon, Elder."

Sorensen grabbed a spoon, scooped out another huge dollop, and licked the peanut butter like a lollipop. Then, he whipped off his shirt *and* his white, silken sacred undergarments, spun a chair on one leg and straddled it.

"I believe I get firsts this time, gentlemen. Short on the sides, and as much of a faux-hawk that you think I can get away with, B."

Young was scandalized at Sorensen being bare-chested in front of everyone, but tried to keep his face neutral. They weren't supposed to be... That wasn't okay. When preparing for his mission, he'd gone through the temple and had taken his Endowments—a covenant to the Church marked by special white garments he promised to wear at all times, save when showering or for some sports, as a sign he would honor his commitment to Heavenly Father. He'd taken that covenant very seriously and only took off his own garments just before stepping into the shower and he put a fresh pair on as soon as he was dry.

Garments were considered to be sacred. Their whiteness symbolized both physical and spiritual purity. The embroidered markings over the nipples and navel as well as the one just above the right knee symbolized the compass and square and the level, respectively, and were taboo to speak of outside the temple. "Sacred, not secret," he'd been taught. Nothing was to come between his skin and his garments. In fact, women wore their bras *over* their G's—which is what most Mormons called them.

Their constant presence again the skin was a steady reminder of those sacred temple vows to honor Heavenly Father, and in turn, it was believed that the garments were capable of providing literal protection from evil and harm. Every Mormon had a story of someone they knew whose lives were saved by the protection of their holy G's. His own father had recounted a story of an engine backfire on base that blasted the mechanics with gasoline-fueled fire. The only person who had come out unscathed, relatively speaking, was one of the men who was also LDS. He had second- and third-degree burns on all skin not covered by his G's. That skin—his shoulders, chest and back, all the way to his knees—had been spared completely.

No one just took them off.

Young looked around at the other guys and registered that no one else seemed to care, not even the greenie. No one seemed to think this was a massive breach in mission protocol, let alone something sinful or dangerous. In fact, Elder May was teaching Romney how to do a complicated handshake involving snaps and chest bumps, and the others were pilfering the contents of Young and Christensen's meager pantry.

"Who's next?" Christensen asked, slapping at a laughing Sorensen's neck with a dish towel.

Guymon whistled and jerked his thumb like the jerk he was and stood waiting for Sorensen to vacate the chair.

"Buzz it all off? Stripe down the middle? Draw a smiley face in there?" Christensen said, snapping the clippers on and off quickly while waggling his eyebrows.

"No," Guymon huffed. "Neat. Clean up the back and sides. Come on, don't be dumb."

Christensen rolled his eyes when Guymon sat, then winked at Young. "I think Sister Cook said she liked a guy with a buzz cut, though…"

Guymon ducked and slapped at Christensen's hand.

"What does Randilyn like?" Christensen pressed. "Friar Tuck bald spot on top, right?"

"Cut it out, Brandon! Just make it neat."

"Yo, I'm next," Romney said, leaving it to the rest of the increasingly loud and rambunctious group to figure out the rest of the order.

Young kept finding ways to skip his turn. He washed the lunch dishes after telling Elder May not to worry about pitching in. He read a short letter from his mother in which she passive-aggressively wondered if he'd been made District Leader yet and then asked him to pray for his father who had just gotten another "very important calling" in the Church. As Elder Gardener nodded toward the chair, Young shook his head. "No, it's okay. You go ahead. I need to write back."

He pulled out his stationery and replied to her, asked for details on his dad's new calling and spent several paragraphs detailing the wonderful architecture in the city, from the rounded rooflines that almost appeared thatched to the ancient buildings still standing after hundreds of years offset by modern glass and steel art museums.

After that, he reorganized the bookshelf holding all of their teaching materials and scriptures—anything to keep busy and to keep his eyes from studying the other boys in the room too intently. Guyman hadn't put his shirt back on, and his pasty, slightly sunken bare chest was disconcertingly eye-catching for its unattractiveness.

The clippers' buzz stopped. Elder Smith bent at the waist and shook his head, knocking a few clumps of shorn brown hair to the tiled floor. He checked himself in the mission-provided mirror that hung near the front door with the words "Can you see HIS image in your countenance?" on a bold yellow-painted plaque below.

"We promised to help move boxes at the library in exchange for a discussion, so we're off," Sorensen said. "Thanks for the cut, B." He and Christensen performed a weird series of hand bumps and finger snaps, ending in a giant bear hug.

"Two weeks left, LaSalle," Christensen said, pushing LaSalle back with a friendly hand to LaSalle's freshly shaved head. "If I don't see you before you head out, you better write."

"Will do, man! Later, guys!"

"That's our cue, too," Elder Romney said, nodding at his companion, Larsen. "We're scoping out a potential spot at Ciutadella Park near the zoo."

"Yeah?" Guyman said, pulling his shirt over his head—he hadn't bothered unbuttoning it and Adam couldn't help but notice how rumpled and messy he looked.

"Get your own spot, dude," Larsen said, shaking his head.

The remaining boys gathered their things and shouted goodbyes until it was just Adam and Christensen. Christensen reached behind his head and pulled his shirt and G's off in one fluid motion; the muscles in his back and flanks rippled. Then he turned the clippers on and stood in front of the mirror to clean up his sideburns.

"Hey, come catch the back for me," he said quietly, pulling the guard off the clippers. "Make sure it's squared off, okay?"

Adam took the vibrating clippers; his insides buzzed to match. Christensen straddled a chair with his arms folded over the back and his forehead resting on his arms. Adam took in the breadth of Christensen's shoulders, the visible musculature, the tawny brown skin, and was hit with an ache so deep in his chest it took his breath away. He wanted to touch that smooth expanse of skin, to feel its warmth against his palm, and he blanched. He absolutely should *not* have such thoughts.

He forced himself to calm the heck down, gently laid a hand on Christensen's broad shoulder and pushed away the memory of how Christensen's body shook when he touched himself in the dark. Instead, Adam squared his shoulders and did as he'd been asked: squared off Christensen's nape.

Christensen stood and looked at the finished job in the mirror. "Could you get back behind my ears? I never get that right."

Nothing bad had happened when Adam touched his companion's bare skin. Registering how warm he was or how firm he felt under Adam's hand didn't cause the floor to split open or demons to pour out to cast him down with the Sons of Perdition. He almost laughed out loud at himself, at how ridiculous that sounded. He *had* half-expected to be struck down, to hear the angry voice of God chastising him for being in the room with someone who had covenanted to wear sacred garments but wasn't, for not being disgusted at touching a half-naked male standing in front of him.

For *wanting* to touch, wanting it so badly.

Emboldened, he stood with shaking hands behind Christensen, who tilted his head down, exposing the taut skin behind his ear. With a bracing breath, Adam leaned forward, cupped Christensen's face and made a few, slow strokes with the tool, forcing himself to focus on how the vibrating comb caught the hair follicles instead of how a muscle in Christensen's jaw jumped at Adam's touch. When he finished, Adam softly blew at the fallen hairs on the skin stretched over the tendon in Christensen's neck, so close he could feel the heat of his companion's body. He immediately snapped off the clippers and stepped back to keep from falling into Christensen's body.

Christensen turned and gave him a steady look, then said, "Your turn."

"What? Um, no, I'm good."

"Your hair's touching your ears. You want people to think you're some kind of granola-eating hippie who follows jam bands? Come on, Elder. I promise I won't jack your hair up, Scout's honor."

"Yeah, okay." Adam straddled the chair, same as the others, but kept his P-Day T-shirt on.

"We already did laundry today, Adam. You're gonna get your shirt covered in hair. What gives? You got a third nipple? Poodle tattoo over your heart? You're not supposed to be allowed to go on a mission if you have tattoos."

Adam barked out a nervous laugh. "What? No. I don't— All right, all right. Don't go shaving designs or anything. No mullets or racing stripes." He pulled his shirt and garments off in one motion, leaving his arms bound by the fabric; he covered his chest with his arms and bunched clothing. If he didn't take it all the way off, he wouldn't be breaking his covenant.

"You *do* have a third nipple, don't you?" Christensen laughed, then tugged at the cloth, pulling Adam's arms free. Adam watched as his last protective barrier was dropped on the sofa. His breath turned shallow, and his heart raced.

Christensen made a point of checking out his chest and abs. "Nope, no conjoined twin, either. What gives, man? Are you... what, shy? You shouldn't be. You're fit as heck. How the heck did you deal with the locker room, dude?"

I didn't want anyone in the locker room to touch me back, Adam thought.

As Christensen walked behind Adam to switch on the clippers, Adam shivered, closed his eyes and tried to stop the repetitive battle between thoughts of how this was wrong versus how desperately he wanted Christensen to get on with it. He wanted *something* to happen.

All thoughts were driven out when Christensen laid a strong, firm hand between his shoulder blades to hold Adam still while he worked. Everything, every thought and feeling, and heck, the very *universe* was centered on those minuscule points of contact between Christensen's hand and Adam's bared skin. Adam chanced a look after a while but shut his eyes again when he was confronted with his companion squatting directly in front of him, squinting at Adam's sideburns to ensure they were the same length. Christensen's breath moved over Adam's lips, they were so close. He kept his eyes screwed shut; his heart beat a wild tattoo in his aching chest.

Christensen's hand suddenly cupped the side of Adam's neck, and, at the shocking sensation of a thumb sweeping softly over Adam's pulse point, he let out a tiny gasp.

"Oh, my gosh," Christensen said, his voice worried. "Did I nick you?"

"Hmm? Oh, no, no, sorry. It's fine. You're fine."

Christensen laughed. His voice was still soft as he teased, "Oh! So, you're just afraid I'm doing a bad job?"

"N-no?"

"Then relax. You look like you expect me to punch you." He patted Adam's shoulder and gave him a squeeze. "Just need to taper this bit in the back and you're all done."

Christensen rubbed the palm of his hand over Adam's head to dislodge any hairs. The friction centered itself in Adam's skull, radiated in sensual ripples down his spine, then settled low with a pulse to match Adam's heartbeat when Christensen leaned over to blow a few pale blond strays off the backs of his ears. Adam's skin stippled with goose bumps. Was he imagining it? Was Christensen making an extra effort to get things just right, making sure every possible stray hair was carefully blown away or brushed off his neck and shoulders with the flat of his hand, merely in order to keep touching Adam? Or did Adam just hope so?

"Okay, man," Christensen said, moving back. "Torture session is over."

"No, it's just…" Adam shrugged, sent his companion a sheepish look, then stood up and looked at his reflection in the mirror. In it, he caught sight of Christensen right behind him with his gaze shifted down as if he, too, was reading the curly script, "*Can you see HIS image in your countenance?*" Shifting slightly, Adam was better able to see Christensen's hard and chiseled chest, the dark hair that spread from its center, the dusky little circles of his nipples.

Brandon looked into the mirror; his gaze connected with Adam's. "Well?"

Adam swallowed thickly, nodding at Christensen's reflection. "I, uh, I like it. Looks good."

"I told you I knew what I was doing."

"I'm glad. I mean, thanks… Brandon." Adam held his gaze in the mirror.

Christensen blinked, then cleared his throat. "Why don't you hit the shower while I clean up this mess? Wait, I don't think I got everything off your neck back there." He brushed the tip of his finger behind Adam's ear, trailing down the thick cord of muscle in his neck and over Adam's shoulder. Adam looked down to avoid seeing their reflections, afraid of knowing that he looked as raw and exposed and needy as he felt. After a breathless moment, he finally turned away to head for the shower. He felt claustrophobic in their empty apartment.

He stood in the water's spray, letting the hot water rush over his shoulders, with his head down and eyes screwed tightly shut. He turned the hot water up even more, needing the heat to replace the sensation of Brandon's fingertips hot and shocking against the tender skin of Adam's nape. He touched his neck where Brandon had; he let his fingertips following where Brandon's had trailed over his shoulder. Then he pressed his hand flat over his erratically beating heart, as if he could still it. He didn't want to think about why his companion gave him such feelings, or whether Brandon might *share* those same feelings. He didn't want to think about *Brandon*; he needed Brandon to go back to being Elder Christensen, Man of God and his mentor.

It would make everything so simple if he could. He wanted—he *needed*—simple, not this growing confusion that clouded his mind, permeated every one of his thoughts, prevented him from simply having faith that everything would be fine, would be as it should.

Instead, over and over in Adam's mind played images of Christensen doing crunches on the floor mixed with how he looked kneeling in prayer, which blended into shadowed movements under a blanket as quiet moans spilled out of his companion played over and over in Adam's mind. He kept his eyes closed as the water poured over his body; the thundering in his ears was not loud enough to silence what he knew Brandon could sound like.

If Adam didn't look at what his hand was now doing in the rush of water, didn't listen to the way his own breath hitched with every wet stroke, it would be as if it wasn't happening.

CHAPTER SIX

"Help them feel you are interested in their good. As they feel greater trust in you, they will feel greater confidence in what you teach them ... building a relationship of trust must be a constant concern." ~ (Missionary Handbook, Second Discussion)

"Humbly kneeling, sweet appealing - 'Twas the boy's first uttered prayer - when the powers of sin assailing filled his soul with deep despair; but undaunted, still he trusted in his Heavenly Father's care. But undaunted, still he trusted in his Heavenly Father's care." Joseph Smith's First Prayer, LDS Hymnal p. 26, Text: George Manwaring, 1854-1889

From then on, Adam no longer shied away from his companion, no longer avoided contact or allowed a moment's guilt for wanting it so much. When they rode on the bus, Adam would find a cramped corner so they would be smashed in together. To get his comp's attention, he would bump shoulders or squeeze Christensen's biceps instead of saying his name. It was as if a floodgate had opened, and he wanted more: more interaction, more of Christensen's attention. Christensen didn't seem to mind, either. In fact, something relaxed even more in Christensen, as if he'd held himself back from being as affectionate as he'd wanted to be, as if he'd been waiting for a signal from Adam.

If he was honest with himself, Adam would be forced to admit that he was trying to encourage more physical contact. He craved it; it just... it *felt* good, being touched, having someone not shy away from wanting to touch him, having someone seek *him* out. It was okay to want to feel good, wasn't it? Okay to want companionship and camaraderie with others? With his companion? It was the two of them against the world, after all. They were supposed to be close.

That was how the other guys treated each other. Adam no longer held himself back. It was thrilling, in a way, to be doing something he'd never allowed himself. Was this how other people lived every day? With joy and ease and camaraderie? He could have laughed at how stupid he'd been, how he'd interpreted every lesson, every raised eyebrow from his parents, as proof he, Adam, wasn't worthy of any form of companionship.

He *was*. And Christensen seemed pleased that Adam had finally dropped the barrier between them, allowing them to grow even closer.

When they knelt for their evening prayers, it was usually at their small sofa in the main room. Adam didn't know what came over him shortly after that P-Day, but, instead of kneeling at the sofa, he continued on into their bedroom and knelt at the foot of Christensen's bed.

"You that tired, then?" Christensen asked. "Just gonna roll over to your bed? Lazy."

Adam laughed softly. "Um, is this okay?"

"Oh, sure," Christensen said genially, dropping to his knees. Adam shifted on the pretense of adjusting his weight and pressed against his companion thigh to thigh.

"Your turn," he said softly, smiling when Christensen took a deep breath and nodded jerkily. His elbow brushed against Adam's on the bedding as he folded his arms and began to pray.

"Heavenly Father, we thank Thee for this day..."

After that night, they often prayed together in that manner. Sometimes they said their own prayers in their minds; other times they shared turns praying aloud. One such night, Adam had a flash to some unknown future where he and his eternal mate would do this very thing, share their intimate wishes and thoughts with each other and their God, and his heart ached.

He hadn't envisioned a woman.

No, the person he pictured bore a striking resemblance to his mission companion. His heart ached because he could never, ever have that in the Mormon Church. It devastated him to think about the bleak future awaiting him. As Christensen's soft voice continued with their prayer, "Help us always to spend our strength in serving Thee..." Adam jolted back to now, to what he was being granted *now*, this fleeting but momentarily perfect life with his mission companion.

"Amen."

Adam lingered at Christensen's bedside, with their legs touching, unwilling to move and unsure of what he expected to happen if he didn't. He told himself, You're waiting for the Spirit to enter your heart. He awaited a sign that could guide him, maybe reveal some insight into what this all meant and why he couldn't help but picture the wrong person with whom he'd spend an eternity. That's all he was doing: holding still, waiting, feeling strangely at peace with whom the Lord saw fit to match him here in Barcelona, though a deeper part of him wanted more.

He remembered a letter the prophet Joseph Smith had written about one of his dear friends, how the prophet had said that it was "pleasing for friends to lie down together, locked in the arms of love, to sleep and wake in each other's embrace."

As soon as the image of being held in Christensen's arms flashed across his mind, he realized that wasn't exactly fitting the definition of a "godly" relationship, that this wasn't the way he was supposed to behave. His face grew hot as he quickly got up and into his own bed, then switching off his bedside lamp.

"Um, g'night," he murmured.

"Goodnight, Adam."

His eyes closed at the use of his first name instead of the formal and expected "Elder," or just "Young" as all the others called him, or the casual "dude" or "man" that Christensen usually used. Strange that his own name could sound so intimate. He bit his lip, flipped over to face the wall, and punched his fist into his pillow to get it into the right shape. Why was he thinking about this? Why couldn't he stop? Why couldn't he be satisfied with the life mapped out for him by his parents and the Church? He forced himself to take a deep breath in and let it out slowly. A half-formed thought kept darting to the surface of his consciousness, but would slip away before he could grab it and throttle it to death.

He woke after a few hours of fitful sleep to a painful erection. He couldn't think of a single hymn, a single scripture, to drive away the carnal thoughts filling his mind. The room was dark, but an outside light gave just enough light for him to make out Christensen's face; he seemed to be sound asleep. All the other guys did… it, he thought, and they'd gotten their mission calls. They even went through the temple. The Lord had allowed it. Maybe… maybe the Lord doesn't really care as much as they say He does.

Nothing had happened to him after that indiscretion in the shower. He'd been telling himself that it was just a by-product of thoroughly cleaning himself. Of course, he hadn't *intended* to do anything. It just happened. Like waking up to messy sheets and pajamas. This, however, this would be intentional. And again he told himself: The others do this; Brandon does it.

Feeling exceptionally bold, Adam kicked the thin sheet off his overheated body, let out a shaky breath and slipped his hand under his pajama bottoms, cupping himself through the silky fabric of his sacred undergarments. He wasn't ready to touch his actual skin, not with his companion in the same room. If he just did this much, it was like… scratching an itch through a shirtsleeve, not… not—

Christensen shifted in his bed, threw one arm up over his head and breathed deeply. Adam's heart skipped a few beats, but Christensen was only moving in his sleep, that was all.

Barely exhaling, Adam drew the pads of his fingertips over the satin fabric with jerky, tentative movements, tracing his hard length. He wasn't quite sure what to do, not just to himself physically but what mental gymnastics he could perform to allow this to happen. He forced himself to breathe slowly. It was just his body, after all; he could touch his own body. That was okay. He held himself in the palm of his hand; the garments made a protective barrier so his flesh wasn't touched. He kept telling himself that would make it all right. As long as he didn't actually *touch* himself he wasn't doing anything wrong. He curled up on his side to hide his body's movements in case Christensen woke up and kept his eyes on his companion as a precaution.

At first he just held himself; the tight grip on that most intimate part of himself was satisfying in its own way. His pulse, aching and bone-deep, beat between his legs and against his palm. His thumb slipped over the rounded crown where a growing wet spot soaked the fabric of his garments. Rubbing a circle over it felt so shockingly good it made his eyes close. His breath stuttered out, and he barely bit back a moan. He could *not* make any noise.

He focused on Brandon's sleeping face and continued to stroke himself over the slippery fabric, squeezed himself at the base only to stroke upward, circled his thumb at the top, worked the moisture gathering there into the material, where he could feel it spread. Adam's eyes had adjusted to the dark, and he noticed every feature on his companion's face, reveled in the freedom to look his fill for once, to take in his companion's imposing frame while asleep.

Brandon slept with his mouth slightly parted. Adam stared at the lush curve of Brandon's full lower lip, at the strong, square line of his jaw, at the long, dark eyelashes resting on his cheek. Adam had to urge to touch them; he wondered what they would feel like if Brandon came close enough to have them brush against Adam's cheek. He turned his face into his pillow and let out a tiny sigh; he ached between his legs and in his chest and wanted so, so much.

Tugging his pajama bottom down to his thighs, he then slipped his hand through the opening in the front of his garments and touched himself fully. He bit his lip to keep a groan at bay—how good it felt to hold himself, how his hips were shifting forward. He was driving himself almost mindlessly through his own hand. It was natural, wasn't it? Wasn't his body doing what it was created to do?

He bit the edge of his pillow and looked across the room once more. Christensen slept only in his garments—he didn't wear pajamas over them as Adam did—and the blankets had shifted, exposing Brandon's white-clad shoulders and chest, stark against his darker skin tone. Adam's hand moved faster; his left hand gripped his thigh through the silky fabric. He bit his lower lip as the unfamiliar sensation of sexual gratification built. The front neckline of Brandon's garments scooped low enough to show the hair on his chest. Through the thin, flimsy material of his garments, Adam could make out the dark circle of Brandon's nipple and had the powerful urge to bite it, put his mouth to it, suck at it through the slippery fabric. He knew the holy marks stitched into the material would frame it perfectly under his tongue.

An unstoppable pressure was building up. Helplessly, he bucked into his loosened fist and looked down in shock at his obscene and unfamiliar and fascinating body. Just before his climax, he glanced up once again at Brandon's sleeping face… Brandon wasn't sleeping anymore.

Brandon's brown eyes stared right back into Adam's blue gaze, and the intensity in his companion's face had Adam climaxing with a jerk and a shudder. Sickening shame flooded him at the grunt he couldn't help but make. As his body's spasms came to a stop, cold sweat broke out all over his body. His lip wobbled, heck, his *hands* were trembling, still holding himself under the fabric now wet with his own come. He'd been caught. He'd been caught doing *that* and by his mission companion. He could be sent *home* for this. He would be disfellowshipped, he was sure. And, everyone would know what he'd been doing.

Everyone would probably guess whom he'd been thinking about *while doing it.*

Brandon didn't move. But then, he also didn't stop looking right at Adam's face. "Hey."

Adam swallowed, willing his voice to work. He wanted to cry. "Hey."

"I was beginning to think you were a machine, or something."

"W-what?"

"I don't know, just, you never did that before that I could tell. You take showers like you're in the Army, too, in and out in less than five minutes. I just... thought that was kinda crazy."

Adam grabbed a few tissues off the dresser jammed between their beds to clean himself up, tugged his pajamas up over his stained garments roughly, stared up at the ceiling and wished he could disappear.

"Are you okay?" Brandon asked, his voice soft and filled with concern. It somehow made this all worse, as if he thought Adam was on the brink of becoming hysterical. "I didn't mean to embarrass you or anything," Brandon continued. "I thought you said you have older brothers?"

"What does that have to do with anything?"

Brandon sat up, propping himself up with one hand. "Are you telling me that you've never busted in on one of them by accident, or been woken up by them doing it, or had one of them bust in on you?"

"Of course not! We don't— I certainly don't... I mean, you're not even supposed to—" Adam groaned and threw an arm over his face, keeping it covered when he heard bed springs creak, signaling that Brandon had gotten out of bed. A weight settled next to his hip, shifting his body into it.

"Adam."

He sighed in exasperation and humiliation. "What?"

"Adam. It's okay."

"Can we not talk about this? Can we just go back to bed?"

Every nerve in his body tingled as Brandon laid a hand on his hip; his thumb casually rested on the crease between Adam's thigh and hip.

"Hey. Hey, Adam, it's not a big deal. Really. It's not to me, I mean. I don't mind. I mean, I don't care."

Adam pulled his arm from where it covered his eyes. Brandon's face showed concern, but there was something else, too. He told himself it was just sleep; his companion looked sleepy. Something in that look made Adam's insides writhe; it was something he'd hoped he'd been seeing in Brandon's face for a while now, something that had begun in the reflection of the mirror when they'd cut each other's hair. Maybe even before that.

"But we're not supposed…" he trailed off weakly. Brandon's thumb made small circles on Adam's hip bone, and it was as if every nerve ending in his body was connected to that one spot.

"Yeah, well, it's easier to ask for forgiveness than permission, right?" It was the standard Mormon joke, pulled out for every occasion from silly infractions like drinking caffeine to, Adam knew, grave sins some of his teammates had committed with girls.

"I don't think you need to, though," Brandon said, startling Adam out of his spiraling thoughts.

"Don't what?"

"Ask forgiveness. It's totally normal. You," he said squeezing Adam's hip before pushing back to his feet, "you are total normal. Okay?"

Adam nodded, staring up at the darkened ceiling.

"Look, I know some of the leaders get really strict about that," Brandon said. "My dad always told us boys that it was actually healthy to do it, gave us medical studies and everything as proof. I know the *Handbook* says it's a sin, but… I really don't think it is. If your body does it on its own, you know? How sinful can *that* be? I… I think the leaders got that one wrong."

Adam didn't know what to think. He bounced between mortification and guilt, worried that he was choosing to believe it wasn't a grave sin because he didn't *want* it to be. That wasn't how sin worked. Also, the idea that the leaders had made an error left him shaky. If they'd gotten *that* wrong, at what else had they erred? He remembered a conversation weeks before when Brandon had wondered the same thing: "Why does God seem to change His mind so much?"

Brandon settled back into his bed with a whispered, "Don't worry about it. It's okay. Goodnight."

For a long time, Adam lay wondering what could have happened if he'd caught Brandon's hand and held it, had kept him there. It was better to think about that than to consider what the Church could have gotten wrong.

———•———

THE NEXT MORNING WAS JUST like every other morning. The sky didn't fall, the Mission President didn't call to tell Adam to pack his things for a dishonorable discharge and the world apparently kept on turning, even though Adam Young had dirty thoughts and, yes, deeds, while serving a mission.

After they dressed and ate, Brandon leaned back in his chair and said, "Let's do something different today."

Adam stared at him, gaping. "But…"

"Nope. I think you're about to freak out on me, so as your trainer," he said, grinning obnoxiously, "I'm making the call that we walk down by the beach. It's cloudy, and it's Wednesday. No one will be there, so you don't have to worry about seeing boobs."

"I'm not worried about that," Adam said, huffing out a laugh.

"I know, just joshing you. Still. I think a break—just an hour or so, okay?—but I think a break will be good for you."

They went to Llevant Beach, the closest beach to their apartment. Brandon was right; few people were there midweek when the weather wasn't warm and sunny, as could happen mid-spring. A mother had brought two little boys, who were kicking around a soccer ball and shrieking and having fun on the expansive, pebble-strewn beach, obviously trying to keep the ball away from the water's edge. An older woman walked a dog, the kind that Adam's father called a "Heinz-57" because it showed qualities of so many different breeds. The woman threw a wet, sandy tennis ball, which her black and brown dog caught, then dropped at her feet with a bark and tail wag until, with a tool, she scooped it up and flung it far down the beach. The dog's tongue lolled happily as it raced back and forth; it cut deep channels in the sand as it skidded to make the catch.

They walked along the promenade, quietly taking in the steady sounds of the ocean waves and the dog barking happily every time its owner praised it. The two children with their mother began begging and pointing at one of the many open-air cafes farther up the beach near the hotels that dotted the shore, the air heavy with their varied aromas. The small family packed their things and left.

A brisk, ocean breeze blew in, momentarily ridding the air of grease and spice. Adam could almost pretend he was down near the Salt Flats the way the Pyrenees Mountains ringed the vista in the distance—if not for the steady movement of the water... well, except for the palm trees... and the bougainvilleas whose dazzlingly rich pink color lined the walk.

Brandon stopped to lean against the safety rail where the promenade met the beach; he smiled and laughed softly when the dog became distracted by some seagulls.

"Is that like your dog?" Adam asked, nodding his chin at it.

"Oh, no. Sally was a German shepherd. That dog there is probably half her size. Who knows what kind of dog that is... Looks like a terrier mix. Cute though." He laughed again when the dog feinted down on its front legs with its tail high and wagging as if it thought it could get the seagulls to play with it.

Brandon cleared his throat. "I don't want to belabor the point. I promise this will be the only time I bring it up."

Adam felt a chill run down his spine.

"But I've noticed that you get really... intense about things. And I don't mean it's a bad thing," he rushed, chancing a look at Adam, who resolutely kept his eyes forward, watching the dog race back and forth. "It's not. And I get it, why you're like that. Maybe more than you realize..." He hesitated, then shifted his feet and dropped his weight onto his elbows while keeping his eyes on the water. "I'm worried about you, Adam. I'm afraid you're going to burn out if you keep going so hardcore."

"I don't… I'm not *trying* to be weird about—"

"Adam, stop." Brandon gripped Adam's forearm, giving it a squeeze. "You're not being weird. But I want you to think about this. We're taught to have perfect obedience, right?"

"Right," Adam replied, his stomach sinking.

"Stop that. I'm not getting on to you, for crying out…" Brandon closed his eyes as if gathering up strength. "Listen to me, okay?"

Adam nodded.

"What have you always heard as an answer when anyone challenges the Church or its leaders?"

Adam didn't respond.

"That they're not perfect." Brandon pressed on. "They're just men. They made mistakes and said and *did* stuff, some things that we don't agree with anymore. They're *not perfect* and neither are you."

"Yeah, but we're supposed to… I'm supposed to be better. I *know* better, so I'm supposed to *be* better."

Brandon sighed. "Yeah. I know. I've been to that Fireside, heard that lecture, too. There is no try. Do or do not."

Adam couldn't help but laugh at the abysmal Yoda impression.

"There he is," Brandon said, chucking Adam on the arm. "No one is perfect. No one. You have to quit being so hard on yourself, Adam. It's eating you up."

Adam slumped against the barrier. His weight was heavy on his forearms where they pressed into the railing.

"You know, you got here that first day and looked scared half to death."

Adam snorted. "That's because I was."

"Yeah, I know." Brandon watched the woman with the dog, then continued. "I meant what I said. You're normal. It's normal. I trust what my dad said on this one." He chewed on his bottom lip, then dropped his hand on Adam's, holding it firmly. "Just... Dude. Don't make a mountain out of a molehill, you know?"

And suddenly, Adam couldn't take it. His eyes stung with the hot itch of unshed tears, and his stomach lurched as he wrenched his hand away because it *was* a mountain. It was insurmountable, this wrong, abnormal thing in him, all the questioning and sinful thoughts, this overwhelming need for something indefinable from Brandon, and all of this happening at the worst time possible.

He could barely find the breath to gasp out, "There's something about... I'm not right. There's something wrong about me, okay?"

"Hey, no," Brandon said, stepping in front of Adam as if sensing Adam was two seconds away from taking off. "No, there's not."

Adam nodded, eyes cast down, because there was. He couldn't look in Brandon's face, sure that Brandon would see, would *know* how much Adam wanted him, wanted something he could never have, something he wasn't even supposed to *want*.

"Adam." Brandon pinched Adam's tie-tack—Moroni with his trumpet calling forth the Saints, the golden symbol on every temple— between his finger, then gave Adam's tie a tug. "There isn't. I get it, okay? I think I know what you're trying to tell me." Brandon held Adam's shoulders and dipped down to catch Adam's gaze. "Feeling... feeling that way isn't wrong, okay?"

Adam was struck mute with horror. Brandon knew? Brandon knew that Adam had... well, the Church called it same-sex— He couldn't finish thinking it. A man was his thoughts.

"Feeling it is like thinking it, and that's the same as acting on it, and I *know* that *that* is wrong."

"Well— Not... Dude, you need to breathe." Brandon clutched Adam's shoulders. "Hey, whoa."

Adam thought his legs might give out. So close to saying it, he was so close to actually saying it...

"Adam. *Adam.* Seriously, are you okay? You're freaking me out, here."

Brandon made to put his arm around Adam, but Adam pushed put of Brandon's grip and scrubbed a hand in frustration over his chest, wishing his lungs would work properly. He wanted to disappear, to walk into the ocean and cease to be.

"Look. Why don't you let me buy you an ice cream? There's a stand right up the beach." After a moment, Brandon nudged Adam, who was now taking shuddery breaths, and cajoled, "Come on. My treat." His voice softer, he pleaded, "Please, Adam. Let me."

Brandon wasn't leaving. He wasn't saying they needed to pray about it. He wasn't even hinting that they needed to call President Jensen. Adam looked into his companion's face and found only worry, not disgust or anger.

"Yeah, all right."

"You can get an extra scoop and everything," Brandon said, slinging his arm around Adam's neck before genially pushing him on. If Brandon knew, if he suspected Adam had those thoughts about him and didn't mind touching Adam, could bear it... Maybe this could still work out. Maybe he could figure out how to fix himself and manage to keep Brandon as a friend.

They didn't speak after that, except to order their ice cream, and settled at a cafe table at the sand's edge where they could watch the water, calm at this time of the day.

Brandon scooped the last bite from his paper cup and stared into its emptiness. "So," he said, clearing his throat. "That, uh, problem you think you have?"

Adam didn't respond. A painful lump lodged in his throat and threatened to choke him.

"Um. So, yeah. Me, too." Brandon dropped the cup on the table with a sigh and looked up; his expression was resolute. "But you figured that out, didn't you?"

Adam stared back; his palms bloomed with sweat. Brandon meant the masturbation thing. It couldn't be... There was no way that Adam's companion was like him like that. Adam was confused, that was all.

"And that means," Brandon said as he grabbed Adam's empty container, "if you're wrong, then I guess I am, too. But the thing is?" He tossed the trash into the receptacle and stood. "I don't think I am. I don't think you are, either."

He stood there, the picture of calm, with his handsome, boyish face shining in the midday sun. "Well, that's the cat out of the bag. Ready to go talk to the masses about Jesus Christ?"

"N-no?"

Brandon's body rocked with laughter. "Me, neither. But we should. We're supposed to. Story of our life, huh?"

Adam watched the water, then said, "Your dad really said it's okay?"

"My dad? I don't think he—" Brandon shook his head, then his confused expression cleared. "Oh. Right. You mean about the... He always told us it was totally normal and not to worry too much about it."

The thing was, Brandon's parents were devout. His dad was Stake President in California. His mom had been the Relief Society President. They were active and seemed to really know their stuff. All of Brandon's family was active, all of his older siblings had served on missions, too. Wouldn't they know?

"Ready?" Brandon asked holding out Adam's messenger bag.

Adam took it and was immediately pulled into a tight hug. Brandon pressed his mouth right by Adam's ear and said fervently, "You're okay, Adam. It's okay."

Adam shivered, trembling in Brandon's hold, until finally he nodded. Brandon held him tighter. Adam responded by sagging into his companion's arms, giving in to the sensation of safety and momentary acceptance. After a while, Brandon pulled away and cupped a hand behind Adam's neck.

"Okay?"

Closing his eyes and nodding, Adam allowed himself to grip Brandon's jacket lapels to hold him in place a little longer. Brandon squeezed his hands and said in a low tone, "Come on. Let's get going, huh?"

Adam nodded and followed.

They wandered the city. They helped a young mother jostling her grocery sacks and small child cross the street safely, but she turned out not to be interested in speaking with them about her eternal future. Some middle school-aged kids asked them who they were and what their name tags were about ("Are you American government employees?") until a teacher shooed them back to the school.

All afternoon, Christensen seemed to want to say something, but stopped. He didn't stop leaning against Adam when they sat down to give their feet a break, nor did he shy away from the little touches he usually doled out to Adam and the other elders: a hand to the shoulder or back, fist bumps, and once, holding Adam's hand when Adam sighed heavily.

"We'll keep trying. Don't give up."

Adam could only nod. His tongue had tied itself into knots at the sight of his hand held in Brandon's while they walked the city streets.

Each seemed to be lost in his own thoughts, even through dinner. They didn't share space as they usually did for evening prayers. Adam needed the privacy, begging Heavenly Father to take these sinful thoughts from him, or if they weren't sinful, to help him understand why he hadn't been able to gain control and master his body.

When he finished with an "amen," he couldn't help but glance across the darkened room at his companion, still kneeling, still praying. He couldn't help how much he wanted to join him, hold him, lie next to him and connect not only on a physical level, but on a spiritual one as well, even more than they already had. He couldn't fight back frustration he felt when he imagined what he was supposed to want—a wife, a temple marriage, an eternal companion—with what he truly did: Brandon. He covered his face, pressing his bicep into his eyes so hard that stars swam behind his eyelids.

"Adam."

Adam couldn't help the pained whimper that slipped out. He could hear Brandon shifting on his side of the room.

"This is what you can't keep doing," Brandon said. "You've got to stop beating yourself up for being human."

"It's not that," Adam said, moving his arm so he could clench the bedding near his hip. "I can't stop thinking—" He shut that down. He'd almost told Brandon that he couldn't stop thinking of *him*.

Brandon crossed the room in two steps and sank down on Adam's bed near his hip so his leg pressed against Adam's hand. Silk and leg hair brushed along the backs of Adam's fingers. He moved his hand in the tiniest of motions to feel the dichotomy of the two more fully and pinched his fingers together to trap a few hairs from just above Brandon's knee. He wished he was bold enough to slide his hand under the fabric and feel the hot, solid heat of Brandon's body against the palm of his hand. Brandon's breathing stuttered. Adam stilled his hand, but before he could pull it away, Brandon pressed his leg more fully into it, sagging his body closer.

"You know I do it, don't you." Brandon made it a statement, not a question.

Adam didn't say anything. His pulse raced, and his breath came short. His fingers gave an involuntary twitch, and, when Brandon didn't move away, Adam allowed himself to draw the back of his index finger in a slow arc along the bared skin of Brandon's thigh. His eyes closed.

"Adam…" Brandon sighed. "I—I'm pretty sure you've watched, listened to me do it to myself, at least." His gaze darted away, cheeks flushed with color. "You can't help it. I mean, I can't seem to help it, that is. Touching myself." Brandon took a deep breath and seemed to make a decision. He looked back at Adam and tentatively traced the waistband of Adam's pajamas at his hip. "You know, I didn't have this problem before."

Adam's head was in a fog. Brandon leaned closer; his fingers made small circles into the exposed thick diagonal muscle at Adam's hip. Adam tried to form a coherent thought and asked, "Before? Before w-what?"

"Well…" Brandon paused, a sheepish grin on his face. "Before you." Brandon's other hand came to rest on his knee, mere centimeters from where Adam still lightly caressed Brandon's thigh with the backs of his fingers. "I tried to get you to understand before, but…" He took a deep breath. "You're like me, aren't you?"

"Yeah, I— Well, not really. You're a better man than I'll ever be."

"No, but, how can you even say that?" Brandon asked, his head tilted. "I've just… I've been thinking about some of this stuff longer. But I didn't mean any of that. I meant like me the other way. I had a, um, a problem before I left for my mission. Problem," he snorted. "That's what my Elder's Quorum Second Councilor called it when I confessed some thoughts I'd had. And he was the one who first—" Brandon hung his head and sighed, "Never mind," and leaned forward to stand up.

Adam shot his hand out and grabbed Brandon's, pulled him back down and was pleased when Brandon shifted to lean closer against Adam's bent leg. The long, hard line of his body was solid and comforting.

"You… you don't have to go. I want to know." Adam shifted to his side and almost curled around Brandon. "What happened?"

Brandon picked at the edge of Adam's bed sheet. "We got… close, you know? Said that he was sorry, that we didn't need to have a court since nothing really happened beyond us becoming 'closer brethren.'"

Adam was thunderstruck. Did that mean Brandon and…? "Did you… with him? Do stuff?"

"No!" Brandon cried. "No, nothing." He flushed completely and looked away. "Oh, my gosh, this is so embarrassing. It sounds so dumb."

"Brandon. You can tell me. I'm not going to judge you, are you kidding?"

With a heavy sigh, Brandon finally answered, "We, you know, cuddled. Uh… to completion."

Adam's heart raced. "How old were you?"

"Eighteen. Almost nineteen. Before I got my call."

"Did you have—"

"We had our clothes on the whole time!"

"No, I don't mean that." Adam glanced at the two of them, practically naked but for their G's. "Did you have feelings for him?"

He looked deeply into Adam's eyes. "I thought I did."

"What, um, what do you think now?"

Brandon shook his head. "That was just, you know, hormones."

Was this just hormones? Adam took in the nervous way Brandon continued to pick at the bed sheet and thought about how he good it was to be in Brandon's company, how safe he felt, how he trusted Brandon not only with his doubts and questions, but with this secret he hadn't trusted himself with. It was like reaching out in slow-motion, his hand coming down, down over Brandon's, stilling its nervous plucking. Brandon let out a tiny breath and turned his hand over, entwining their fingers.

"Did, do you remember me mentioning that men were sealed in the temple to other men in the early days of the Church?" Brandon asked, his voice low. Adam nodded his head. "Sometimes... men were able to express their love for other men back then. After Cooley—that's the guy from my Elder's Quorum who I got 'close' to. After him, I did a lot of looking into stuff to try and understand what was going on with me. Books and websites and stuff, and they were written by members, mostly. Journal of Discourses, other stuff."

A huge weight lifted from Adam's chest even as his heart rate jumped to an alarming speed. He thought he was the only one who had wondered about that historical temple quirk, had wondered if men being sealed to each other—the way married couples were sealed to one another—meant what he had never been able to let himself imagine, a possible future for himself where he could feel happy and complete, too.

"I— Yeah. I did know that about the temple. But I didn't think it was so they could..." Adam couldn't look in Brandon's face and finish that sentence.

"It was mostly an apprenticeship thing, a kind of adoption situation. It wasn't... gay marriage." He cleared his throat. "But I think, because of some of the letters I've seen, that there may have been some for who it was just that. They could use it to like, hide out in the open, you know? And if the Church brought it back, then guys like us..." Brandon's voice fell to a whisper. The darkness of their shared bedroom was a protective bubble. It was almost as if Brandon's voice was quiet in order to maintain the illusion, keeping this just between them, as if not even God could hear them. The thought of God not knowing Adam's thoughts and feelings was a huge relief.

"It wasn't like, like love for all of them, of course," Brandon continued, his fingertips drawing along the length of Adam's hand, over his palm and up to each pad in a soft caress that made Adam's hand spasm, made him want to reach out and clutch Brandon's hand and press it to feel how fast Adam's heart was beating. "But yeah. For a few of them, because the rite existed, it was that, it was... They wanted to be together. My great-great grand uncle was sealed for time and all eternity to Joseph Smith in the Nauvoo Temple, actually. For him I know it was supposed to be just like a wife. That's what he wanted it to be like. I found some letters he'd written at my grandmother's. He never married a woman. Didn't want to."

Adam struggled to align this information with everything he'd been told to believe. They were teetering on the edge of a huge crevasse, trying to cobble together a safety net using the gospel they'd studied so fervently and in which they'd invested their lives. He shifted and rested an arm on his own knee; his index finger brushed the edge of Brandon's garment on his upper arm. Brandon began to worry a new place on Adam's bed sheet, a place closer to Adam's waist. Every little shift brought them closer to each other, to something bigger than just this moment.

Adam closed his eyes, confused by how much hope was building. Everything he'd ever been taught told him that what was happening was wrong, what he was feeling, what he was *wanting* was *wrong*. Men weren't supposed to... *He* wasn't supposed to want this, any of it.

Brandon's warm hand on his leg broke through his chaotic thoughts, making everything clear.

Brandon exhaled softly, saying, "It's in the Bible, you know. 'The soul of Jonathan was knit with the soul of David, and Jonathan loved him.'"

Adam could see the page in the Old Testament book, 1 Samuel, as if it was lying right there in front of him. It was scripture—that had to make it okay, because what he felt, this tenderness and affection for such a good man was just what was in that Bible verse.

He opened his eyes. He took Brandon's hand in his, finally daring to look into his companion's face. With a sigh, Brandon brought their foreheads together and ran his hand through Adam's close-cropped hair.

Adam barely breathed. Every nerve-ending was alight where Brandon was touching him, but he managed to say, "It can't be wrong, Brandon, not when it feels like this. Even Joseph—"

Brandon rested his lips on the edge of Adam's mouth and whispered, "It can't be wrong. It's, it's not. The scriptures even say, 'Then Jonathan and David made a covenant, because he loved him as his own soul. And Jonathan stripped himself of the robe that was upon him.'"

Adam held Brandon's face; his thumbs traced the hard edge of Brandon's jawline. His heart beat wildly. His voice quiet and choked with emotion, he quoted back, "'And David arose, bowed three times and they... they kissed one another.'"

Their lips met in a chaste, simple press. They held each other, mouths barely touching. Brandon ran his hands up the silky fabric to hold Adam's body more fully against his, and the intimacy of it broke whatever dam was left in Adam. It had to be right, these feelings he had, this need and desire, because it was for *Brandon*. With a low noise, Adam nuzzled Brandon's cheek before bringing their mouths together more intimately. They each pulled on the other, embracing more fully. Adam didn't know what he was doing, but instinct took over. He slanted his head to deepen to kiss, needing more and unable to stop the low moans buzzing in his throat when he felt Brandon's tongue tracing the seam of his mouth.

Brandon's wide and strong hands clutched at Adam's back and slipped lower until they grabbed the hem of Adam's pajama top and garments in an attempt to pull them up and over. Adam stopped him, however, by leaning back, breaking their kiss.

"I... I can't." Adam looked down, couldn't quite meet Brandon's eyes. Brandon shifted on his knees, and Adam could see how hard he was, how much he wanted this, wanted *him*. Adam wanted it too, but... Maybe... He bit his lip, already tender and a little swollen, and said, "It's just, I can't take them off yet. I'm not ready for that. But... here." He pulled his pajama top off, feeling naked in just his garments. Brandon cupped the back of Adam's head and drew him back to his mouth for a more languid kiss.

"It's okay. It's okay. I don't mind. I get it, I do. I just feel greedy, I guess."

Adam had never felt more whole nor more afraid. Brandon's hands slipped under the silky fabric, "I want to feel you against me, though." He moaned when Adam shivered. They positioned themselves on the narrow twin bed so that they wouldn't crush each other.

"Can you just take the bottoms off? Not your G's but the other?" Brandon whispered into his ear. Brandon teeth dragged lightly over Adam's earlobe and sent shudders down his body.

He tugged the cotton fabric down. Brandon assisted by kicking the pajamas off Adam's feet and to the floor. The white of their garments stood out in the night's darkness as if they were illuminated. Instead of feeling exposed, Adam felt private and wonderful as Brandon's hand drew across Adam's hip bone and grazed the edge of his body where it pushed through the opening of his garments. He couldn't resist the urge to thrust upward to feel more of that friction.

This was okay. No, this was more than that. It was wonderful and good, and all good things were a sign of God's love for His children. That lesson had appeared over and over in Adam's life, and he'd been told to train his eyes and his spirit to look for moments of goodness, to seek them out. Well, this was maybe the best, the most fulfilling moment of his life yet, the most complete he'd ever felt.

As Brandon nuzzled his neck, Adam breathed hotly into his ear, "'Let me not be ashamed, O Lord; for I have called upon thee. Into thy hand I commit my spirit.'"

"Spirit, huh?" Brandon bit his earlobe and dragged the pads of his fingertips up and down Adam's length, quoting back with barely contained joyful laughter, "'For day and night thy hand was heavy upon me; my moisture is turned into the drought of summer.'"

Adam laughed quietly and pushed Brandon's chest with one hand. Brandon held it in place for a moment, his smile mischievous and happy, then dashed into the bathroom and brought a bottle of lotion. He grinned and, after climbing back into bed alongside Adam, asked, "Still with me? With this? Tell me no; if not, it's okay."

Mind swirling, Adam nodded. "Yeah. Yeah, I'm still with you."

When Brandon took Adam firmly in hand, Adam's entire body trembled. Dragging the tip of his nose along Adam's hairline, Brandon said softly, "'O taste and see that which is good.'" Brandon traced the barest edge of his mouth against Adam's before dipping in with his tongue and kissing him languidly.

Adam groaned and lay back against the pillows when Brandon broke away from their kiss. "Oh my gosh…" It had felt so good, touching himself in the quiet dark, but this… This was something he couldn't describe: the feel of someone he cared for so much holding him, touching him so intimately, *wanting* him.

Brandon stopped to squeeze lotion into his palm. Adam lightly ran his hand up Brandon's taut flanks. His head was spinning, and this all seemed a dream. Everything was coming together in the most amazing sensations his body had ever known, yet it still felt spiritual, otherworldly. All his life he'd been taught that bodies coming together was something holy, sacred, that it meant something much more than simple physical pleasure. Everything happening now was proof that that was so wonderfully, joyously true.

He'd never felt more like himself, and because he'd been trained to look for answers in God's word in everything he did, he couldn't help but recall certain scriptures that had meant so much to him. He felt wild with want and desire and sheer happiness, and it was strange that he wanted to laugh as much as moan when Brandon touched him like that, wasn't it?

Brandon must have sensed Adam's manic thoughts, because he stopped with his hands resting on the tops of his own thighs. "Adam? Should I stop? I will if you need me to."

Adam hooked a leg around Brandon's waist and grinned. "Stop? 'O continue thy loving kindness unto them that know thee.'"

Brandon laughed, ducking his head. He glanced at Adam from under his thick eyelashes, and Adam's breath was taken away once more. As Adam looked his fill, Brandon was clearly aware of how transfixed Adam was. Smirking, Brandon took himself in hand and jutted his hips forward. "'Behold the perfect man, and behold the upright.' For lo, it is mighty."

Adam's face blazed red even as he laughed out loud.

Brandon continued his ministrations and punctuated each sentence with a wet and deep kiss. "'My loins are filled...'" He gasped against Adam's mouth when his knuckles brushed against Adam's belly. "'Lord, all my desire is before thee and my groaning is not hid from thee.' Oh, my gosh, Adam, I just need to touch you, please?" He collapsed to his side, taking Adam back in hand with a cut-off moan.

Adam stopped his thrusting into Brandon's hot grip, opened his eyes, and finally allowed himself to touch Brandon in the same way. He circled his hand around Brandon's girth and marveled at the silken weight of it in his palm. "Oh, my gosh... You feel so good." It was probably so stupid and obvious, but Brandon didn't seem to care what Adam said, given the gasps each stroke of Adam's hand pulled from him. Adam almost wanted to stop, wanted to throw his arms around Brandon's shoulders and just *hold* him, hold this feeling still just long enough to help control how fast his heart beat, how tremendous his need was.

"'M-my heart was hot within me.'" He quoted back, trusting other people's words more than his own. "'While I was musing the fire burned; then I spake with my tongue.'"

With a delicate, almost tentative, lick, he traced Brandon's mouth before kissing him; their hands struggled to find a rhythm they could both maintain. Panting, Brandon broke away and dropped his forehead against Adam's neck. "I want to do more than just this with you. I want to do everything. I know that's... a lot. I wanted you to know."

Adam closed his eyes, stilling his hand as unbidden memories of incessant lectures on self-control flooded his mind. "Oh, Brandon, we can't. Not, not yet. Maybe not at all? I don't know. I just... This is a lot already. Isn't this good, though? Am I not—"

Brandon's warm hand caressed his face and quickly drove out all other thoughts. The exhilaration he felt now superseded any sense of right or wrong that might have lingered.

Brandon kissed a trail from Adam's ear to his collarbone. "I know, I know. And you are. You're..." He kissed the tip of Adam's chin. "It's fine, really. Better than fine, honestly. It's just that we're finally doing this, and I don't want to stop. Come here." Brandon shifted, then pulled Adam on top of him. "Rest your head on my shoulder?"

Adam straddled him, bracing his weight on his elbows next to Brandon's head and taking the time to look to his heart's content. Brandon, fingers entwined and slick with lotion, wrapped them around them both. Adam had to bite down on Brandon's shoulder to stifle his broken moans as the slippery feel of Brandon's palm worked in tandem against Adam's. A roaring built in his ears as Brandon made the same quiet noises Adam had heard so many times in the middle of the night, until Brandon moaned quietly, his body trembling. The roaring in Adam's ears built to a crescendo until his body let go, a giant pressure finding release all along his spine until the hairs on the crown of his head were standing on end.

He pressed his mouth to the side of Brandon's neck as he tried to get his breathing under control. His heart pounded and his mind buzzed as Brandon draped a leg over his and flung an arm around Adam's waist, holding him close, keeping him there, keeping them together.

Brandon nudged Adam's cheek until Adam kissed him, slowly, tenderly, feeling as if every secret desire in his heart was laid bare before this young man who meant so much to him. After a moment, Brandon looked at him, and said in a somber voice, "Behold, the Bridegroom cometh."

With a pointed look at the mess cooling between their bodies, he broke into laughter, Adam joining him before a cold rush of panic filled his body.

"Okay, I... I think that may have crossed a line."

Their laughter subsided.

"I'm sorry," Brandon said. "I ruined it, didn't I?"

Adam looked into his companion's earnest face and smiled softly. "No, no, it's okay. We were just joshing around before, right?"

Brandon's smile was so sweet and grateful that it made Adam's chest twinge. As they continued to lie together, Brandon made good use of their close proximity to trail kisses and soft bites down Adam's neck, something Adam didn't think he would ever tire of. How did people not kiss and touch all the time?

Brandon tightened his leg around Adam's; his entire body sagged into the mattress. "So. Zone transfers are in two weeks. I got the call about it earlier tonight."

Everything came to a standstill. Adam checked Brandon's face for any hint of a joke. "Do you know if we're being split up?"

Brandon kissed him softly on the lips. "I don't know. Obviously I don't want them to, especially not after all this... They usually don't move people around here too much except for when people go home or there's a problem, so I'm hoping not."

Adam fought his growing panic. Transfers meant interviews with their leaders. Interviews meant questions that probed into private matters between companions. It was *required*. They wouldn't understand that it was okay, what he and Brandon were feeling. Maybe they didn't know that it wasn't wrong. Adam certainly hadn't until tonight. But then, maybe he'd just given in to what he wanted to happen, maybe he just wanted it *not* to be wrong?

Even now, in Brandon's arms with Brandon's warm breath on his neck, he still couldn't help questioning its rightness. He'd been well-trained to always assume his own guilt, after all. He couldn't quite wrap his mind around what had happened, that they'd just done all of that to each other. *With* each other. Good gosh, he was on a *mission*, for crying out loud. He couldn't make sense of what was happening between them, still didn't know if he wanted it to happen again or... No, no he definitely did want it to happen again, but he still had that sense of shame, that overwhelming sense that he should repent for who he was and what he'd done and act as if none of it had happened at all.

Brandon rolled to his side and pulled Adam up against him. His hands skimmed lightly over Adam's back, his arm, and trailed over the nape of his neck before he dropped a tender kiss on Adam's exposed skin. The intimacy shocked him at first, giving way to warmth and a sense of peace.

Good things were from their Heavenly Father. This... this was something good. Wonderful, even. Good things were from God, and God was love. God was goodness and happiness, and he felt those things more strongly when he was with Brandon than he'd felt anything else in his entire life.

He kissed Brandon softly at the corner of his mouth and settled deeper into his companion's arms. He felt safer and more like himself than he could remember as they lay together in silence, drifting toward sleep.

He decided. He wanted it to happen again. He wouldn't feel ashamed of this. God was love.

CHAPTER SEVEN

"And if ye shall ask with a sincere heart, with real intent, having faith in Christ, he will manifest the truth of it unto you, by the power of the Holy Ghost." (Moroni 10:4, Book of Mormon)

Adam woke to Brandon snoring softly a few feet away in his own bed. He smiled to himself at the memory of their legs hanging off the mattresses while both of them tried to find a position that would be comfortable for the entire night. Because they were both large-framed and their beds were so narrow, Brandon had had to go back to his own bed. Adam swung his legs onto the cold floor and scrubbed his face. While they were warm in their own beds, he could easily let himself believe he'd imagined last night. The dark bite mark on Brandon's shoulder was a harsh reminder that he hadn't. Their suits would cover the mark.

He got to the business of making breakfast and calling in to the mission home, as they were required to do with regularity. That attended to, he sat down to dig into his meal. He looked up from his eggs and the Book of Mormon opened next to his plate to see Brandon joining him with his own plate. Brandon shot him a grin.

"Hey. 'Morning. Thanks for the eggs. Any assignments today?"

Adam pushed the jam toward Brandon and, suddenly shy and unsure, buried his face in his scriptures. "Nope. Just the usual."

"Well. I think we need to continue this trend of doing the unusual."

Adam's face grew hot. He looked up; the fork trembled in his hand. "W-what?"

"Well, there are loads of tourists at the Gaudí temple right now, you know, La Sagrada Família. Could be a good place to go fishing today.

Plus, we can make sure we've seen all the sights before we're transferred to the boonies."

An awkwardness fell over the two of them at the word "transfer." The rational part of Adam's mind, the part that his father and the Church had carefully crafted to put himself and his own wants and needs last, thought it would be the best thing for them, while the newly awakened emotional part was overcome with sadness at not having Brandon as a companion. He couldn't picture anything about his mission without Brandon at his side.

They finished breakfast in silence, straightened up the table and spent the required hour in silent personal scripture study. Elder Christensen checked his watch. "Time to get a move on. Do you want to lead?" He knelt in the center of the living room and looked up at Adam with a calm face.

"No, that's all right, you go ahead." Adam knelt with his arms tightly folded against his chest. Guilt and worry began to take root.

Christensen waited, breathing deeply with his eyes closed before he began their morning prayer. "Our Dear Heavenly Father, we thank You for this day and for the hope of finding those who would benefit from Your Gospel in their lives. We thank Thee for our health, for our minds, and for each other."

A tremor shot through Adam at the use of "each other."

"We ask for the blessing of clarity so that we may feel Thy spirit move through us. That we may be inspired by the promptings of the Holy Ghost and have the strength to act on those promptings. We ask for our hearts and minds to be opened to one another, that we may work together to bring joy and hope to Your children and… and ourselves. Bless our leaders to have the strength of mind and spirit to lead us. Help us always, in this we pray, in the name of Jesus Christ, Amen."

"A-amen," Adam answered. He sat on his knees, trying to catch hold of the lucidity that had been so evident last night, that surety that what he and Brandon had done together was something good, something right. Darkness seemed to be growing inside him, and his first thought, his first instinct, was to believe that it was the Spirit leaving him because of his iniquity. He should ask for forgiveness, but asking for forgiveness meant that he knew it was wrong, and more importantly, it meant that he would commit to never doing it again. That's what repentance was.

He opened his eyes, seeing Brandon's tie-tack: the angel Moroni sounding his trumpet, a symbol for members of new revelations, of preparation for the Millennium, and of course, of repentance. He didn't know if he *wanted* to repent. He didn't know if what was happening between them was even something to repent *for*.

"Elder? You ready?"

Christensen stood over him, his hand outstretched. Adam bit his lower lip and took it.

———•———

ELDER CHRISTENSEN STOPPED IN HIS tracks, jammed his hands into his suit pants' pockets and whistled at the giant cathedral's nativity façade; Adam followed suit, minus the whistle. It was unlike anything Adam had ever seen, like something from *The Lord of the Rings*. Even with the giant cranes—the building had been under construction for over a century now—it still looked like something ancient, something from fantasy. Huge spires jutted from what had appeared to be drops of mud until he was able to get closer and see the sheer volume of detail, the angels and saints with their musical instruments, and prayers embedded in the textured material that made up the outside. A person could spend a week looking at twenty square feet of it. They both stared at the enormous structure for several minutes along with the throng of other tourists.

"Kinda makes the stories about the Salt Lake Temple taking forty years to build sound like nothing in comparison, huh?" Brandon said, voice filled with awe. "You know they won't even be done with this until—"

"Thirty years from now, yeah, I know," Adam replied tersely. He automatically bristled at the negative statement about the Salt Lake Temple. He'd been conditioned to take offense at anything perceived as negative against the Mormon Church. It was ridiculous to react this way; one was a piece of art and the other was a House of the Lord. Being irritated with himself just made him crankier, though.

Christensen looked at him sideways. "You all right?"

Young nodded curtly and dug in his backpack for their proselytizing materials. It was stupid to be so defensive about a building. It didn't matter. And if he would just be realistic, he argued with himself, he could recognize that nothing he'd ever seen could compare to the intricate details and the enormity of the Gaudí temple. He was feeling a bit protective, that's all. Whether for himself or his religion, he couldn't quite say.

They stood outside in the bright sunshine offering greetings and smiles and pamphlets for those who would take them. Not many did. They were at a famous Catholic structure, after all. They helped a few older women carry heavy bags, watched a Russian couple's dog while they went inside for the tour and were offered bottles of water by a passing group of nuns.

They sat on the edge of the rounded stone platform at the edge of the Nativity entrance to drink their water. "You know," Christensen gasped as he screwed the cap back on, "I've always had a hard time accepting that nuns would be barred from God's presence, given that they've devoted their whole lives to Him."

Young spun the plastic ring at the mouth of his bottle and nodded, taking in the concept as Christensen continued.

"Which is why I don't really believe that He would."

"You don't?" Adam sputtered. "You can't just… *not* believe that! What on earth are you here for, if it isn't making sure we baptize these folks so they *can* get to the Celestial Kingdom?" That was what Mormons knew was the highest level of heaven, the one where you would dwell in God's presence.

Christensen turned to look him dead in the eye. "Honestly? I came to test my faith. I'm here to see the world, to learn." He shrugged. "Those ladies live their life in service of God. We're just a couple of kids, really, and we're presuming to know more than they do? That one nun looked ancient. I'm having a hard time believing all the things that don't sound very Christian to me, Adam."

Young was seriously worried now. "Elder, do, do we need to talk to someone? The Mission President could be up here in an hour, and—"

He glanced at his messenger bag where he knew his mission cell phone was—authorized use, only—when Christensen grabbed his hand after pasting a smile on his face. "I'm sorry. I'm fine. Sometimes I just wonder if what we're doing is right, that's all. 'Suffer the children to come unto me,' is what Jesus taught, and I just, well, I just have a hard time accepting that He would turn His back on people who live their life for Him just because they haven't added their names to a certain team's roster."

Adam squeezed Brandon's hand, then dropped it. "But He won't completely. They just won't reach the fullness of His promise, of their own eternal salvation."

Church Doctrine was very clear on that, that heaven comprised three kingdoms. Only the most righteous, those who lived His principles, who served missions, regularly visited the temple, married in the temple for all time and eternity, paid a full tithe, only *those* people would achieve Heavenly Father's highest blessing: Eternal life and progression. Only those people could become like God Himself. It wasn't as if the nuns would be thrown in Hell. Mormons didn't believe in Hell. They just wouldn't progress eternally. Even as he thought that, it didn't settle right with him.

"It just seems... cruel. Like a parent picking a favorite," Christensen said, thumbing at the label on his water bottle.

That rankled Adam. Not that Brandon had said it, but because it finally put a finger on the concept, making him understand what about it had always seemed unfair. That concept drove him to desperation to understand his own faith. He didn't want to be left behind in a lesser Kingdom of Heaven, and had subconsciously believed that he would— his family would move on and up, being better and more devoted than he was.

"Yeah, that's something I have to deal with here on earth already. I don't want to have to deal with that forever, too," Adam laughed, though it didn't ease the tightness in his chest.

Christensen smiled, knocking his knee into Adam's. "Yeah. Sometimes I just can't swallow it all down. I'm just not going to say 'yes' without thinking some of these things through anymore."

Adam searched his companion's face. "You're not going to turn apostate on me, are you?"

Christensen laughed at that. "No. But come on. Are you telling me that you don't question things inside that head of yours, Still Waters? Don't even act like you're not constantly thinking about this stuff in that big square noggin of yours. I mean, we both know you don't say much out loud."

Adam huffed a quiet laugh.

Brandon tapped the side of his dress shoe against Adam's. "'The glory of God is intelligence,' after all. I know we've been told to blindly obey, but I really think we're supposed to question stuff, too. Especially the stuff that seems unfair or unjust. If we stumble, we can pick ourselves up again with a better understanding. All those perfect Peter Priesthood guys back home did everything automatically. They didn't know why they were doing it, they just *did*. I want to know without reservation. Can you understand that?"

With a jolt of embarrassment at realizing he'd been one of those automatic followers that his companion had just derided, Adam completely understood Christensen's point of view. He'd wanted that himself, but until now had believed himself spiritually weak for even thinking about it. But here was one of the strongest, kindest, most spiritual men he knew voicing his deep-seated fears and needs. Adam knew that wasn't easy. "Yeah. Yeah, I can, actually."

"I'm really glad we ended up together, Adam. For lots of reasons, but that's a big part of it, too."

The sun warm on their faces, the buzz and hum of tourists and locals all around them, the faint music from a cafe across the street faded into nothing as Adam looked at his companion's earnest expression. Mormons didn't call it destiny but fore-ordination: that before they came to this earth, certain spirits lined up, choosing to be family, friends or loved ones. He'd never given it much thought. After all, his family didn't seem as if they'd choose one another on earth, let alone in the Spirit World.

But here, now, he could imagine a thread, gold and shining, so thick, so strong it was more like a rod that connected his heart and mind to his companion, who may not understand all the parts that made Adam who he was (and after all, *Adam* didn't understand himself completely) but someone willing to learn who he was. And Adam was certainly willing to learn all that made Christensen who *he* was, as well. In that brief moment, he was so grateful to his Heavenly Father for ensuring that they found one another that he felt he might cry. For all the unique lives that had been on earth, all the spirits waiting in the pre-existence yet to come, that they found each other now, in this place, at just the right time...

Christensen looked at his watch. "Hey, it's getting on. We need to check in."

Adam couldn't let the moment pass without marking it somehow. He leaned his weight into Christensen's shoulder, closed his eyes and said softly, "Dear Heavenly Father, thank you for blessing me. Amen."

Christensen smiled at the pavement and answered softly, "Amen."

They walked the few miles back to their little apartment in pleasant silence, and while Adam called in to report their activities for the day, Christensen made their dinner. In what was becoming common in their private time, they talked about contradictions they had found in their studies as they ate.

"Faith. It's a test of faith," Adam said. "Any time we don't understand something it's... Well, that's what my dad always said," he finished lamely.

Christensen rested his forearms on the edge of the table with his head hanging down. "Would you do something for me? Would you give me a blessing? I'm having a hard time clearing my thoughts after, you know, everything. It... it feels like my soul is sick."

This would be the first time Adam performed the rite on his own. He knew himself to be fully qualified to do so as a holder of the Melchizedek Priesthood, but it was odd not to have his father or Quorum President leading the prayer. It made it real, his Priesthood. He coughed. "Um, yeah. Of course. If you're sure you want me to be the one to do it, that is."

"Adam, I think I need it to be you."

Christensen looked as though he wanted to reach across the table and touch Adam's hand, and that sent a thrill of both excitement and trepidation through him. It seemed Brandon thought better of it at the last moment when he instead stood and positioned his dining chair in the middle of the kitchen. He sat ramrod stiff with his eyes closed and his hands folded in his lap. Adam took a deep breath and took the bullet casing-shaped vial from his key chain and spun the lid. The sacred oil inside had been blessed by one of the Apostles at the last General Conference. If Brandon was feeling sick or afflicted...

He stood, wiped his trembling hands on his dress slacks, picked up the vial again and attempted to clear his mind. He allowed a few drops of oil to land on Christensen's head; they added a slick sheen to the crown of his dark hair. Young placed his hands lightly on his companion's head, fought back the urge to massage Brandon's scalp and began the prayer.

"Elder Brandon Christensen, by the power of the Melchizedek priesthood that I hold, I anoint you with consecrated oil in the name of Jesus Christ. I also leave a blessing upon you."

In his mind he could hear the familiar words his father and his older brothers had spoken so many times before and tried to emulate the prayers they'd given, but could only focus on the heat radiating from Christensen as it warmed his hands and made his toes clench.

"I leave a blessing upon you that your heart will be healed and your spirit won't be broken."

Christensen shifted in his chair, and Adam let the weight of his hands rest fully on his head, finally giving in to the urge to allow the tips of his fingers to thread through Brandon's dark hair.

"I pray that you will be given the answers you so desperately and earnestly and *righteously* seek."

His whole body vibrated; he didn't know the source of his words, but knew they were meant for him as well.

"I pray that you will feel whole and know your purpose both in this mission and in life. I do so in the name of Jesus Christ, Amen."

Brandon murmured "Amen" and reached up to hold Adam's hands in place. After a moment, Adam realized that Brandon's thumb was moving back and forth along Adam's pulse point in his wrist. Adam untangled his hands from Brandon's hair and laid them on Brandon's shoulders and gave them a squeeze. He was not ready to break whatever connection they'd had.

There was something almost marital in what they had done, something uniquely intimate. Adam had seen husbands give their wives and children blessings in time of sickness and trouble. Adam's father had often called General Authorities Gerald knew to lay a blessing on any member of their family when the need arose, most likely assuming their higher authority would be a greater insurance against evil influences or for healing. He'd always looked forward to the day when he would be asked by his loved ones to pray for them, to bless them, and he'd always been exhilarated by the promise of such an honor.

Brandon stood and took Adam's hand in both of his. His face had a soft glow; he seemed peaceful and resolute. "Thank you for that. I feel better already. I'm going to shower first, if you don't mind?"

Adam stood still, watching Brandon walk away and strip out of his suit, his shoes, his clothes and, finally, his garments, leaving them in a heap on the floor as he crossed naked to the bathroom. Were their holy undergarments truly powerful vestiges of God, clothing that could protect him from evil as he'd always been taught, or was there something in the person that made them worthy of God's love, and did that love gave the person protection? Understanding crept into him even as his mind tried to dance around the real question he was unable or unwilling to ask himself.

It seemed so natural practicing his religion with this man, sharing faith, and even more natural was the night before, what they'd shared in his bed. Surely God, who commanded his children to "love one another" was a God of *all* forms of love?

On the heels of this thought came the memory of lessons his father had taught him about the *correct* forms of love, how anything that debased God's laws came from the wicked, the unworthy. Adam thought of his father's reaction if he ever found out what he had done. He could see his mother's horrified face and the look of disgust from his brothers, hear the whispering of his shame in the halls of the church. There was no question in his mind that, if that happened, if his father or mother learned about what he and Brandon shared that he would be excommunicated, cut off from his family and from eternal joy. There would be no highest Kingdom of Heaven for him. He would be barred from God's complete love, from eternal progression, barred from an eternity with his family.

And all for having tender feelings for his missionary companion.

Deep in thought, he sat on the edge of his bed still wearing his suit with his hands hanging loosely between his knees . Brandon came into the room wrapped in a towel; his voice brought Adam out of his thoughts.

"You okay?"

"Yeah, just thinking things through."

Brandon opened a drawer and pulled out a fresh pair of garments. "Well, maybe don't do it so hard. Looks like your head is about to explode."

Adam looked up to find Brandon grinning, but his eyes quickly shifted downward as Brandon bent over to step into his garments. Adam quickly looked away. "Sorry," he mumbled. "That can't be helping things. I don't know what's wrong with me."

He stood to leave, and Brandon grabbed his arm. "There's nothing wrong with you."

"That's not what my dad would say. That's not what the other Elders would say. That's not what our rule book says."

"Well, maybe there's something wrong with all of them instead of us." He held Adam's arm a bit longer, then dropped it. "What were you thinking about when I came in?"

Adam heaved a huge sigh, leaned against the door frame and rubbed one hand through his sandy blond hair. "You. I don't understand what's going on between us. One minute I think we're the greatest priests ever and I feel so filled with the spirit when we're out there preaching, meeting people, trying to do what we've been commanded, and the next minute I'm thinking of how I wish you would—"

He blushed and looked at his shoes. They were in need of a shine. He'd think about that instead of thinking about Brandon kissing him again, touching him like last night. "Never mind."

"That's what I keep thinking about, too, both of those things. Can't stop thinking about it, really. Especially the other stuff."

Adam, caught off guard, looked up. Brandon crossed the room to lean against the other side of the doorframe, opposite him.

"It can't be totally wrong, Adam. I get why we're taught not to have sex before marriage. Our bodies are sacred, a gift not to be used casually. I get that. And I actually agree with it. You don't want to make babies by accident, especially if you're not married. You don't want to just be all casual about sex so it loses all meaning." Brandon reached out, dragging the backs of his fingers down the length of Adam's arm before letting it fall at his own side. "But last night I felt closer to Heavenly Father than I've felt in a long time. Probably not since I baptized Sister Chus, to be honest. And that's another thing. We're taught that any sin will close the door to our success out here, but I'm the only one who's baptized anyone. The only one who got us any further discussions. The other guys? They get invited over for the novelty. They're not being taken seriously. You and I both know it."

Adam nodded.

"So why is it that I'm the way I am, and I'm the guy who brought someone to the fullness of the gospel, too? How could that be if I'm full of sin?"

Adam thought about all Brandon said. He wanted so desperately to find the puzzle piece that would fit into the dogma he'd been taught as truth, the one thing that would make how he felt be okay and not an abomination. He wanted to find that one thing that would make him feel right hours after the moment and not just while in it.

His brows knit in concentration, Adam said, "Yeah, it's like it shouldn't feel good if it's so wrong. Not that..." He heaved out a sigh. "I know that just because something *feels* good doesn't mean it *is* good. I mean that it does in here." He looked into Brandon's face while he rubbing the center of his own chest. "Does, does that make any sense?"

Brandon squeezed Adam's shoulder, smoothed the flat of his palm down Adam's tie and stopped just below where Adam's heart pounded.

"It feels right because I, I think it is. And... I can't help thinking," Brandon said, slipping his fingers under the silky material to squeeze the hidden clasp from Adam's tie-tack, and the back of his hand was hot and electric on Adam's belly even through layers of dress shirt and garments, "that some of the things we've been taught aren't right."

Adam's breathing grew shallow. Brandon loosened Adam's tie, and every brush of his fingers on Adam's bare neck made his body feel heavy; he could feel the pulse beat between his legs, could feel the hairs on his arms stand on end. "Things? W-what things?" His voice dropped to barely a whisper, reverential and quiet as if they were in church.

Brandon left the tie loose on Adam's neck, but began undoing the buttons of his shirt one by one. His eyes were intent on the task. "It's like all the rules we missionaries are told to obey, all one hundred and sixty-seven of them. All the lines we have to toe; the check marks we have to make every single day. I think… They're keeping us busy so we don't notice all the great stuff out there. All the happiness we're denying ourselves."

Brandon drew his fingertips under Adam's dress shirt outlining his pecs. His thumbs traced the sacred markings sewn over the nipple; Adam closed his eyes and exhaled slowly.

His voice shaking, Brandon said, "It's like the Church is about the *Church* and not about Heavenly Father."

Adam bit his lip, moistening it. A well-conditioned part of his mind wanted to argue, to yell that what Brandon said was blasphemous. But the part of him that was just waking up and noticing the world for what it truly was heard a concept he'd not been able to articulate on his own, something that rang true. And hadn't he prayed that very day for answers? For the truth?

Leaning forward, his hair tickling Adam's faintly stubbled chin, Brandon exhaled a hot breath along Adam's bared neck. "This, what's happening between us, this feels like that scripture, 'In my distress I cried unto the Lord and he heard me.'"

Adam, eyes closed, buried his hand in Brandon's dark, wet hair, his weight resting against the door frame. "I… I think He did hear us. Brandon, I think He's answering us."

With a low noise, Brandon tugged at Adam's shirt, pulling it off his arms, leaving him in his G's. They stood there, holding one another, breathing deeply. A droplet of water fell from Brandon's hair onto Adam's hand. He brought it to his mouth to suck it off, then traced another droplet as it ran down Brandon's temple and caught it in his mouth before it could fall off Brandon's jaw.

"You feel like an answer," Adam murmured. "Like a revelation."

Brandon shook his head. A needy whine slipped out of him before he surged forward to catch Adam's mouth in a passionate kiss. He rucked up the hem of Adam's garments to stroke Adam's belly while tracing Adam's ear with his tongue. Adam held on tighter, lost to the sensations of being touched, being held, being understood, reveling in the sensation of Brandon's skin warm and smooth under his hands. It was so easy here in this private place he and Brandon were making for themselves. So easy just to *feel*, to believe it was okay. It seemed right, this shared emotion between the two of them, as if it was true. He believed it, he did.

Cupping the back of Brandon's head as Brandon continued nipping and kissing along Adam's neck, he said, "Oh, my gosh, Brandon that feels so—" He pulled on Brandon's hair to bring his face level with his languorous smile. "Can you, um, give me a hand?" he asked, looking down between their bodies. He knew how it could feel and he wanted it again, wanted everything he could have.

Brandon yanked the garment off and unbuckled Adam's belt as Adam tugged off Brandon's towel. Brandon paused, leaning back a little as if he knew Adam needed to look his fill. Adam's gaze roamed over the hard planes of Brandon's body, skirting the thick, dark hair at the base of Brandon's groin until he realized he didn't have to look away. He *could* look. Brandon *wanted* him to look. And it was so clear in the way his body began to respond that this was what *he* wanted. This reaction, this hunger building was nothing like the reaction to accidentally seeing the dirty pictures of naked girls the guys passed around in the locker room back at the U.

He'd never wanted those girls. He'd never wanted a smiling, dutiful Mormon coed on his arm, either. *Brandon* was who he wanted.

Their lips crashed together. Desperation for one another built as Adam kicked off his pants and remaining garments. They fumbled back to Brandon's bed and took their hands from each other just in time to avoid falling onto the mattress.

With a strength that made Adam's insides twist hot and liquid at being so easily manhandled, Brandon flipped Adam onto his back and straddled him. His eyes were heavy with need and his damp hair stood in crazy spikes from being roughly handled. He ran his splayed hands from Adam's shoulders to his hipbones; his thumbs tickled the mat of light brown hair in the center of Adam's chest and raked through to where it thinned into a trail below Adam's navel.

He kissed and licked a path from Adam's neck to his navel as Adam tried to calm the frenzy building inside him. "Can I try something?" Brandon asked, shimmying down Adam's body.

Dumbfounded, Adam nodded, not really sure what he was agreeing to, but trusting Brandon no matter what it was.

Brandon's hand spasmed against Adam's side as he nodded. "Okay." He then proceeded to blow all the circuits in Adam's brain when he put his mouth… With a body shaking shudder, Adam jerked underneath him, shocked and overwhelmed. Too much, that was too much. His hand was in Brandon's hair guiding him back toward his mouth for a kiss that would let him calm down.

"No? I thought—"

Adam shook his head and kissed Brandon gently. "I just… it's a lot."

"I've never done this before, you know," Brandon murmured against Adam's lips.

Adam's barked an incredulous laugh. "You think *I* have?"

"Well. I'm glad we're doing this together, then."

The corner of Adam's mouth quirked up. "Yeah. Me, too."

"Will you let me? Trust me, okay?"

Adam took a deep breath and nodded. As Brandon kissed back down his body, Adam felt the last remnant of his prudishness, his closed-off nature, fall away. Brandon accepted him, accepted this. He wanted it as much as Adam did. With an impish grin, Adam asked, "How does it go? 'Even as you desire of me so it shall be done unto you.'"

Brandon stopped what he was doing and laid his cheek against Adam's hipbone, laughing. He bit the thin skin stretched there, then soothed it with a kiss. "I thought this wasn't supposed to be funny, what we're doing."

Adam's laughter ebbed, leaving him smiling, languid in his happiness. "I think that's a part of the whole 'joy' thing we've never had." He ran his fingertips through Brandon's hair, shocked at himself for not caring that he was lying naked in a bed with another man, a man who just happened to be his missionary companion.

With a cocked eyebrow, Brandon asked, "So do you want me to suck this thing or not?" before dissolving into laughter. His shoulders shook with it. Brandon stilled, however, when Adam—head spinning with what was about to happen—linked their hands together, dragging them back down to where he ached. Adam moaned and jerked when he felt Brandon's mouth engulf him, hot, wet and unlike anything he could have imagined, *had* never imagined.

It took a moment or two for them to figure out how it all worked; Brandon's teeth scraped the underside once, and Adam hissed in pain. Brandon made it all better in short time, then entwined his hand with Adam's. Adam's toes curled up in the sheets; his mouth worked soundlessly as he allowed himself to experience the simple pleasure of another person's body, the body of a person he cared for so deeply.

A powerful orgasm was building, and Adam didn't know what to do. His body didn't want to stop, but he knew instinctively that he should warn Brandon. He stammered, "Brandon I'm going— I can't help it!"

Brandon knelt over Adam, kissing him tenderly as his hand took over, as Adam's body clenched, as he gave in to it, unable to stop the desperate noises, as he flushed all over with the heat of Brandon's heavy-lidded gaze.

Brandon touched his fingertips to Adam's belly with a sort of reverence and awe. He fell onto the narrow space between the wall and Adam. He buried his face in the crook of Adam's neck as Adam gasped, trying to catch his breath as he came down.

"I see why that's called something holy. Holy moly..." Adam sighed, draping his arm over his heated face.

Brandon laughed against Adam's neck, tickling him.

Adam turned his head, smiling sadly. "We can't go on like this, you know."

The color ran out of Brandon's face.

"These beds are too small for us."

Adam popped to his feet. He was embarrassed by the mess on his torso, but quickly ignored that when his eyes moved to Brandon lying on his back, completely naked and still very interested. He'd seen naked guys in the locker room, but the unspoken rule there was to avoid lingering glances and to keep eyes chest-high or higher. He'd seen naked girls, too, by accident, before flipping the channels on his brother's remote to something more chaste and honorable in case someone walked in. He had felt weird for not being turned on by the girls. He understood why, now.

The long, powerful lines of Brandon's body in repose, the breadth of his shoulders and how they tapered into slim hips, the dark thatch of hair at the base of his groin, his thick thighs, muscled from playing sports and walking everywhere—all that made Adam's mouth go dry.

He wanted. Oh, how he wanted. But not like this. Well, not on a single bed barely large enough for one large young man, let alone two.

"Come on. Get up and put your shoulder to the wheel, Elder," Adam said, grabbing at the bed frame under his mattress.

Brandon grinned and got to his feet. They made quick work of shoving the two beds together to make a bed large enough to accommodate them both. They flopped onto it, not quite touching. They had fully committed to something now, and it both frightened and exhilarated Adam.

He swallowed thickly and asked, "Do you want me to... you know."

Brandon threw his arm over his eyes and cupped himself. His voice sounded breathless as he answered, "Yeah, I mean, you know... if you want to."

Adam sat up and put his weight on one hand as he looked down at the body being offered to him. Brandon was a thing of beauty, his body hard and chiseled, naturally tan, but darker on his arms where his short dress shirt sleeves came to an end. Adam wondered if it would be possible to ever grow tired of looking at him. Trying to calm his nerves, Adam drew his fingers over the defined muscle at Brandon's hip. If he did this, it would mean he completely accepted who he really was.

He kissed the center of Brandon's chest and made his way down the length of him; his heart pounded and his mouth flooded with saliva at the clean, slightly musky scent. Brandon bent his leg, holding Adam tightly to him. Adam looked up and saw Brandon, his chest heaving, staring down at him, with eyes heavy-lidded and his thick lashes shading his dark brown eyes. Adam watched Brandon's reaction as he tried to copy what had been done to him, tried to give back what he'd been given. Brandon arched and licked his lips; one of the little noises he made when he touched himself slipped out.

After a few minutes, Adam's jaw began to ache; was that something a person got used to? The thought of doing this enough to become used to it excited him. As he gave in to the pleasure of giving *Brandon* pleasure, he became bolder. He allowed himself to acknowledge that he wanted this. He wanted a man, wanted *this* man. He loved the smell of him, the taste of him, the hard planes of Brandon's body, the strength of his character, the breathless way he gasped Adam's name.

Adam had an urge to taste everything, to explore everywhere, to memorize every hitch in Brandon's breath and the way his skin tasted and smelled and the silky texture of Brandon's skin stretched hot and petal soft in places. He didn't know where this newfound daring had come from. He only knew that he wanted to hear Brandon make *that* noise again, the noise that said Adam did something that Brandon really liked. That was a good sound.

He smiled, pressed a gentle kiss to Brandon's belly and his eyes closed in bliss at the sensation of Brandon's hands in his hair holding him just where he wanted to be.

———◦———

THEY WEREN'T MUCH FOR PROSELYTIZING the next few days. They slept in, entangled in their sheets and each other, hitting the "snooze" button on the alarm clock well after the required wake-up. They didn't forget to call in at the appointed time, though. That would have brought trouble down on them, and they still believed they only had a short time before transfers were announced the next Sunday.

Sometimes they came at each other shyly, touching and exploring each other's bodies with reverence; other times they were like animals, biting and grabbing, shoving the other against the wall in desperation to be together, to touch and rut their bodies against one another until they climaxed, shaking, sated. Adam, on occasion, would feel pangs of guilt for giving into temptation so easily, but each night they would kneel side by side, like a real couple, an eternal couple, and say their prayers together before climbing into their modified bed, and his life was everything he'd wanted but never believed he could have.

While doing what they were supposed to be doing and proselytizing in one of the city's plazas, they ran into Sorensen and May. The two had partnered up now that LaSalle had finished serving and gone home. Sorensen taught Adam a new handshake, blocking what they were doing from Elder May.

"No way, Greenie. You have to be in the trenches for at least four months before you learn this one."

Adam laughed and asked May, "So! How is it living with this guy?"

May blushed and shrugged. "Eh. He's all right, I guess."

Sorensen threw his hands up in the air. "I am *sorry* about the bathroom. Jeez."

May mumbled, "I'm just saying, lock the door."

"Dude. You saw me go in with a magazine. Universal freaking sign for 'Gonna be a while.'"

"Well, I didn't know! I wasn't paying attention. Just, for frick's sake, light a match next time."

Christensen, his face somber, said, "This is what comes of home-cooked meals drying up. Digestive nightmares. Wait, did they dry up?"

It was Sorensen's turn to blush. "Brother and Sister Moreno love me, okay? They're worried about me losing LaSalle, and they happen to show concern through multiple courses of really delicious food."

"That's not all they love," May mumbled.

"What?" Adam asked.

"Nothing, don't listen to him. He doesn't like anything with spices or flavor. He's a mayonnaise kind of dude." Sorensen fake punched Christensen's chest a few times. "Hey, so how goes it out here today, B? Any luck? We've had doors slammed left and right."

"Sewing those seeds," Adam and Brandon said in tandem, then laughed at each other.

"See, this is what we need to strive for, May," Sorensen said. "If I'm going to extend, we better end up like the dynamic duo over here, or I'm going to blame you."

May chewed the inside of his cheek, not saying anything.

"Ah, ignore him," Sorensen said. "He's just mad he didn't get a rebreather in his last care package."

"Gross, Elder," Brandon said. Adam watched May out of the corner of his eye as Brandon and Sorensen caught up on district news, noting how May looked angry about something, something that probably wasn't just being forced into smelling the commode after his mission companion stunk it up. Come to think of it, there was something off with Sorensen, too. He seemed... diminished. Adam suspected it was from missing LaSalle. They'd been well-paired, too.

Sorensen and May waved goodbye and moved off; their body language was stiff and uncomfortable. Brandon sighed and hung his arm around Adam's shoulder, pulled him close and caused Adam to forget anything that wasn't directly related to how he felt with Brandon at his side.

"I'm glad we never fought like that."

Adam looked over in surprise. "I can't imagine us ever fighting, can you?" He took a chance, glancing around to see if anyone was watching them. On the contrary, people seemed to be avoid looking at them. Adam whispered, "I can imagine other things I could do with you, though."

"Oh, yeah?"

Adam's face spread in a wide grin.

Brandon made a big show of checking his watch. "Will you look at the time? We should probably head back."

"Yeah, let's head home."

Home. Their little apartment certainly had begun to feel like a home. All his life he'd been taught that finding an eternal companion to love, honor and cherish, a partner to worship with, was one of the most important things he must do on this earth. It was essential to enter the highest kingdom of heaven, after all. The fact that the companion he had chosen was the same sex was irrelevant for the time being. For the first time in his life, Adam Young felt complete, a real person with real feelings, not an automaton going through the motions. As the Mormon hymn went, "his spirit, like a fire, was burning."

They attended the Sunday service as usual, choosing to sit in the back corner together instead of finding a family that needed an extra set of hands to help control the kids. Part of Adam simmered with shame and guilt in the familiar setting, hearing the songs from his childhood, going through all the rituals of sacrament and prayer that reminded him of growing up in his father's house, all while sitting next to Brandon and knowing what they had done to each other only hours before.

But another part of him looked at the congregation and saw the Spanish families cooing over their spouses, giving each other little kisses, smoothing hair off of sweaty foreheads, the husbands putting their arms on the bench behind their spouses and their fingers tracing over the delicate, softly-rounded shoulders of their wives. He saw the approval of that love and yearned to feel the same acceptance, though he understood that it was an impossibility in the modern LDS Church.

At least he could allow himself to feel what they must feel, if only privately. He shifted in the pew so that his shoulder was flush against Brandon's and imagined how it would be to have Brandon's arm around him or his arm around Brandon, to pull him close, to kiss the side of his head just for the joy of being allowed to do it because he was moved by the spirit and full of love.

The congregation stood for a benedictory song. Adam knew the song inside and out, and began singing in his deep baritone without paying much attention to the words. He listened instead to how Brandon's clear tenor blended with his own deeper voice—how well they meshed. As the last verse of the song began, Adam began to pay attention to the words.

"All the hopes that sweetly start, from the fountain of the heart, all the bliss that ever comes to our earthly human homes, all the voices from above sweetly whisper: God is Love."

His voice cracked on the last low note, and he sat down quickly, fumbling in his bag to hide the emotions he couldn't hold back. *All* the hopes. *All* the bliss that ever comes. There was no parsing that word, all. So why couldn't... He huffed out a frustrated sigh and choked back a lump in his throat.

Brandon bumped his knee with his own. "Hey. You okay?"

Adam flipped the pages of his quadruple scripture set and nodded briskly. "Yeah. Just—" He flashed a smile he knew was wobbling on the corners and said, "We'll talk later, promise."

Brandon, his face all concern, nodded. He looked around the room before he looped his index finger around Adam's pinkie and tugged it. "Okay."

The Mission President approached them after Sacrament service. "Transfers are happening tomorrow, but you both know that, right?"

Adam's heart seemed to join the sour lump in his throat. He tried to swallow past it as he nodded.

"You two aren't going anywhere, just bringing in a new companion for Elder May," their Mission President said. "No reason to shake things up too much, especially since I'm going back stateside. Boy, doesn't that make my wife unbelievably happy!"

They looked up at him in shock. New companion for May? What about Sorensen? And President Jensen was going home?

"Young, you haven't heard anything about this?" The President looked at Adam with surprise. "I thought your dad would have told you.

Gosh, I guess he really is a stickler for that rule about not distracting your child on a mission, eh?"

Adam forced a laugh. "Yeah, that's my dad. A stickler." He swallowed and asked, "What, uh, what does this have to do with my dad?"

"He's the new Mission President! He and your mother moved in Friday, just two days ago. You're saying they didn't tell you?" he asked, head tilted and eyebrows close together in apparent disbelief. "Huh. You know that he knows a bunch of the General Authorities, and, since you were the last bird to leave the nest, they thought it would be a nice treat for your mother and an honor for your dad."

Adam was dimly aware that the man was still talking, but it sounded tinny and far away. A roar filled his ears. His face was hot, his hands were like ice, and the weight of Brandon's hand on his shoulder seemed enough to crush his bones to dust.

CHAPTER EIGHT

"If the investigators have not yet committed themselves [...] these commitments must be among your major objectives. [...] Identify anything that might be holding [them] back. Make plans for helping them overcome any obstacles." ~ (Instructions to Missionaries)

Adam didn't remember their bike ride home from church. His mind swirled with terrifying thoughts of his father's angry face, his mother's disappointment and an almost overwhelming sense of shame. He suddenly snapped to attention when Brandon gave his shoulder a small shake in front of their apartment building.

"Adam! Hey, it's going to be okay."

Adam's head gave an infinitesimal shake; Brandon, appearing confused, pressed further, guiding Adam through their front door. "What? What's got you like this? We'll handle it."

"No. It's not going to be okay. He's going to know." Adam buried his face in his hands and moaned. "He's going to kill me."

Brandon laughed at that and started rummaging through the cabinets, getting started on dinner. "He's not going to *kill* you, Adam, what on earth? And, my gosh, he's not going to know anything. Also, you don't have to say anything. I certainly won't be volunteering information. You can count on that. I mean, when we're home, we can talk about how we want to handle it..."

His voice drifted off as Adam laid his cheek on the Formica table, the coolness of which soothed the heat in his face, and watched as Brandon pulled out noodles and a condensed soup can. Brandon, coming from a tight-knit and loving family where his parents apparently accepted everyone, didn't understand; Adam had *heard* his father say he'd kill "any son of mine who turned queer" in a priesthood meeting after the Church made its official statement about children of gays and lesbians being denied the blessings and promises of the Church, of baptism. He remembered his father's smug satisfaction when the Church doubled down on their LGBT stance in November of 2015, saying children of gay and lesbian couples would be denied baptism and the blessings of the Priesthood until they turned eighteen and denounced their parents, rejecting them as family in the eternities.

He knew just how his father would react.

"You don't get it, Brandon. He'll *know*. Oh, my gosh… What have I done? I did this to you, too."

Brandon dropped the can opener, grabbed the back of a chair and spun it around to sit next to him. "Hey. *Hey.*"

Adam looked up, sure his face was a perfect picture of the complete misery and fear threatening to swallow him whole.

"Don't think I'm not scared, too, all right?" Brandon said, his hand on Adam's forearm.

Adam dropped his chin on Brandon's hand. "It doesn't seem like you are, though."

"Dude. I know what's at stake here. Forget that it's highly likely that I'll be excommunicated, with my whole family shamed by me being sent home early. Do you think I want everyone back home to know I'm being sent back dishonorably for… fornicating?"

Adam laughed wryly at the archaic word the Church used.

Brandon sighed. He had a sad smile on his face as he said, "And we haven't even done that, yet. Just the lead up. Not that they would see it differently, but still."

Adam's heartbeat sped up at the casual use of "yet," which didn't help matters. The last thing he needed to think of right now was that one extra act they'd both been too shy to try. He certainly didn't need to imagine Brandon, naked, smashed up against the kitchen counter, with the muscles in his back and shoulders rippling under his smooth, tanned skin, or the hitches in Brandon's breathing when Adam gripped his backside with both hands, kneading the thick muscle there...

He didn't need to think of that at all, not when his *father* might show up at any moment with all the authority of the Church behind him, ready and willing to destroy all of the happiness he and Brandon had created for themselves in their few months together.

That sobered him up.

"Besides," Brandon said, standing up and crossing to the kitchen, so his back was to Adam. "I don't want anyone to think of what we're doing, because it's for us. It *about* us. It's our business, ours and God's. It's not... I don't know. We'll figure it out. Something."

Adam looked on as Brandon opened cans and mixed ingredients. Brandon shoved the dish into the oven, set the timer—a goofy rooster whose head spun around that had been a surprise in a care package from one of Brandon's sisters—and sat next to Adam.

Adam took Brandon's hand, linking their fingers. He found it oddly comforting and ironic that their CTR rings—"Choose the Right," the acronym serving as a reminder to follow God's laws—lined up side by side. "So... what do we do?"

Brandon leaned back in his chair and hooked Adam's ankle with his own. "I don't know. I don't want to change anything, you know? I like this, how we are."

Adam's heartbeat slowed; calm was trying to win out. Brandon did that for him. "Yeah, I do, too. And, well, me, neither. I don't want to change anything. But I don't know how to hide how I—"

He cut himself off, his face flushing, and pushed away from the table to create a little distance.

Brandon stayed in his seat, looking at his empty hand. "What were you going to say?"

Adam paced back and forth, rubbing his hands through his hair. His body thrummed with nerves. "It doesn't matter. Never mind. Let's just focus—"

"It does matter. What were you going to say, Adam?" Brandon stood then and turned to look at him with a half-smile. "What was it?" Quietly, Brandon asked, "Please."

Adam couldn't look away, even though he wanted to; he'd never said anything like this to another person. He knew his face must be beet red; his hands wouldn't stop shaking. "I don't know how to hide how I feel."

Holding perfectly still, Brandon barely breathed out, "Feel about what?"

Adam thoughts twisted, trapped between the overwhelming need for Brandon and the fear of eternal damnation that his father and the Church had planted in him. He forced himself to look into Brandon's eyes. Brandon was being brave about this. Adam could, too. He could see in Brandon's face something similar to the need and fear coursing through Adam, and that helped. He took a deep breath and started unraveling the oppressive knots of fear that had been tangled up inside him for years.

"How much I feel for you. I think that people look at us and they know."

Brandon somehow was closer to him now still with that half-smile, half-afraid look. "What will they know about us, Adam?"

"That we... We're..."

Brandon was moving toward him, backing Adam against the wall. Brandon reached out with one finger and drew it along the edge of Adam's missionary name tag. Adam couldn't breathe; all he could focus on was the heavy weight in his gut, the lightness in his chest where his lungs struggled to draw breath, and Brandon's long, dark lashes framing his intense gaze.

"That we love each other."

Brandon's breath came out in a long sigh. He pulled Adam into a tight embrace, murmuring against his ear, "If you weren't going to say it, I thought I'd have to deck you."

A laugh that bordered on an hysterical cry burst from Adam; that heaviness in his gut melted away with every sweep of Brandon's hands along his back.

"Oh, come on, Elder," Adam said, pleased with how steady his voice sounded. His arms tightened around Brandon's torso. "You know I could totally take you in a fight."

They rocked gently from side to side, laughing softly. The timer went off; Brandon pulled away and held Adam's face. His smile was blinding. With a small sound of pleasure, he kissed Adam softly and turned to finish dinner. Adam set the table, the both of them moving through the small space with ease and comfort. He settled at the table and watched Brandon make a "Missionary Salad"—iceberg lettuce and cheap, bottled dressing from the "American Foods" shelf at the local market. The scene was so oddly domestic and felt so right.

It felt right because it *was*. It was *right* and it was *good*, this life they had here and especially how they felt about each other.

Brandon sat across from him, grinning. "And how was your day, sweetheart?"

Adam laughed softly and held Brandon's hand, took in how neatly their hands fit together, allowed himself to just be happy. He squeezed Brandon's hand and murmured, "My turn." He gave a quick blessing over the food, and they both dug in. After a few bites, he asked, "Wouldn't it be great if it could always be like this?"

Brandon swallowed, "I'd prefer something not from cans, myself."

Adam kicked Brandon's shoe under the table. "You know what I mean, you jerk."

"Yeah." Brandon smiled; his cheeks were tinged pink. "I do. And yeah. It really would be."

They both looked at each other for a long time. Adam was the first to break eye contact, almost overwhelmed by how easy it was, by how easy it could be, if only they weren't trapped by a system of rules that wanted to turn what they shared into something hateful and wrong, something ugly and shameful.

There was nothing ugly about Brandon, not to Adam. There was nothing shameful in the way they looked out for each other, cared for one another. Nothing hateful in their easy manner with one another, nothing wrong about them and what they felt, *nothing*.

Soon enough after coming home from their missions, they'd be pressured by their church leaders and parents into getting married, starting their own families and moving on to the next stage of life. Adam could see himself happily following that prescribed path if only he could have Brandon by his side. If only.

He pushed the food around on his plate. "I don't know what to do about this, Brandon. I don't want to tell him, tell *them* anything. They won't understand and they'll make it something sinful. But…"

Brandon leaned his head against the wall, closed his eyes and nodded. "But I don't want to act like this isn't who I am, Adam, that this isn't what I want. That *you* aren't what I want."

Adam held his breath. "I am?"

"Yeah, you nerd." Brandon gently kicked Adam's foot. "I mean, I already know you snore—"

"I do not!'

"You do; it's *hilarious* that you think you don't. And I know that you change your socks three times a day—"

"I only have wool socks. We're by the *ocean*, Brandon."

"And you think no one sees how good you are, how good you're *trying* to be—"

"I'm not— I'm just—"

"But I do. I see you. I see who you are, who you want to be. I *know* you. The real you, Adam. Not the person you were told you had to be, but who you really are."

Adam was laid bare, stripped of all pretense and carefully chosen mannerisms under Brandon's unwavering but thoughtful gaze. Instead of feeling exposed and scared by that laser focus, he was exhilarated. Someone knew who he was, who he *really* was. And they still wanted him.

"You're always putting other people first," Brandon said. "You always do things for other people instead of yourself. But I like that you let me take care of you. I like that you let me in."

The corners of his mouth twitched, but Adam managed to fight down the dopey grin he knew was trying to come out.

"And if I'm doing it just right," Brandon said, eyes mischievous as he put his weight on his elbows, leaning in to say softly, "your eyes roll back, you start breathing heavily, and your stomach muscles tighten up right before you—"

"Okay, there! That's enough of that, huh?" Adam, blushing furiously over bedroom talk *not* being restricted to the bedroom, pointed at his mostly empty plate. "I mean, tuna noodles, am I right? Some good stuff, right there."

Brandon laughed, squeezing Adam's arm.

"Baby steps, okay?" Adam said, his cheeks hot. He'd never seen his parents *hug with both arms*. A person couldn't talk about... about orgasms in the light of day. At the dang dinner table. He still had on his missionary tag, for crying out loud. "I mean, it's not like..." He coughed to clear his throat, aware that he was starting to get aroused by the way Brandon was sitting back in his chair, with his hands looped together behind his head and staring at him with a dirty grin. "It's not like I don't like that stuff. It's just, you know."

Brandon sucked on his teeth, clearly fighting back a laugh. "It's just, well, tuna noodles. Right."

"Jerk," Adam said, but there wasn't any heat to it. He was so new to this, and that left him wrong-footed and prone to feeling stupid and prudish. He *was* stupid and prudish, even he could admit it. That just added to the whole embarrassment thing—how obvious his immaturity was.

He gathered the dirty dishes and turned on the water. Before he could get started on the cleanup, Brandon was there with his hands on Adam's hips and his mouth at Adam's neck. Adam dropped the soapy scrub brush into the sink and gripped the edge of the countertop;

he pushed back into the warmth and comfort of Brandon's body as Brandon pressed forward against him.

Adam sighed as Brandon held him close and his mouth whispered into Adam's skin, "You have to know how much I want you, Adam. But not just that, the physical stuff. It's how much you mean to me."

"That's how it is for me, too. Brandon, you have to know that, too."

"I do. It's just cute how flustered you get."

"I'll show you cute," Adam said, turning in Brandon's hold and surging forward to kiss him. If he stopped all the embarrassing and wonderful things coming out of Brandon's mouth by doing so, that was just a side benefit.

They got as far as ties off and dress shirts unbuttoned before the phone rang. Adam jumped back from Brandon as if he'd been hit with a cattle prod. Brandon sighed and grabbed the phone as Adam got his clothes back to rights. A phone call on a Sunday night could only mean the Missionary President or their Zone Leader with new instructions.

"Mm hmm. No, that's an honor, sir, thank you. We'll go over the particulars tomorrow, right. See you then. *Hasta mañana.*"

Brandon hung up the phone, stared at it and calmly reported, "I've been made the new Zone Leader. We meet with the new Mish-Pres tomorrow." He looked up, and his face was void of all color. "Looks like I get to meet your parents right away."

Zone Leader. It was considered a huge honor, one that came with a lot of responsibilities. It meant that he and Brandon would almost always be saddled with another missionary to help handle all the extra tasks Brandon would now have, that Brandon would be the point man for the other missionaries, that their phone wouldn't stop ringing and that they'd be with Adam's father for a good chunk of the time.

They'd be with his *dad*. His father. He and Brandon, the guy he was falling in love with. Oh, gosh, a *guy*. He flashed back to a conversation between his dad and another priesthood holder discussing one of the apostle's answers to dealing with homosexuals, particularly when on a mission, how that church leader had actually said, "Sometimes you might just have to lay them out, a solid punch in the mouth. Although life's road might be lonely for those of same-sex attraction, happiness can be found in the Church by faithfully following its teachings."

Adam was beginning to doubt any chance of finding lasting happiness through the Church's teachings. He clung to an idea from the letter Brandon's mother had sent him, the one that said they should focus on how it felt to follow what they believed, how doing what he believed his Heavenly Father wanted him to do was always the right choice.

Now, his instinct was to believe what he and Brandon shared was love, was real. And God is love. All the bliss, all the goodness in a person's life was a gift from God. The scriptures said it, the hymns said it and his heart believed it.

He couldn't reconcile the Church teaching that gay and lesbian Mormons were fundamentally flawed and unworthy of God's blessings for being what God had made. It seemed as if his choice was quickly being narrowed down to being with Brandon, being himself and being grateful to his Heavenly Father for bringing such a blessing of love into his life and lose his membership and all that came with it or follow the Church's teachings and being miserable for an eternity. The two choices just couldn't work together. So really, it came down to where he chose to put his faith: in love or in the Church.

CHAPTER NINE

"And by their desires and their works you shall know them." (D-C 18:38)

"Reconcile yourself to the will of God" (2 Nephi 10:24)

"In the Church, we enjoy the companionship of other members. We mutually help and inspire one another to live as Christ lives. This companionship gives strength to endure the challenges of daily life and to avoid temptation." - 6th Missionary Discussion

The next day found them going about their usual morning routine and setting aside their laundry; it was Monday. P-Day. Instead of having a relaxing day hanging out with the other missionaries in the beautiful late Spring weather, they would be inside meeting with the new Mission President.

Adam examined himself in the mirror as he finished with his tie, looking for anything his father might criticize. Brandon came out of the bathroom in cargo shorts and a UC-Davis T-shirt, clothing acceptable for them to wear on P-Day—*not* acceptable to meet the new President, though. Not in Adam's eyes, at least.

"Brandon, you have to wear a suit."

"It's my one day off! Besides, I don't have anything clean," Brandon said, kicking his hamper with the side of his foot. "Laundry day, remember?"

"My father doesn't believe in days off. Look, I've got a shirt left; you can wear that."

"Hey," Brandon said, squeezing Adam's shoulders. "It's going to be okay, Adam. We're good missionaries. We have a great reputation with the local members and the other guys, too. It's just another day, okay? He's the Missionary President today, not your father. Just treat him like you did Brother Jensen. Deep breath, man."

Nodding, Adam huffed out a harsh breath and tried to calm down. He grabbed his shoeshine kit, dropped onto their small sofa and put a mirror finish on his Sunday shoes. Brandon eyed him but didn't say anything, just buttoned his borrowed shirt and smoothed his hair back. It was a little loose at the neck, but Adam hoped his father wouldn't care.

They took a bus to the Missionary President's designated house in northern Barcelona, near the Parc de la Trinitat. A small green space across from the bus stop was lined with more of those delicate-limbed trees Adam now knew were jacaranda trees, heavy with beautiful purple blossoms. There was nothing comparable to them in Utah, but he was too nervous to enjoy their unique beauty.

They arrived at the small iron gate and pressed the buzzer. A tall, stiff, grey-faced woman with the appearance of beauty lost years ago opened the door and crossed the small courtyard. Adam fidgeted with his sports jacket and fought down the urge to smooth his hair at the sight of the woman's displeasure.

"Oh. Hello, Adam."

"Mother, good to see you." Adam tried to ignore Brandon looking back and forth between the two, knowing his companion wasn't used to the formal way the Youngs interacted.

"Well, your father wants to see you; he went through the zone records and saw that you've not had a baptism yet." Her mouth was pressed into a thin, tight line. Her gaze flitted over Adam's face, as if she was sizing him up since the last time she'd seen him and found his appearance wanting.

"Sorry, Mom," Adam mumbled as they entered the house. "It's not easy out here."

"Nothing worthwhile is. Don't track any of that road trash in; I've been sweeping it out of this courtyard all weekend," she added, shooting the overhanging trees with their purple blooms a filthy look, as if daring them to try to make a mess of her borrowed home.

Brandon stepped in front of her and stuck his hand out, "Hello, Sister Young. I'm Elder Christensen. It's nice to finally meet you."

She looked baffled, but took his hand. A stern voice boomed out from deeper inside the house. "Is that the one missionary who managed to do the Lord's work here?"

Adam's father emerged from the back room, tall, imposing, for all that he was soft in his expansive middle. His cheeks were ruddy and his mouth was pressed into a firm line as he looked Brandon up and down. Adam could tell Gerald liked what he saw in Brandon when his father stuck out his hand with an approving nod, saying, "President Young, son."

The two shook hands; Adam stood to the side, shuffling back and forth as he waited to be acknowledged. His father's focus was still only on Brandon, however.

"Not rubbed off on my boy yet, have you?"

Adam thought his face might melt at the images that conjured up and coughed to cover his distress.

"Well, give it time, give it time." President Young huffed; the sound was sharp and agitated. He finally turned to Adam and gave him a small, tight nod. "Son."

Adam nodded at his father. "Sir."

Brandon looked between the two of them and interjected, "I have to tell you, President Young, your son *has* rubbed off on me—"

Adam thought he just might strangle *himself*.

"I mean to say," Brandon continued, figuring out the innuendo he'd used, "that he's a *great* missionary. Very dedicated. He keeps me on my toes. We've made a lot of contacts because of him." Brandon gave Adam's shoulder a squeeze in an attempt to pull him into the conversation.

"Is that so?" Adam's father said, not sounding as though he believed a word. "I suppose your reports do have you both evenly split. Well, let's see about turning those contacts into full-tithe members and then I'll get excited. Adam, you go help your mother carry some of those boxes from the hallway so we can get this place in order. Elder Christensen? Follow me, I want to talk about some of your fellow missionaries. I've heard some stories that have me very disappointed..."

They wandered off. Brandon chanced a look over his shoulder; his expression was an apology. Adam sighed and grabbed a box as his mother walked back in. "Where do you want this, Mom?"

"In the bedroom, of course. It says so there on the side."

AFTER A FEW HOURS OF laboring, incurring several tsks and pained sighs from his mother for not instinctively knowing what she wanted, all of the boxes were in their right places. Brandon and President Young had finished. Brandon came out of the office looking green around the edges and more than a little shaken.

Adam's father looked normal, which was to say, gruff and no nonsense.

"I expect someone of your reputation to set the perfect example, Elder. I want the rest of the boys in this mission to look to you for the proper way to behave. You are the standard bearer. Son?" he asked and turned to Adam. "You know I expect nothing less from you than perfection. You've got it in you; your brothers and even your sister had successful missions full of baptisms, so don't shirk your duty. You two run along now. I'm sure you have laundry to do and contacts to make."

Gerald Young turned his back on them to look at a pile of letters. Their meeting was over. Adam nudged Brandon with his elbow and walked out.

"Don't you want to hug your mom? Say goodbye?" Brandon hissed.

"No. She's not expecting that, anyway."

Safely outside, they walked to the bus stop a few blocks away. Both men were silent for a few minutes as they navigated the busy roads back to their apartment.

Brandon broke the silence with a long whistle. "Man, you were *not* kidding."

"That was a good day," Adam laughed, although it lacked any humor. "He wasn't actively listing each of my shortcomings. No, this time he just hinted at them. Passive-aggression at its finest."

Brandon shuddered. "I—" He shook his head and kicked at a mound of purple jacaranda flowers piled along the curb. "I thought you were *exaggerating* about them. I just… Wow. I mean, no offense, but that's your *mom?*"

Adam thought about the little notes of encouragement, the candies and cheap, puffy stickers Brandon's mother stuck into each month's care package for Adam and him and felt a familiar longing. He could hardly believe Sister Christensen was real, she seemed so warm and loving. Brandon's dad, too, would put comics and doodles in the packages. He was especially fond of photocopying comics from the local paper and adding winks and smiley faces. Well, Adam just didn't have that, that was all there was to it. He was happy that Brandon had a family who seemed to be proud of him.

As they waited for their bus to arrive, Adam dropped onto the bench and asked, "So what did you two have to talk about for almost two hours?"

Brandon covered his face and let out a frustrated noise. "Oh, my gosh, Adam. It's awful. Probably one of the worst things that could have happened. Poor, dumb, stupid guy." Brandon punched his fist into his open hand. "So stupid!"

"Feel like letting me in on whatever this is?"

Brandon looked at Adam, his face visibly pained. "It's Sorensen. He got busted with a girl."

"What? What are you talking about, he's the last guy I'd ever think—"

"I know. Honestly, and this is just me reading between the lines of what your dad showed me. I think it just *looks* bad. I don't think he really did anything, not, um."

The "not like we've done" went unspoken. They shared a meaningful look and waited for an older woman to finish reading the posted bus schedule out loud. When she noticed their name tags, she hurried along her way.

"That family who kept having them over for dinner had a daughter," Brandon continued.

Adam rolled his eyes. "Of course they did."

"No, it's not like that, really. I'm sure of it. Well," he laughed bitterly, "no, I'm not, actually." He stared at the light midday traffic and worried the inside of his cheek with his teeth. "So, frickin' Elder May is the one who ratted him out. May discovered him writing letters to someone, and you know how we're really supposed to be writing through our Church email accounts?"

Adam nodded. It was how the Church could keep track of those who might be breaking rules by discussing "non-spiritually uplifting topics" like dating and movies and current events.

"But if you're writing home to your folks or brothers and sisters, it's not that big a deal. Well, clearly there were a bunch of letters going out. That raised May's suspicion, and when Sorensen was in the shower, May snooped and read one, saw it was for a local girl, and I guess they were pretty racy. Long and short of it, May ratted him out to the old Missionary President, Brother Jensen, a week ago. Jensen didn't want anything on *his* record so he left it for your dad to deal with."

Adam looked horrified. "What are they going to do? I mean, they were just letters, right?"

Brandon shook his head. "He's being sent home. They had a court set up for this morning, evidently. He's probably been disfellowshipped; your dad didn't say. I can't imagine them ex'ing him over some letters, though."

"You don't know my dad," Adam replied, horrified to think of Sorensen, bright, funny, dedicated Sorensen being dishonorably discharged, but he feared that was *exactly* what happened. "Maybe, *maybe* if he'd been writing to his girl back home, they would just give him a dressing down or something. But knowing my dad, he would have assumed Sorensen was acting on whatever is in those letters if she's here in town, especially since he's been over to her flippin' house so many times. Oh, my gosh. What a stupid… When is he leaving?"

"Left. Just after lunch today. Your dad and another church leader showed up out of the blue early this morning and told him to pack up then and there, then had the court."

Adam grabbed a nearby lamppost. His stomach may have been twisting before, but now it was in absolute turmoil. That reaction over romantic letters?

Brandon worried a loose paving tile in the road with the toe of his shoe as the bus pulled into their stop. Sighing heavily, he said, "Come on, we better head back. He gave me a list of things to do as long as my arm."

———•———

OVER THE NEXT SEVERAL DAYS, Brandon had so many responsibilities thrust upon him that he was unable to go door-to-door tracting with Adam, who instead went by himself on "splits" with another group of missionaries. Everyone had blackballed May. No one would talk to him beyond common courtesy, not even Guymon.

"So the thing I want to know," Gardener asked, hands shoved deep in his pockets as he rocked back and forth, "is what kind of companion just goes straight to leadership instead of keeping it within ranks?"

"Look," May said, getting visibly heated.

"No one asked you to speak, Greenie," Guymon spat. Adam got the impression that Guymon was glad not to be the source of everyone's derision. "And yeah, Gard. That's a real good question."

"I have lots of questions," Gardener continued, his voice vibrating with anger. "And honestly, I think I might write LaSalle and ask him how long it had been going on."

"That's a good one," Guymon said, the boring little sycophant that he was.

"Because if I wasn't allowed to so much as talk to that hot chick from Amsterdam who kept finding us at Las Ramblas, then how the heck is Sorensen being allowed to freakin' hook up with Spanish girls and in their dang homes, too?"

"Wait, what?" Guymon shoved Gardener's shoulder. "That's not—"

"Please, like you don't want to suck face with Cook."

"Guys," Adam said, raising his voice. "You're not helping."

"Yeah, well we can't all be perfect little Peter Priesthoods like you and Christensen, can we?"

Adam's face flushed. He definitely wasn't the poster boy for perfect behavior.

"Look, I did what I was supposed to do, okay?" May said, trying to push his way into the knotted group the others had made. "Don't be mad at me for following the rules."

"How does it go?" Gardener asked. "Exception to the rule? Rules were made to be broken? You didn't have to be such a freaking *narc* about it, May. You have to assess the situation. If he was just writing letters, who the heck even cares? He was a good guy, and you wrecked his whole life. Did you even think about that? About his mom waiting to have a big welcome home party? About how everyone in his ward is going to know he got sent home because hey, what's that? Where's the Return Missionary Sacrament Service? Oh, right, can't have one, because he's been freaking disfellowshipped."

Adam feared that punches might start to fly, so he redirected May to the other side of the square, where some older men were using the checkerboards on picnic tables, and tried to get the words "you wrecked his whole life" to stop reverberating in his head.

"You should have come to Brandon," Adam muttered, shoving May onto a bench.

May looked him up and down, snorted and looked away. "Yeah, okay."

Adam's skin crawled with the barely-hidden disgust on May's face. May was a little jerk, a rule-abiding, thoughtless creep, mad that Adam was siding with the others. He was sure of it.

Because President Young expected so much of Brandon, the only time that Adam saw his companion now was at night and for breakfast. Adam was constantly teamed with the others. After that first incredibly busy and disorienting week, Brandon sighed into his breakfast. "We're going to have to be smart about things, Adam. About what we're doing."

His spoon paused halfway to his mouth, Adam looked up, unsure where Brandon was going.

"I don't know if your father or any other of the guys might show up here without us being prepared. We need to put everything back." He tossed his head toward the bedroom door.

Oh. The beds. Adam nodded. "Yeah, that makes sense." He glanced up to see Brandon sitting there with an unhappy look on his face. "Gonna miss it, though."

Brandon smiled at that, looping his ankle around Adam's under the table. "You know the rule: 'Only sleep in the same *bedroom* as your companion.'"

Adam laughed, delighted at the mischievous glint in Brandon's eyes as he stated the next rule in the old missionary handbook, "'But do not sleep in the same *bed* as your companion.' Oops."

That glint Adam had enjoyed watching winked out as Brandon's face turned somber. He didn't move his leg, though.

The feeling of being connected to something larger than himself, the fire that had been lit inside Adam was slowly being extinguished. Word about Sorensen had spread fast, and everyone was on their toes. The missionaries he now spent his days with were dull and mindless.

Everyone was scared of messing up and now did everything by the book with no discussion. Even Ketchup was somber and less irritating.

Adam stopped paying attention to the things he was required to say to strangers and began operating on rote; he stopped hearing the steady stream of "*No me gusta*" and "*Gracias, no*" when homeowners opened the door and saw the familiar white shirt and black name tag.

Brandon was becoming so stressed by all the extra work he had—not to mention the stress of spending so much time with an increasingly demanding President Young—that he was barely eating, and he certainly wasn't able to get to bed at the same time as Adam. Days began passing into one another with nothing to distinguish them.

One night while lying in bed listening to Brandon talk in the living room on his mission-appointed cell phone to one of the northwestern region's branch presidents, Adam realized that he wasn't committing anything that the Church would consider a sin, now. How funny that he wasn't feeling *any* renewed sense of the Spirit or happiness, no greater connection to his religion or to his Heavenly Father as a result. Now, feeling disconnected from it all, he moved through his mission untethered and unsure—the way he had when he'd first arrived at the MTC.

Adam lay in bed at night watching Brandon toss and turn and mumble in his sleep. His experience now was almost exactly what he'd feared his mission would become before learning what it could be. Now the remaining seventeen months stretched long and wearisome before him. Where was the joy? Where was the connection to something greater than himself?

A few weeks after the change in personnel, Adam and Brandon had a surprise break. They woke to heavy rains and electric storms rolling off the ocean—storms that were expected to pummel the city all day. There would be no leaving the house; there was no point.

They looked at each other over the empty breakfast dishes. Hints of smiles formed on their faces.

"Better make a quick call to Sister Guell and let her know we aren't making the meeting with their contact today." Brandon was on his feet and at the phone in a split second.

Adam opened the front door and, through the narrow opening of their building's courtyard, looked at the bruise-colored sky. A jet of electricity sparked and crackled across the clouds. "Whoa."

Brandon came up behind him, slid a hand up his back and buried his fingers in Adam's hair just above his nape. Adam grabbed the door handle and swung it shut, and there was Brandon. Their lips were together, their hands struggled to pull off their suit jackets without losing contact, their feet tripped over each other to find something to lean against.

"Missed you," Adam breathed, his hands working on the front of Brandon's slacks.

"Didn't think," Brandon gasped, stopping to pull his half-buttoned shirt and G's over his head and tossing them to the floor, "that I'd get to be with you again, thought he'd transfer you or something."

They both stilled at that. Brandon cupped Adam's cheek and drew his thumb softly over it. Adam turned his face and kissed Brandon's palm, sucking on the fat pad at the base of Brandon's thumb, reveling in how amazing if was to know the entire day stretched in front of them with nothing to do but to be together. Adam braced his elbows against the wall, bracketing Brandon between them and traced Brandon's lower lip, exhaling into his mouth when Brandon gripped him and pulled their bodies closer.

Adam understood the urgency building in Brandon; it matched his own. While deepening their kiss, he impatiently ground his body into Brandon's; he was almost mindless from the heady sensation of their bodies connecting so intimately through the soft fabric of their remaining clothes. With an impatient noise, Adam stepped away and tugged his dress shirt and G's off, then helped Brandon do the same before pulling Brandon back into arms, leaning their weight against the wall as he went back in for another deep kiss. As they touched and loved one another, Adam couldn't help how his body sought the heat of Brandon's, nor how his hands gripped Brandon's soft, dark hair, as pressure, wonderful, fulfilling pressure built inside him, and he finally felt right and whole now that they could be themselves, be together in each other's arms.

As they got their breathing under control, chuckling softly and peppering one another's faces with kisses and murmured words of love, Adam was overcome by want, but it was beyond something base, something physical. He wanted so much: wanted to spend all day with Brandon at his side; wanted to dress in regular clothes and explore the city, hand in hand. But more than that, he wanted them to proudly affix their name tags and search until they found an investigator, someone who was in need, and find a way to share this overwhelming joy and happiness he felt when he and Brandon were together, the sense of completeness he had when he and Brandon tackled a difficult problem and came out on the other side feeling stronger and more connected. He wanted to pour into that person the peace and love and righteousness he felt for his Heavenly Father, that feeling that was so amplified when Brandon was at his side. He wanted to watch Brandon in his temple clothes baptizing that someone, wanted to stand at Brandon's side as they confirmed that person with the Holy Ghost, making them a true child of God, and then he wanted to lie down every night at Brandon's side, wake to him every morning, tackle every problem, the two of them, together.

Adam didn't know how to ask for that, didn't know if he could, and it was all too much.

Brandon caught his breath, too far from where Adam's heart was racing. He pulled Brandon into his hold and kissed him, murmuring, "Don't go away again, okay?"

Brandon dropped his forehead on Adam's shoulder. "I don't ever want to."

Adam pressed kiss after kiss onto Brandon's temple, breathing him in, and sighing happily as Brandon's arms snaked around Adam's waist more tightly. "I missed that so much."

"Me, too," Adam replied.

"Can, can we try something?"

"What? What is it?"

Brandon drew the edge of his teeth along the tendon in Adam's neck, making Adam's skin break out in shivers. He sucked a wet spot high on Adam's neck under the hinge of his jaw and said, "It's just, I missed you so much. I didn't know if we could do this again."

"Brandon, I want to do everything with you. Just ask."

"Will you let me inside you? *Be* inside you? I'll totally stop if you want me to, okay? I just want to try, if you'll let me. Or, the other way? I'm okay with that, too, I think. I-I can't stop thinking about it."

Adam, lightheaded and breathless, swallowed thickly. It was something they'd never done, hadn't even talked about. He chewed on his lower lip, prompting Brandon to soothe, "No, I'm sorry. Forget I said it. It's too much."

"I… Brandon, I didn't say no." Pulling back a little, Adam pressed the flat of his hand to Brandon's bare chest, just over where Brandon's heart was beating. Brandon covered Adam's hand with his own.

"You can say no," Brandon said. "I've just wanted… I really want you. Like that. If you want. We can do it the other way, if you'd rather?"

Adam almost lost his footing at the image that brought to mind. He shivered and drew Brandon back. "I don't want to say no, though. I've been thinking about it, too, I just couldn't… Yeah, I really want to, Brandon. It's just… I'm not really sure how it all works."

Brandon's face went red. "Before my mission I may have seen some, um, websites that explained how to do it."

"Yeah?" Adam said, face heating. His body was rapidly showing interest again. He closed his eyes and took a deep breath to force himself to calm down and think; both fear and excitement coursed through him. When Brandon continued to wait for an answer, he knew what he wanted: not to wait a moment longer, not when it seemed like ages since they'd been able to be together. "Show me, then."

"Oh, my gosh, Adam." Brandon swiftly covered Adam's body with his own, nuzzling his cheek along Adam's thick shoulder. "I promise," he said. "If you don't like it, don't like *anything*, just say it, okay?"

"Brandon," Adam said, turning to hold Brandon's face. "It's okay. I want you to. I want *you*."

"Yeah?" he asked as his hands massaged lower and lower. A thrum of energy raced up Adam's spine as Brandon kneaded and massaged his backside. "You sure?"

He couldn't help but drop his head forward, nodding a yes, nor could he help the moan that escaped when Brandon's fingertips trailed all the way down Adam's spine. He hadn't realized how many nerve endings were there, how sensitive his body was, as Brandon continued to gently touch him in an attempt to get Adam to relax fully.

After several moments, Adam realized something they'd forgotten. "Wait," he said. Brandon immediately pulled away so that Adam turned to give him a kiss. "No, it's just that we need... like, lotion or something? Oil?" Adam blushed at using the word "oil;" it sounded so licentious, so tawdry. So *sinful*.

"We don't have any more olive... oh. Um, hold on." Brandon left, went into their bedroom, and came out a few minutes later looking sheepish. He had what looked like a large, golden bullet on a keychain in his hand; Adam decided hearing the word oil wasn't as blasphemous as seeing where Brandon would be *getting* it.

"It hasn't been blessed yet, this isn't my normal one," Brandon quickly explained. "I would never—" Brandon cut himself off, looking nervous.

If Adam wasn't in trouble before, he certainly thought he would be now—using unconsecrated holy oil as... Well.

That didn't mean he wanted to stop. Not at all. For now, however, he wanted the security of Brandon's arms around him as they experienced this together. Adam wanted to chase the excitement building, wanted to feel how different being with Brandon like this could be.

When Brandon drew Adam back into his arms, sighing with evident relief, Brandon said, "I love your deep voice, have I said that yet?"

Adam's heart stuttered at the use of "love." It was still so new, this understanding of what his feelings really were, but the word was so right, the perfect expression for the way his body came alive when close to Brandon. It was the perfect word to describe the overwhelming need to share everything from his day to his thoughts to his life with his companion.

Companion... Brandon was that in every way, too. Considerate, tender, funny, uplifting, challenging. He was everything Adam envisioned for an eternal partner, and now, now they were sharing that one last act that other couples whose relationships were sanctified by God and their Church were allowed, and it was everything beautiful and wonderful and overwhelming, their bodies coming together in the most intimate of ways, and Adam trusting Brandon completely.

And that was how he knew this was love, and that it was good. He trusted Brandon with his heart and this moment and beyond, all that it meant, and knew Brandon was trusting him, too. He was overcome with emotion, a feeling larger than he thought his body could even contain as he marveled at how this was love, this was the two of them learning how to say with their bodies what their hearts had been feeling for so many months, now. Adam was struck all over again with the knowledge that there was a reason this was considered a holy sacrament, that this joining of bodies was something beautiful when shared between two people who loved each other. And he did. He loved Brandon with all his heart, and it was more than the carnal pleasures of the flesh, which, as he gasped and groaned, held safe in Brandon's arms, was wonderful, more than he had imagined it could ever be.

But this act was something he couldn't imagine sharing with anyone else. This was something to be saved for the person he loved.

He clutched at Brandon's arms encircling his waist, and held on tight, filled with amazement that they'd found each other, that they were in each other's lives, that they *loved* each other.

They were meant to be together, at this time, in this place, and suddenly it was more than he could stand, not kissing Brandon, not breathing Brandon's air, so he turned and caught Brandon's mouth with his, whispering all he could find words enough to say as they moved together, the center of the universe beginning and ending where their bodies joined so perfectly.

Adam's body was racing toward completion. He dropped to his forearms and in his mind flashed memories of the two of them sharing meals they'd cooked for each other, sitting side-by-side as they read scriptures and pondered the deep mysteries of faith and of themselves, kneeling together as they held hands and prayed. "Please," Adam cried out as his heart filled to bursting. "Brandon, it's so much…"

"I know, I know, me, too." Brandon gasped, burying his face in the crook of Adam's neck once more.

The wind drove the rain against their one window, but Adam couldn't be bothered to pay attention as Brandon began dropping open-mouthed kisses along his shoulder, couldn't care about the crack of lightning when Brandon's palm was white hot against Adam's chest, covering Adam's racing heart, wasn't focused on anything but the way his body felt alive and whole, full and happy and finally like himself, like he wasn't alone, like he was finally, blissfully *right*.

Brandon's body gave a spasm as he clutched at Adam's chest, holding him tightly, and it was overwhelming, so overwhelming that Adam's toes curled. Pressure and pleasure were building inside him until he thought he might start to cry. He wanted this sensation to go on forever, but it needed to quickly come to an end before it grew into something too huge, almost terrifying in its intensity.

His breathing ragged, Brandon pressed his cheek into the back of Adam's head. His body shook as he stammered, "Oh, *G-God*… oh, my God. I love you so, so much, Adam!"

Adam's vision narrowed, and his ears rang as he climaxed. His body sagged happily into Brandon's strong hold as he tried to catch his breath, tried to find air enough to say the words back.

Cold air swirled against Adam's legs and broke through the fog of lust and love and pleasure that was drowning his brain, but he didn't register it as anything important, certainly not as important as how it felt when Brandon wrapped his arms tightly around Adam, shaking and trembling as he murmured, "I love you, Adam. I *love* you." Nothing was as important as that.

Adam clutched at Brandon's hand as he tried to find a way to speak past the lump in his throat. His eyes stung and his heart almost burst from his rib cage. No one had ever said they loved him. He brought Brandon's hand to his mouth and dropped kiss after grateful kiss to his palm, his wrist, his knuckles. It was perfect.

A door slammed shut.

"What in *God's* name are you doing to my son?!"

The cold air. The hastily shut door. Every muscle in his body froze. Brandon tensed, then there was horrible emptiness. Adam's back was suddenly cold, as if Brandon had been pulled off him. Adam turned around, his hands in front of himself to hide his nakedness. Brandon was scrambling to his feet from the living room floor. His father *had* pulled him off, then, thrown him.

"What did he do to you, son? Are you all right? What in the hell is going on here?"

The Mission President was in his house. His *father*. He'd seen…

"Go get some clothes on, you despicable…" President Young was shaking, glaring at Brandon and pointing at him. "I should punch you right in the mouth, you filthy perverted… degenerate. How someone like you could have been made a Leader— Disgusting!"

Adam's vision swam; his ears roared as if he was underwater. He could see Brandon stammering, trying to pick his clothes off the ground, and his father, oh, his *father*! President Young's hair stood on end, his jowls were shaking, his eyes were rolling wild in their sockets as he took in the scene.

Brandon, his face panicked, tried to explain, to say something. Adam couldn't move, couldn't make out Brandon's stammering. His worst fear had come to pass, and he was awestruck by the horror of it all. His face was hot as Brandon tried to plead, reaching out to President Young only to be slapped away.

"And Goddammit, Adam, cover yourself! Absolutely obscene! What is *wrong* with you, not defending yourself against.... against a pantywaist! How could you let him *do* this to you?" Brandon tried to say something, but President Young whirled, his fist raised. He shouted, "I'm not speaking to you!"

Brandon quickly jumped into his pants and threw his shirt over his head. Adam's father grabbed him by the elbow and dragged him out into the storm. He didn't bother to shut the door. The wind blew rain into the open doorway. Adam, naked and terrified, stood shivering far enough away that he wasn't affected, not by the cold or wet. Nothing seemed to be able to reach him, he was so deeply locked inside himself, unable to face the enormity of the situation. He blinked as he noticed a pair of dress loafers knocked askew against the wall and realized that Brandon didn't have on shoes.

He heard a car door slam before thunder boomed in the distance. His father came raging back in the doorway, shouting, "What have you done? I *always* knew there was something wrong about you..." He snorted and shook his head. "This will kill your mother." He jammed a finger into Adam's face; Adam cringed from it as far as he could as he father spat, "In my mission? You do this in *my* mission?"

His father slammed the door with such force the frame cracked along the top. Adam began heaving in air. His vision was beginning to narrow; stars danced at its edge. His hands shook uncontrollably. Ruined. Everything was ruined. Something that had seemed so wonderful, so *perfect*, something and someone he'd waited for his whole life had been ripped away and made into something *ugly*, forever tainted by his father's presence.

He looked down at his nakedness and was ashamed.

CHAPTER TEN

"WHAT A PRECIOUS THING IS a good [missionary] companion. He becomes your protector in times of trouble or temptation." (President Gordon B. Hinckley, LDS Church News, July 4, 1998)

"FOUR OF THE SWEETEST WORDS that every mission president likes to hear are: 'I love my companion.'" (Rulon G. Craven, The Effective Missionary, p. 56)

"THY LOVE TO ME WAS wonderful, passing the love of women." (2 Sam 1:26)

"YEA, I HAVE LOVED THEE with an everlasting love: therefore with lovingkindness have I drawn thee." (Jer 31:3)

ADAM KNEW HE'D SHOWERED BECAUSE he was holding a damp towel in his hands. He knew that his father had come back to grab Brandon's things, because the closet was open and there was a hanger on the floor and Brandon's duffel bag was gone from its usual place. He knew he wasn't alone because he heard whispered voices coming from the living room.

His mind was foggy with terror; his stomach roiled with acid. The muffled voices from the other room were unclear. He wasn't ready to face his father, to face what had happened to Brandon, to face what this meant for himself: Eternal damnation, cast into Outer Darkness, left behind for all time and eternity without his family, but more importantly, without God.

"Yes," a voice was saying, "Elder Christensen. *Brandon* Christensen. I know, I know, I guess you just can't tell sometimes, can you? I never in a million years would have *thought*..."

At the sound of Brandon's name Adam snapped out of his stupor. They were talking about Brandon, and Adam had to know where Brandon was, had to get to him, had to try to explain why he'd just stood there, motionless. He'd let Brandon be dragged out and hadn't said a single word to help. Brandon must *hate* him. His face crumpled. He hated himself.

Adam peered into the front room to see his father standing in his shirtsleeves, his tie loosened and his hair astray, listening to another church member who was sitting on their small sofa making travel plans. Brandon, it appeared, was being sent home immediately.

The man on the phone looked at Adam; his face barely hid his distaste for whatever he believed Adam to be, for whatever his father had explained he'd walked in on. But Adam didn't care about that or the angry red blotches on his father's face. He only cared about Brandon. If he could fix that problem, he wouldn't care about his own fate so much.

He walked up to his father, detached enough not to be offended when Gerald Young took a step back, and asked, "Where's Brandon?"

"*Elder* Christensen, Adam, although he won't be that for much longer. Why didn't you tell anyone that your companion was a... a you know?"

Adam ignored that line of questioning. "What's going to happen to him?"

The man on the phone covered the mouthpiece and said, "He invited darkness into his spirit. Same-sex attraction," the man said, speaking as if it hurt his mouth to spit the words out, "cannot be acted upon; it's a grave sin. You both knew that. He won't remain a member of this Church. The revelation President Monson received was very clear. You can be SSA—" Adam knew the term the Church preferred to LGBT.

"—but you cannot act on it. You must obey God's commandment until he can fix you in the next life. As for me, I wish they still did electro-shock therapy up at BYU like they did back in the seventies..."

Adam's ears thrummed. His father moved as if to lay a hand on Adam's shoulder, but pulled back at the last moment; he clearly didn't want to touch his son. Adam thought he might scream if his father *did* touch him.

"Did, did he overpower you, Adam? That's what happened, isn't it? You never were first string, didn't seem to have it in you. Your mother was too soft on you."

Adam looked into his father's face and saw nothing but hostility and revulsion. He'd never seen love there, not really. Now he knew what love looked like, how it felt, how it filled his heart with joy, how it made him feel whole and capable and ready to tackle the world.

"No," Adam replied. "That's not what happened. He didn't... *attack* me. Dad, he *loves* me."

"That's not possible. Gays don't *love*, they only want to give in to their selfish needs. You can't make a family if you're *gay*. That young man has rejected Christ's teachings, rejected the *prophet's* teachings. Selfishness never brought happiness."

Reality came screaming back, almost knocking Adam off his feet. He couldn't help himself. He laughed. "You're... you're so stupid. Oh, my gosh. You don't know anything! You don't know *anything* about happiness." He closed his eyes to get the awful picture of his father's face out of his mind. He finally understood what happiness was, and it wasn't to be found in anything in that room with him now.

The hard slap across his face snapped him out of it. "Don't you ever speak to me like that again," Gerald hissed.

His father's shoulders heaved, and his nostrils flared with the force of his panting breaths. President Young looked over his shoulder and saw that the other man wasn't paying attention, he'd moved into the kitchen to write down flight schedules.

Gerald began to slap Adam about the head, shoved him back into the bedroom, then kicked the door shut with his heel. Adam threw his hands up to defend himself, as he'd always done.

"I oughtta knock your head off your shoulders, you ungrateful, disobedient, disrespectful little fa—!"

Adam shoved his father off before he could utter that one word. He put all of his anger and disappointment, all of his frustration with never having been accepted or loved by his parents into that push. His father careened into the door with a heavy bang and slid off his feet, breathing heavily. Adam stood, wild, furious, trapped, but still defiant. He scanned the room for a weapon, something he could use to defend himself. His father watched, eyes widening and hands going into a defensive pose, not unlike Adam's had been just moments ago.

It sobered Adam enough to keep his hands by his side. He didn't want to be anything like his father.

"Now, you listen to me," Gerald said, clearly still trying to maintain a voice of stern authority as he got to his feet. He tried to loom over Adam, but they were finally the same height; Adam was younger and far more fit than his aging, paunchy father, and, though he never wanted to be the kind of man from whom people cowered, he relished the flash of fear in his father's eye.

"You know that was disrespectful to me." Gerald smoothed his shirt front in what appeared to be an attempt to maintain self-restraint. "Let's not let things get out of control any more than they already are. Get dressed; get your things for the night. You can't be left alone; you know that. You're going to stay with Brother Ramirez and his family where they can keep an eye on things."

Brother Ramirez must be the man on the phone.

"Tomorrow we'll get this sorted out. Dammit, we'll have to hold another effing court. My own son!" Gerald punched the door behind him with a meaty fist. He opened it and looked over his shoulder. "Don't you open your mouth until I tell you. Don't you say one word about what happened here unless I tell you the word to say, is that understood?"

Adam didn't nod. He stood there, defiant and unyielding, staring at the open door until he heard his father leave. Then he dressed and threw his things into his suitcase and bag. Brother Ramirez, the driver from his first day in the mission field, waited at the door with a wary look on his face.

"Let's not talk about what happened, shall we?" Brother Ramirez said, avoiding eye contact. "My wife is very sensitive; she doesn't need to be exposed to all this sordidness."

Adam followed behind him. The wind caught the door to the apartment and swung it shut with a loud bang. There were tree limbs and debris in the street from the storm; the sky was yellow and green, the distant clouds were dark as the storm moved farther along the coastline, but the damage was done.

———•———

Two weeks. It took two weeks for everything to be sorted out, leaving Adam trapped in the basement spare room of a house he'd never been to. Sister Ramirez brought him his food on a tray in his room with a regretful, but kind and motherly, smile. Adam didn't mind not sitting at the table with the rest of their family. He wanted to be alone.

No one would tell him what was going on. No one dared mention his former companion's name within earshot. He had no idea what his father was saying about Brandon, how the mission's "best and brightest" just up and left without anyone knowing what happened, or where Adam was and for what reason. Adam figured his dad was claiming he was sick, based on the snatched bits of conversation he heard from the hall outside his room. It would be one of the few ways his father could avoid immediately reporting about Adam's indiscretions.

He wished he knew how Brandon was doing and whether Brandon's family had allowed him back home. Brandon's family was so close;

Adam would be devastated to learn he'd ruined that for his companion. Adam had built up a fantasy about Brandon's mother welcoming *him* into the family, too. She'd seemed so loving and open in her care packages and letters: She'd send treats for the other guys, candy bars and notes for Adam. He remembered how Brandon always went soft whenever he read anything she'd written him and her thoughtful consideration for their questions. Adam hoped she hadn't let her love for her son be affected, if only for Brandon's sake. He couldn't imagine a mother who was so warm, so tender with kids who weren't even her own turning from her son, but then, he also couldn't have imagined himself or Brandon being in the situation they now faced.

He started writing Brandon at least ten different letters before realizing that no one would mail it for him, nor did he know where Brandon *was*. He didn't have access to his organizer where all of his addresses were kept. Was Brandon at his house in California? Had he been sent somewhere? Kicked out? That seemed unlikely, it really did. Brandon's family so clearly loved him.

"And he loved me. Loves," Adam said, correcting himself. He was on his fourth round of pushups, stuck in the basement with nothing to do but focus on himself. At least he had moved past his inability to look at who he was, at how he thought and felt and what he truly believed, both in spirit and in himself. "I love him. Love comes from our Heavenly Father, and love can never be wrong."

He hummed "God Is Love" through the last five reps, powering through them as if they were nothing.

Finally, his father came to retrieve him. He refused to make eye contact with Adam.

"Your court is in an hour. Get dressed appropriately."

A thrill of terror raced through him. He would have to stand before his leaders in the priesthood and explain in detail what had happened so they could determine the severity of the sin and act as mouthpieces of Heavenly Father with regard to Adam's punishment. To tell those people anything about the life-changing experiences he and Brandon shared would cheapen them. The thought of saying anything to those strangers so they could dissect every touch, every whispered word of love, to find and assign wrongdoing was horrible. *That* would be the sin.

"You'll come back to your mother's and my home in the north part of the city. It'll be held there. Now, listen," he said, chancing a quick glance at his son, "I don't want you going into too much detail. No one wants to hear that sick stuff, you got it? Let's just have you explain how Christensen hypnotized you, and you were overpowered and can't remember anything but that. Everyone talked about the boy's charisma, so that'll help. Elder May even said something about it, that he felt it, too."

Adam blinked at that. Elder May?

"They've told me that if that's the case, they'll let you off with a warning," Gerald continued, "but you'll have to stay supervised for the remainder of your mission. It's a burden on your mother and me, but..."

His father's voice faded. Stay? Stay and act as if nothing had happened? Continue toeing his father's line, trying to teach people doctrines and ideas that he didn't think he believed in anymore? As for his court, Adam knew that his father would be in the room. How could he tell that group of men what had really happened? But even worse was the thought of *lying* about it, lying about what Brandon meant to him. How Brandon had given Adam the freedom to let himself grow, to think for himself for the first time in his whole, pitiful, controlled and mapped-out life. Brandon hadn't hypnotized him; Brandon had set him free. He owed Brandon *everything*.

"... absolutely shamed your family. Your mother knows nothing about this, so you keep your trap shut. She thinks you're just sick, contracted some weird virus or something, and your comp knocked you around." His father gave him an appraising look. "That's not hard to believe. Jacob—" That was Adam's next oldest brother, six years Adam's senior and built like their father. "—used to put you in a headlock pretty easy." His father sniffed. "You never fought back. Should have guessed back then."

Adam balled his fists at his sides and stared at the gap in his father's shirt where it struggled to stretch across his expanding belly.

"Get your things; you'll be coming back to our place, regardless. I'll be waiting in the car."

When they arrived at the Mission President's house, Adam was told to wait in the hallway while Gerald made phone calls in his office. He sat on an uncomfortable straight-backed chair and awaited his fate. A glossy LDS magazine on a console table caught his eye; a stack of letters sat in a messy pile next to it. Adam absentmindedly flipped through the stack and stopped at a thin postcard with a picture of the ocean on it, taken at Llevant Beach. He tried to turn it over to see who it was from; a bit of the stamp had curled over, and, as a result, the card was stuck to another letter, a bill from the looks of it.

He ripped the letter away and read the postcard's back. His eyes watered. He read it several times. His father's door opened and Adam quickly shoved the postcard into his pocket.

"Well. Let's get this over with, then. They're ready to talk to you."

Adam smoothed his hair and checked his tie in the hall mirror. His father took an exaggerated step away from him as he approached the French doors. "Remember what I told you. You were weak, and he overpowered you, got it?"

Adam looked up at him. His father backed farther away; worry lines creased his forehead.

"No, sir, Elder Christensen did not overpower me," Adam said, his chin up and his shoulders square.

"It's all right, son, this is a court of love. Heavenly Father doesn't want you to lie to us."

"I know," Adam said, smiling wryly. "That's why I'm not lying."

"Now, look—" Gerald, *President* Young choked back his temper with a cough. "Everyone here understands how you can come to idolize your companion. We were all missionaries, all of us were green at one point, right?" The men all nodded, their pale, aged faces showing varying degrees of pity and shock.

"We understand that he was someone all you fellas admired," his father continued, "We have the confessions from the others, how he was everyone's favorite, how he hoodwinked you all into thinking he was a good, worthy man. But something went wrong. We all know you're supposed to be obedient to your leaders, but he was *wrong*. You don't have to cover for him anymore. You can tell us how he used force and no one here will judge you."

Adam scanned the group and knew that they most certainly *would* judge him. But he didn't want to lie anymore, not to himself and not to the world. "He didn't force me to love him."

A few of the men's jaws dropped open. President Young looked ready to explode. "You don't know what you're saying."

The corner of the postcard poked Adam's hip through his thin dress slacks. "I do. I know exactly what I'm saying. I love him, a man. The best man I've ever known, really. And we love each other. I willingly let him make lo—"

"That's enough. That is *enough!* I will not have that sort of language in my house. Get out of this room. You are making a mockery of this court. We'll call you in when we've made our decision." President Young pointed at the door.

Adam gladly walked out. He paced in the kitchen waiting for the deliberations to end. His father's fake-leather covered organizer was lying on the counter. His throat tightening, he flipped to the day after he and Brandon had been caught. A note was scribbled in the margin, "Home. Ex'd. No contact with A."

An address was written under that; Adam recognized it as Brandon's home address. He'd been sent home? Had they taken him back? He flipped forward looking for any more notes, anything that would tell him how Brandon was doing, if he was okay, if he hated—

"Elder Young?"

One of the men from the council poked his head out of the office doors. "We're ready for you, son."

Adam's mind was in a haze. He drifted back into the room, knowing that whatever judgment they passed didn't matter, not really, not now when he'd finally let himself be completely open and honest with who he was and he could let that satisfaction, that peace, act as a buffer to their consternation and piety.

The man who'd called him back in cleared his throat and began speaking in a monotonous tone; Adam recognized it as the way all the leaders in the Church gave their Sunday talks and classroom lectures. It lulled him further into a detached state. It was all so... silly. So much anger and rage, so much time and energy wasted because two men loved each other. He couldn't help but smile.

They *loved* each other. They were good people who loved each other, and God is love.

"A disciplinary court is a court of love. One of the most loving things the Church can do for a person is to relieve them of the burdens of their covenants through excommunication and disfellowship. It is not done to punish but to help them. We, as your leaders, are anxious to reach you and encourage you to the righteous path of repentance. The Church has been very clear about the Law of Chastity, and that so-called gays and lesbians are violating that sacred law if they act on their sinful inclinations. They, and those acts, are subject to the discipline of the Church. This council has, through thoughtful prayer, been led by Heavenly Father and the Holy Ghost. You are to be disfellowshipped. You are still a member. You may not keep your temple recommend. You may not use any facet of your priesthood. You may not partake in the Sacrament, nor may you offer public prayers. We encourage you to continue paying a full tithe so as to not compound one sin with another..."

Adam's gaze drifted out the window. His father's house had a limited view of the ocean. If he focused, he could hear Brandon's laugh the day they'd walked down to the beach that morning when all of this began and he remembered how they'd watched a dog feint and play with a couple of seagulls in the wet sand, how they'd confessed who they were to one another, how they'd trusted each other.

Brandon had bought him ice cream and held him until Adam calmed down, terrified by his own nature.

"...reinstated as a full and righteous member of the Church so long as you never engage in any form of communication with Mr. Christensen so long as he remains immersed in sin."

The man sighed and straightened a stack of papers on his desk. "Gentlemen? Would someone care to offer a prayer? If—"

Adam interrupted, "I'm sorry, you said I can't ever talk to Brandon again? My *eternal salvation* depends on this?"

The man looked affronted at the meeting not running smoothly. "Yes, that's correct. You are never to interact with that young man again. Those are the conditions that Heavenly Father has outlined."

"Then I refuse to accept them."

Silence fell over the room.

"What did you say?" Gerald hoarsely whispered.

"I refuse," Adam said, turning to him. "You can't tell me that I can't ever speak to someone. That's not anywhere in the scriptures. That's not a part of repentance. Christ didn't teach his followers to hold a *grudge*, what the heck? And I love him. I'm going to see him as soon as I get home."

"Not while you live under my roof you won't!"

Adam smiled then, the first genuine smile he'd been able to produce since this whole nightmare began. "That won't be a problem, *Dad.*"

The man who delivered his verdict stood then, his hands flat against the table, his face red, filled with anger. "Then you reject this priesthood council's decision! And by doing so, reject Christ! Excommunication is the only way to solve this matter."

The other men in the room murmured agreement.

"Fine," Adam said, putting his hands in his pockets; his index finger traced over the edge of the postcard. "I'll wait outside. Tell me when I'm leaving."

"You can say goodbye to your dorm, to your car and your family, then, because I'm not—"

He turned his back on his father, who was now visibly shaking with pent-up rage, and closed the door behind him.

————◆————

NINE HOURS LATER HE WAS sitting on a plane. His suit and tie were jammed into his carry-on bag along with all of his G's. He was happy to find that he was comfortable in only jeans and a T-shirt, though it was odd not wearing the familiar G's after so many months, after so many years of being taught that they were a spiritual and physical barrier from evil.

When they'd arrived at the airport, Adam's father had shoved his passport hastily into Adam's hand; he must have been under the impression that gay was "catching."

"Your brother Seth will be waiting to pick you up. You're going straight back to the house where he and Claudia are house sitting. You are not to leave the house without your brother accompanying you. You are not..."

Adam tuned him out. He had no intention of meeting Seth at the airport. His father got him to security and turned away without another word. As soon as Adam was on his own, he found a working pay phone. The person at the other end, in a voice Adam had longed to hear for months, happily agreed to accept the charges so Adam could relay his flight information.

"Have a safe flight, dear. We can't wait to hug the stuffing out of you."

Adam smiled at the soft, maternal voice and hung up. It was going to be expensive to speak any longer, and he'd already cost those he loved enough. All that was left was the flight back.

Now, his heart light and his face aching from the joy he couldn't contain, with the sense of freedom soaking into every particle of his being the farther the plane carried him, he pulled out the postcard that had been re-directed to his father's house from his old apartment in Barcelona.

Adam:

2 Sam 1:26, Jer 31:3
Call me when you leave. I'll be there when you land.

Come home to me.

All My Love, B

He held the postcard in his hand and smiled as he looked out the window at the ocean miles below.

EPILOGUE

———

"THERE ARE, BY MOST ESTIMATES, 5,000 kids experiencing homelessness in Utah at any given time. Roughly 42 percent of them identify as LGBT, and most come from Mormon households. This means, of the 450,000 people in Utah between the ages of 15 and 24, a projected 22,000 to 35,000 of them will experience homelessness at some point." Chadwick Moore, 'The Ghost Children of Mormon County,' Advocate, April 26, 2016

"EACH CHILD SHOULD FEEL IMPORTANT. Parents need to show they are interested in what their children do and express love and concern for their children. […] The family is the most important unit in The Church of Jesus Christ of Latter-day Saints." Gospel Principles, Chapter 36, pages 209-210, 211

"BELOVED, LET US LOVE ONE another: for love is of God; and every one that loveth is born of God, and knoweth God." 1 John 4:7

"OH MY GOSH, MOM," BRANDON said, pulling on the back of his mother's rolling office chair. "Get off the Internet."

"But, honey," she said trying to scoot forward, but failing, "there are boys and girls just like you talking about how they're doing now."

"At least get off Reddit." Brandon let go of her chair and laughed softly as she pulled herself forward to her desk.

"Like this young lady here. Fell in love on her mission while she was in France, came out to her family and… Oh."

Sandra Christensen closed the lid to her laptop.

"Maybe not so much like me?" Brandon asked.

Sandra fell back in her chair and stared up at the ceiling. "I just can't understand how many kids have been…" She sighed. "Well, yes, I can. I just can't understand how so many *parents* can choose the Church over their babies."

Brandon leaned down, kissed the top of his mom's hair and rest his cheek. He could smell her perfume, the same scent she'd worn his entire life, and it made his heart ache with how lucky he felt. He'd been terrified on that long plane ride back to the United States, but at his long layover in Chicago, he decided to get up and walk around before the plane took off again. He found his mom and dad speaking fervently with the gate attendant.

"Sandra! Bob!" he called out, remembering his mother's instructions never to call out "Mom" in a crowded room because fifteen women would look up.

"There he is!" his mother cried, and Brandon's soul sank at the sight of tear tracks on her face. "Come here, come here," she said, pulling him into her tiny but fierce embrace.

Then his dad was there wrapping his considerable arms around them both, kissing Brandon's head and saying, "We got you. We got you, kid; it's okay."

Brandon hadn't been able to hold back the choked sobs that had been threatening to pour out of him ever since he was shoved, shoeless and terrified, into the back of a car and told he would never see Adam again.

"I know you hate me. I know it."

"What?" Sandra asked. She grabbed Brandon's face in her hands, her thumbs smoothing away the tears he couldn't help at the sight of his folks, and said, "Now you listen to me, Brandon Marshall Christensen. You are my son. And there is *nothing* you could do to make me hate you, do you hear me?"

He nodded, still unsure.

She pulled him back to her; her arms wrapped like a vise around his waist; her cheek pressed against his belly, tiny and warm and… and *there*.

The gate attendant cleared her throat. "Um, I see you found each other. Why don't we just let the three of you get back on the plane before regular boarding?"

"Thank you," Bob said, guiding them to the gangplank with a hand on their backs.

It was unreal. They even had seats on either side of him for the final leg to California. "What are you two doing here? I'll be in Sacramento in a few hours. Wait, how could you afford this?" His family was not well-off. Plane trips had been few and far between in Brandon's life.

"Sister Johnson?" Sandra prompted. "Up the street? Mark's mother?"

"Uh, yeah?"

"Stewardess. She put us on standby so we could get here."

Brandon covered his face with his hands. "Oh, my gosh. Does everyone know?"

"Know what?" Sandra asked. "We called her and said there was a problem, you had to come home, and she took care of the rest. She sends her love, by the way."

"Mom," he said, lowering his voice to a whisper as a stewardess walked past for her pre-boarding check. "Everyone is going to know, and they're going to just hate me. They're going to deny you and Dad callings and—"

"Don't you worry about that, Brandon," Bob said, raising the arm rest dividing their seats to pat his son's knee. "There is nothing more important than family. Haven't we always been taught that 'Family is Forever'?" His dad's smile twisted sadly at the Church's mantra. "Now, you listen to me here." He twisted in his seat and took Brandon's hand in his, a hand that always felt so strong, had always made Brandon feel safe and cared for, as if his dad could do anything, could fix anything. "Son," and his voice broke. "Your mother and I have known you were… were gay for years."

Brandon made a noise of protest, but Bob barreled on.

"We've known since middle school, and we've still loved you. Do you understand?" He ruffled Brandon's hair and smiled softly. "Your brothers and sisters know, and they love you. We are a family, and we're going to be a family forever. Isn't that what we promised when your mother and I were sealed in the temple? What did I tell you about making promises?"

"That you better mean them," Brandon replied.

"Exactly. You think I don't mean what I say?"

"Honey," his mother said, pulling on him so he could see her tanned, gently-lined face. She had more grey in her close-cropped hair than he remembered, more lines around her eyes, but they were the same kindly brown they'd always been, "We're just so happy you're coming home." Her voice wobbled as she said, "We missed you."

He put his face against his mom's neck, and the familiar smell of her perfume opened the floodgates. His dad rubbed his back as he cried and cried.

Now, he was back in his overcrowded home, and his mom was gearing up for one of her rants. It was adorable. For a woman barely over five feet tall, she had the energy of at least six people.

"Mom," Brandon said, spinning her chair around again. He and his brothers loved how portable she was. She shot him her best put-upon face.

"What?"

"Adam got a letter today. From someone in his family," he said.

"Oh? Oh! Well. Is it good?"

"I don't know," he sighed. "He won't open it."

"Who's it from? His mother?"

Brandon thought of the grim-faced woman he'd encountered in Spain and the way judgment and unhappiness poured from her. He thought of his mom never letting him out of her sight from the moment they'd found each other at the airport in Chicago, how she fussed over him and his siblings, demanding kisses and hugs, tickling them and smoothing her hand over their heads and cheeks. He realized he hadn't seen Sister Young touch Adam once, not a hug or, heck, not even a handshake. She was the least maternal person he'd ever met, but then, his own mother was pretty much the best. Anyone would fail in comparison.

"No," Brandon replied. "It's from one of his brothers. The doctor, or the neurology student at the Y, I should say."

"At the Y, huh? Hmm." She used her sneakered foot against Brandon's leg to twist her chair side to side. "So you don't think it's going to be a good letter?"

"I don't know how it could be," Brandon said. "But I say this because he's obviously feeling tender. Just… maybe lay off the PFLAG stuff for a bit. He's still getting used to everything."

"Aren't we all?" Sandra said, grinning as she kicked at Brandon's shin. "Well, sounds like tater tot casserole is in order. You said he loves those peanut butter bar cookies, right?"

"He *really* loves them when you put the chocolate drizzle stuff on top."

"Oh, he does, does he?" Sandra asked. "I seem to recall a certain someone I gave birth to loving that, in particular."

"That's why we're so perfect together, huh?"

Sandra's face softened. "I just want to hug him and not stop."

"Me, too."

"Hugs are great. Just remember the house rules, please. I don't mind that you boys feel what you feel, but I wouldn't let your siblings and their significant others mess around under my roof, either, if they weren't married."

"Yes, ma'am."

Sandra got to her feet and stretched her arms overhead. "Well, it's getting close to supper time, anyway. Dad'll be home soon, too. You make sure Adam knows he can come talk to me if he wants, okay?"

"Kay, Mom. Love you."

She beamed, her eyes watery. "I love you, too."

Brandon wandered through the messy basement, popping his head into the tiny bedrooms his dad had built down here to accommodate their growing brood and looked for a head of blond hair amongst the brown. He found Adam replacing lightbulbs in the food storage—a large room off the stairway with floor to ceiling shelves in which the family stored their one-year food supply. Brandon leaned against the doorframe smiling as he watched his boyfriend's expression while he delicately unhitched the long fluorescent tube.

"These freak me out," Adam said. "I think it's the humming. Hey."

"Hey," Brandon answered. He ran the flat of his hand up Adam's back and squeezed Adam's nape. Adam's eyes fluttered shut, then snapped open, and he looked around.

"You don't have to keep doing that," Brandon sighed.

"It's…"

"Hard, I know."

Adam snapped the tube in place and propped the burnt-out light against the wall. "I'm just not used to it being okay."

"My parents aren't going to freak out if I have my hand on you, Adam."

"What about your little brothers and sisters? Mary doesn't like me."

"Mary doesn't like anyone."

Mary was the youngest Christensen sibling, nine, and going through what Sandra called her 'sneaky age.' "All girls just look suspicious when they're in the fourth grade. It's terrible. I don't know why the CIA doesn't round them all up and have them be international spies until they get their periods. They'd be a force to be reckoned with."

"So do you want to go tonight?" Brandon asked, smiling as Adam backed him around the corner where white buckets of flour and other baking supplies were stacked.

"How is this thing tonight not church?" Adam ran his finger along the knit collar of Brandon's T-shirt.

"It's just at *a* church. It's not *the* Church. Besides, I have a feeling that talking to people one-on-one will be more fruitful than filling out applications online."

Adam grinned. "You just get overwhelmed by money stuff."

Brandon snorted. "Well, yeah. Habit."

"Community college, summer jobs, our own place. That's the plan."

"Well, that's if you get into UC-Davis, too," Brandon said. "Sorry you're not a local. Tuition isn't cheap otherwise." His academic scholarships coupled with California residency tuition was the only reason he was able to attend college in the first place. Now that Adam's family had cut him off, there was no way Adam could afford to go back to school; Adam's athletic scholarship wouldn't cover all the costs. Plus, that would mean Adam going back to Utah, which he was set against.

Brandon's family had been pretty adamant that Adam wasn't going to go back, either.

"Son," Bob had said on the drive back to their hometown of Vacaville from the Sacramento airport—Sister Johnson had put Brandon on standby to meet Adam in Salt Lake City along with Bob and his sizable girth in case any of Adam's family had tried to strong-arm Adam into going back to Provo. "I want you to think long and hard about how going back to Utah is going to affect you. You'll be in the shadow of the Mormon Church everywhere you go. Do you have a support network at all? Anyone in your family you can trust to stand by you?"

Adam had shaken his head no.

Bob's mouth flattened into a thin line as he nodded. "Right. Now, everything Brandon's told us about you, every note you've sent the family while you boys served, I just can't in good conscience let a kid like you get thrown back into that... that pit of shame."

Adam looked down at their entwined hands. "I feel like I'm ruining your family," he muttered.

"We've been over this," Brandon said, drawing Adam into his arms, who stiffened until apparently realizing no one was going to shout at them. "Every time we wrote our questions for my folks, any time I expressed a doubt, they'd pray about it as a family here. They'd look into our questions and only found more themselves."

"That's what I mean," Adam cried.

"My family does everything together, okay? Even if it means finding our own faith, a new one."

The day after Brandon came home, the local church leaders had arrived with their somber faces and instructions for Brandon to come to the stake center for his own official "Court of Love" to be officially excommunicated; President Young, in his fit of pique, hadn't held one back in Barcelona.

"We won't be doing that," Sandra said.

"Sister Christensen," the Bishop said, his voice a warning.

"Sandra," she corrected. "I'd like to be released from my calling in the Young Women's Presidency," she said, and it was only because Brandon knew her so well that he could hear the emotion she tried to control as she spoke. "Bob and I have already written our letters to the Church office requesting that our membership be revoked."

"Sister *Christensen!*"

"Sandra." Her expression was firm. "Tom, I know you're a good man. I know and love your wife to pieces. I also know that you—heck, like we all did because we didn't know any better—spread that horseshit about gay marriage for Prop 8."

Brother Johnson, the stewardess's husband, shifted uncomfortably on his feet at their front stoop.

"My husband and I feel we've had personal revelation about the Church and about our faith. We don't believe the Church is being run by our Heavenly Father any longer. You can tell the ladies in the Relief Society not to bother with the cards and visits. We no longer consider ourselves Mormons."

She shut the door with a trembling hand.

"Well. That's that," she'd said, and burst into tears.

Brandon held her in his arms and cried, too. "I'm so sorry, Mom. I'm so sorry."

"I'm not," she'd said into his tear-stained shirt. "I love you. I love you and your brothers and sisters, I love your father, and I'm sure I'll love Adam. We'll get through this."

Now, Brandon held Adam in his arms and repeated his mom's words. "We'll get through this. Just like we've gotten through everything."

"Nowhere to go but up, right?"

"Right."

AT DINNER, BRANDON MADE A point of squeezing Adam between himself and Mary. Brandon's older sister Joanna, twenty-two and living with her college friends, had joined them for dinner. Brandon's older brothers, Jack, twenty-five, and Bob, Jr., twenty-seven, lived in the Bay area a few hours north. Still, even minus two people, it was a squeeze.

The family held hands as Bob began to bless their dinner.

"Heavenly Father, we're so grateful to be gathered as a family to eat this wonderful meal you and my wife have blessed us with. We're so grateful to have Adam and Brandon with us, that You have shown us how magnanimous You are with Your love, that You have chosen our family to learn the true fullness of Your gospel, how love is love is love."

"And that mom put extra cheese on the tots," Brandon's twelve-year-old brother Bill added under his breath.

"And the extra cheese," Bob added. Everyone tittered, even Adam. "Help us always to serve one another as well as all of Your children, gay, straight, crooked or bent. In this we pray in Jesus' name. Amen."

"Amen" resounded from around the table as plates began to be passed. Brandon looked at Adam, who was nervously eyeing a scowling Mary.

"Make sure she gets a corner piece," he whispered, grinning as Mary's eyes went round and large when Adam scooped out a corner and put it on her plate instead of his own. "You just made a fan for life," he said, nudging Adam's shoulder.

Mary asked, "Are you going to marry my brother? The kids at school say you can if you want to." There was a challenge! Adam looked like a deer caught in the headlights.

Bob answered. "Mary, marriage is pretty serious. It's also not our business." He smiled from the head of the table at everyone crammed on benches and the Christensen's mix-and-matched chairs. "But I think I speak for everyone when I say that if that was something you two decided was the right thing to do in, oh, five years or more, that we'd support you."

Everyone at the table laughed or nodded.

Brenda, Brandon's sixteen-year-old sister, said loftily, "I'm not ever getting married. I live with boys. You're all pigs."

Bill replied, "Maybe you'll marry a girl."

"Maybe I will. Girls are way less gross than boys are."

Mary leaned into Adam and said loud enough for Brandon to hear, "Brenda never washes her gym socks. She says it's 'good luck.'"

Adam laughed and covered it with a sip from his glass of water.

Brandon leaned back in his chair and watched his ridiculous family, all of them loud and smiling and ribbing each other, everyone always in each other's space, and had never been happier to know that family meant always having each other's backs, too. They may not all understand what had happened on Brandon's mission—Bob and Sandra said that it was private and up to the boys' discretion what they shared about it—but they still loved their brother. And they were coming to care for Adam, too.

Adam leaned down. Mary whispered fervently in his ear about... who knew, but it was important if the serious expression on Adam's face as he nodded along was anything to go by. Brandon noticed how Adam cut the crusty browned bits off his own serving and put it on Mary's plate, and the happiness expanding inside him was so tremendous that he thought he might break open.

Of course Adam, the youngest and most disaffected in his own family, would understand how Mary, the baby of the family, might feel neglected. It was hard being in a big family, especially one filled with large personalities. He put his arm behind Adam's shoulder and gave it a squeeze.

John, seventeen and with obnoxious Justin Beiber-styled hair, crooned, "Look at the lovebirds."

Adam blushed and leaned out of Brandon's hold. Brandon cut his brother a dirty look.

John seemed to realize what he'd done and stammered, "H-hey, man, it's cool. I didn't mean it like… I was just joshing you guys." He closed his eyes, then said, "So, look. Adam. I was hoping you might come hang with me tomorrow up at the gym? Coach said something about me maybe moving to special teams. We lost our free safety and I think he wants me there now. So, maybe you could show me some stuff to focus on?"

Sandra smiled at her plate.

"Uh, yeah. Sure," Adam replied, his cheeks flooding red. "Yeah. I can show you some drills."

"Were they ones you did at the U?" John almost knocked his plate to the floor, he leaned forward so fast. Everyone knew John's goal was to make the football team at USC. Adam nodded and they were off, with Bob cutting in to ask Adam about different players and techniques.

"The cute ones are always gay," Brenda sighed.

"Thanks," Brandon said, flicking his bangs back and laughing.

"And full of themselves."

ADAM WAS PRACTICALLY BOUNCING UP and down in the passenger seat. Mary had worked her way up from the third bench in the back of the family van to being draped over the console, chattering with Adam a mile a minute for the last half-hour of the drive as they got closer and closer to the beach and its parking.

"You guys remember to stick close, okay? Pay attention to where I'm camped out," Brandon said, signaling to park.

"Dude, it's not our first time," Bill said, nodding to Adam. "It's his." Bill rolled his eyes, grabbed his backpack and took off down the beach at breakneck speed with Brenda hot on his heels.

That left Brandon and Adam (and Adam's new shadow, Mary) to unload the coolers, beach umbrella and towels. Adam stood watching as Brandon got their little camp set up. When it was clear Mary had no intention of leaving Adam's side, Brandon said, "Mary. Bug off."

"Hey," Adam said laughing. "Don't be mean."

Brandon rolled his eyes. Adam didn't understand what it was like to have a little sister, but he'd learn soon enough. "Mary, we want to make out."

Mary looked scandalized. Brandon had a suspicion that she had a big crush on Adam. Better nip that in the bud.

"Go find Brenda. Tell her I said to buy you an ice cream. I know Mom gave her a ten."

Mary's eyes narrowed as she muttered, "Knew it," and took off after her siblings.

Adam plopped onto the towels and looked around before pulling his shirt off. "It still feels so weird," he said, rubbing his bare skin.

"I don't think I mind as much anymore," Brandon said, pulling his shirt off, too. They had been forbidden to wear their temple garments after being excommunicated. Sometimes Brandon missed them, what they meant, but not today. "It's so hot."

"Mm," Adam agreed. "Hey. I don't mean this as a come-on, but would you put sunscreen on my back? I'm so pale I usually just burn to a crisp."

"Why isn't it a come-on?" Brandon asked, snapping off the cap. "You know you can come onto me."

Adam choked.

"I didn't mean it like *that*. Wait…" Brandon rubbed his hands over Adam's broad shoulders and kissed the freckles that dotted them. "Maybe I did."

They hadn't been able to be together physically since Spain, but they were working on getting their own place once Brandon went back to school in August. He missed the feeling of Adam sleeping next to him, the touch of his lips, the way his deep baritone sounded when he was turned on; he missed the intimacy of being in love with another person and physically showing them. Adam was so easy to love, too. Any expression of it from Brandon, heck, from any of Brandon's family, and Adam beamed for hours. It made Brandon want to spoil him, to cherish him, to proudly walk down the street with Adam's hand in his and declare his love for anyone to hear. He never wanted a day to go by without Adam in it, and hoped that one day they could have what his own parents had.

Sandra and Bob constantly hugged and kissed, teased each other, danced in the kitchen when "their song" came on, went on their Friday night "date nights" which the kids all knew was them getting In-N-Out and driving to make-out point. They were so embarrassing. It was awesome.

Adam wasn't used to people being demonstrative at all and seemed shocked if he happened to catch Sandra and Bob kissing or being tender with each other. It was as if he'd walked in on them doing something private and not just being a couple still in love after thirty years. It was hard to keep from touching Adam as much as Brandon wanted to, as much as his parents and siblings were comfortable with, but he was trying to respect Adam's shyness, not just with physical affection but that they were both men. Living where they did in California, just sixty miles southeast of San Francisco, meant the Christensens had been around gay and lesbian couples before. It wasn't like living in Utah, where most people were LDS, and those who weren't were deeply entrenched in the culture. The Christensen family didn't seem to be *shocked* by seeing two men holding hands or kissing one another. They just maybe were irritated by it being their brother. Then again, Brandon thought it was weird to see John following girls around town like a little puppy.

Adam tugged Brandon's hands off his shoulders, wrapped himself up in Brandon's embrace and leaned his weight back into him. "It's not the same as in Spain."

Brandon's heart lurched. "What?"

"The ocean. It's not the same. It's... different. The water, the waves. The beach is, too. I didn't know it was like that."

Brandon pressed the flat of his palm over Adam's heart where it beat steady and sure. "It's a different ocean."

"We're different, too."

"We are."

"We're better." Adam pressed a kiss to Brandon's hand, and leaned his weight back more fully. He seemed to be gathering himself to say something important as he asked, "Brandon?"

"Mm?" Brandon dropped tender kisses along Adam's temple, in his soft hair.

"I love you so much."

Brandon squeezed his arms, his face close to bursting from the force of his smile. He replied, "I love you, too."

"I... your family." Adam's voice had gone watery. "I really love them, too. Your mom..."

"She's the best."

"She really is. I don't know what I would have done without them."

"But that's the thing," Brandon said. "You don't have to. You're family now. They'll never let you go."

Adam's breathing hitched and he clung to Brandon's arm over his chest. "And family is forever."

"It is."

Adam murmured "love you" one more time. They sat together as the sounds of the waves crashed against the shore, as kids playing tag ran back and forth, and as someone's music drifted over them. No one cared that they were two men in an embrace. No one gave them dirty looks.

They were two men, in love, with at least one of their families who loved them as well, and now were free from an organization that wanted them to feel ashamed, wanted them to wallow in despair, to spend their lives alone until God "fixed" them in the next life.

They were in love, but more importantly, they knew they were loved, by each other, by Brandon's family and, they both believed, by their Heavenly Father.

It was going to be okay. They had faith.

THE END

GLOSSARY OF TERMS

Apostate - A member who openly disagrees with Church leaders and doctrine, in public or private. Considered potentially cursed or condemned and an enemy to the Church. Often results in ex-communication.

Apostle - The highest priesthood office of the Melchizedek priesthood in the Mormon Church, Twelve apostles, called a Quorum, act as the governing body of the Mormon Church. The prophet and President is always an apostle

Bishop - Clergy who oversees a ward, non-paid position that is assigned arbitrarily. Ecclesiastic training is not required. The position usually lasts four to seven years.

Calling - A job given to a member such as Bishop, choir director, or nursery aide. Typically unpaid and untrained beyond sharing of teaching materials commissioned by the LDS Church. It's considered an insult to God if you do not accept a calling.

Church house/Ward house - Building where Sunday meetings and other weekly religious meetings and activities are held. They are typically built from a standard blueprint within the U.S.

Court of Love/Disciplinary Council - When a member commits a sin considered grave, the Church holds an ecclesiastic trial during which the member is tried for alleged violations of Church standards. If a member of the LDS Church is found guilty of an offense by a disciplinary council, he or she may be excommunicated or their church membership may be otherwise restricted. Disciplinary councils are also referred to unofficially as disciplinary councils.

District Leader - A missionary who runs a small geographical subset within a mission and reports to the Mission President.

Endowment - A temple ceremony that prepares members to become kings, queens, priests, and priestesses in the afterlife. It includes a ritualistic washing and anointing, symbolic gestures and acts, and ends with the member receiving a "new" name for use in the temple and in the afterlife. After completion, the member will begin to wear sacred undergarments.

Eternal life - Spelled with a capital E, as opposed to eternal life to denote the difference in quality of one's afterlife. Capital-E Eternal denotes one who has achieved the highest order of Heavenly Father's glory. The other refers to general immortality.

Excommunication - The penalty for "grave" sins such as murder, incest, homosexuality, and apostasy. Notices of excommunication can be made public, especially in the case of apostasy. Those "exed" have their names removed from the Church as members (both on Earth and in the temple/ the afterlife) and cannot partake in the sacrament.

The Family: A Proclamation to the World - Statement delivered to the world in 1995 that the LDS Church believes marriage only to be between a man and a woman, and that gender is assigned before birth and cannot be changed. This was sent to the Hawaiian Supreme Court prior to their vote on legalizing "gay" marriage in 1997. While not official canon, Apostle Boyd K. Packer, speaking as one who holds the highest keys of the Melchizedek priesthood as a "prophet, seer and revelator and special witness of Jesus Christ", advised members during General Conference in October 2010 to treat this proclamation as direct revelation from God.

Garments - Also called "G's." Considered sacred, these undergarments are to be worn day and night, symbolic of the covenants made in the temple to honor a commitment to God. It is believed that they protect the wearer from sin and danger. Women must wear bras over their garments, as nothing is to come between the skin and the material. They have "sacred" markings on the nipples, navel, and one knee, symbolic of a level, compass and square, commonly understood outside the LDS faith to be rooted in Freemasonry, of which Joseph Smith was a third-degree Master Mason.

Heavenly Father - God, a distinct and separate deity from Jesus Christ and a member of the Godhead. Mormons tend to avoid saying "God" outside of hymns or scripture, as it's believed to be taking his name in vain. Also, the belief is God is our spiritual father and we are His children. Jesus is literally the Son of God, separate and whole.

Holy Ghost/Holy Spirit - A distinct and separate non-corporeal being, and third member of the Godhead. He was chosen to be so for the sake of bearing witness to individuals of the truthfulness of the Gospel and of Jesus Christ by "entering" a person's spirit and bearing the truthfulness of God, Jesus, and the Gospel.

Institute - Religious training program organized and operated by the LDS Church for college-age members. In Utah and parts of Idaho and Arizona, these classes can be taken on local college campuses or in special "Institute" buildings just off campus.

Jesus Christ - The literal Son of God, and second member of the Godhead. He died on the cross and was resurrected as a flesh-and-blood being three days later, which time was spent preaching to the Native American people Mormons calls Nepites and Lamanites. Jesus is considered to be the literal head of the LDS Church.

Lamanites - One of the peoples of the Book of Mormon. Originating in Jerusalem, they are descendants of a man named Laman, who broke off from his brother and prophet Nephi. They were cursed with dark skin because of this iniquity. Mormons believe Native Americans are their living descendants.

Law of Consecration - First announced as a revelation by Joseph Smith in 1831, it existed for the support of the poor and to ensure that all members would be "equal according to his family, according to his circumstances and his wants and needs." Echoes of this still exist today in the modern church through the use of a Bishop's Storehouse, a member-based welfare system that can be quite effective.

Law of Adoption - A temple ritual practiced in Latter-day Saint temples between 1846 and 1894 in which men who held the priesthood were sealed in a father–son relationship to other men who were not part of nor even distantly related to their immediate nuclear family. Dr. D. Michael Quinn, highly-acclaimed and excommunicated Mormon historian, noted in his epic work, "Same-Sex Dynamics Among Nineteenth-Century Americans: A Mormon Example", that during his last two years of life, Joseph Smith sealed men to other men in the Nauvoo Temple, a practice Brigham Young altered post-Joseph's death to follow the "father-son" adoption rite instead of the "brother to brother, locked in the arms of love" concept originally used. See Bibliography for complete citation.

Melchizedek Priesthood - the priesthood authority of the Twelve Apostles of Jesus, as well as Old Testament prophets, higher than that of the Aaronic authority of John the Baptist and of the Levites. This has the offices of Elder, Seventy, High Priest, Patriarch and Apostle.

Mission - Geographical administrative area where LDS men and women dedicate their time for up to two years in an attempt to convert people to Mormonism. Missions are paid for by those who serve and not by the Church. If one cannot afford a mission, the local church will encourage members to fund it.

Mission Field - Anything outside of the state of Utah. Typically used as a colloquialism.

Missionary Training Center - The MTC, as it's called, is the training facility in Provo, Utah where missionaries learn the skill of proselytizing and, if going abroad, their new language. There are smaller MTCs located throughout the world, but it's most common for new missionaries to arrive at the original location.

Nephites - Hebrew descendants who were inspired to build a ship in 600BC and travel to what is now North America. One of the peoples of the Book of Mormon. They all died out and no record of them exists historically. Other than, of course, the Golden Plates in which they recorded their history, carried to Upstate New York, buried, and was later discovered by Joseph Smith. The Golden Plates were taken back into heaven after Joseph "translated" their ancient language.

November "Leak" - The Mormon Church operates at the micro-level through a "Handbook of Instructions," as the ecclesiastic jobs are unpaid and untrained. An update made, leaked in November of 2015, featured a new and direct policy with regard to LGBT members, who the Church refers to as "SSA" - Same Sex Identifying. Children of "SSA" parents will not be given a "name" in the Church, nor will they be allowed to be baptized, receive priesthood blessings, or be called to any leadership positions including serving a mission. An exception can be made once the child has reached adulthood and commits to serving the church and renouncing their LGBT family. Those who are actively "homosexual" are officially considered apostates.

OMH - "Oh my heck." Mormons don't swear, unless it's fealty or to their own honesty.

Outer Darkness - The Mormon version of hell, and the worst outcome for any soul. This is where "sons of perdition" are cast. Note: Hitler does not reside here in Mormon lore.

Pre-existence - Like Milton's Paradise Lost, Mormon Doctrine believes in a War in Heaven where Satan and his followers were cast out of God's presence. We all were spirit before we became flesh on Earth, and while the Church says it isn't doctrine that we chose our families and certain friendships before we were born, they did teach that at one point, including that people who weren't valiant in the War in Heaven would be cursed with the mark of Cain, a.k.a black-skinned. (See: *Mormon Doctrine* by Bruce R, McKonkie, Prophet Spencer W. Kimballs' many essays and talks, *Journal of Discourses*, Brigham Young, the reason why blacks weren't allowed to have the Priesthood until 1978, *Saturday's Warrior, My Turn On Earth*, etc.)

Priesthood - The power and authority to act in the name of God for the salvation of Mankind. Only males twelve-years-old and older who are vetted as "worthy" are ordained a priesthood holder.

Polygamy - A religious practice of men marrying extra wives. Women are not allowed to marry more than one male. In the LDS church, this was considered the highest commandment until they were threatened with Federal action in 1890 and ordered to cease the practice, which drove it into secrecy but did not stop the practice. It is still considered an important commandment and the "revelation" to continue this practice continues to be listed in their set of holy scriptures.

Seminary - Religious study organized and operated by the LDS Church for teenagers. In Utah and several locations in Idaho and Arizona, these classes are available to LDS members in lieu of other school classes in buildings across the street from their local high school. Those in the mission field typically attend at the church building or their teacher's home before school begins, such as at 6:00a.m.

Smith, Joseph - Founder and first prophet/President of the Church of Jesus Christ of Latter-day Saints and a polygamist. At the time of his murder, he had close to forty wives, one of whom was fourteen when they married.

Sons of Perdition - A person who will not partake in the afterlife. See: Section 76 of the *Doctrine & Covenants*. Key elements: they are fully aware of the fullness of the Mormon Gospel and reject it, thus being banished to brimstone and Satan. Again, Hitler is not a son of perdition.

Stake - Several wards combine to make a Stake, headed by a Stake President and his two counselors.

TBM - True Blue Mormon, one "born in the covenant" to active parents who were married and sealed in the temple. A "TBM" would attend all Sunday and Wednesday meetings, attend Youth activities and conferences as well as Seminary and Institute lessons.

Temple - a building dedicated to be a House of the Lord and considered the most sacred building on earth. One cannot attain the highest glory of God without participating in the temple's rituals.

The Y - BYU, Brigham Young University, also known as "The Lord's University" unless you attended the University of Utah. Located in Provo, Utah and wholly owned by the LDS Church.

Ward - Geographically-assigned congregation, headed by a Bishop. On the chance of small numbers in the geographic region, this would be considered a Branch, still headed by a Bishop.

Zone Leader - In the mission field, this is the missionary who oversees the day-to-day activities of the various districts, and reports to the Mission President.

ADDITIONAL WORKS CITED

Craven, Rulon G. *The Effective Missionary.* Salt Lake City, UT: Deseret Books, 1982, p. 56. Print.

The Doctrine and Covenants of the Church of Jesus Christ of Latter-day Saints. The Pearl of Great Price. Salt Lake City, UT, U.S.A.: Church of Jesus Christ of Latter-day Saints, 1982. Print.

"The Family: A Proclamation to the World," Liahona, Oct. 2004, 49; Ensign, Nov. 1995, p. 102.

"Handbook 2: Administering the Church." Handbook 2: Administering the Church. Web. 30 Jan. 2017.

"Hymns of the Church of Jesus Christ of Latter-day Saints." Salt Lake City, UT: Church of Jesus Christ of Latter-day Saints, 1985, p. 87, 249. Print.

"I Hope They Call Me on a Mission." The Church of Jesus Christ of Latter-day Saints. Web. 30 Jan. 2017.

Packer, B.K. "For young men only." U.S.A. The Church of Jesus Christ of Latter-day Saints, 1976. Brochure.

"Preach My Gospel: A Guide to Missionary Service." Salt Lake City, UT: Church of Jesus Christ of Latter-day Saints, 2004. Print.

Quinn, D. Michael. *Same-sex Dynamics among Nineteenth-century Americans: A Mormon Example.* Urbana: U of Illinois, 1996. Print.

Smith, Joseph. *The Book of Mormon: An Account Written by the Hand of Mormon upon Plates Taken from the Plates of Nephi.* Salt Lake City, UT: Church of Jesus Christ of Latter-day Saints, 1981. Print.

Smith, Joseph. *King Follett Funeral,* Eulogy. Nauvoo, IL. Apr. 16, 1843. Speech.

Young, Brigham, John Taylor, G. D. Watt, and J. V. Long. *Journal of Discourses*. Liverpool: F.D. and S.W. Richards, 1854. Print.

ACKNOWLEDGMENTS

I WAS VERY FORTUNATE TO be raised by my father, who allowed me the space to come to terms with my own religious beliefs. I was also incredibly fortunate to have a father and step-mother who passionately collected the neglected and disaffected, who set an example for me to be kind. Kindness and an open heart will always be the right way to live, no matter your God's name or flavor.

I am incredibly grateful to all the women in my church who took me under their wings and loved me such as Sisters Bennett, Gougler, Fowler and Bertrand, the latter going the extra mile to pick me up at 5:45 a.m. to make sure I was able to attend Seminary, even when her own daughter skipped like a normal teenager. They set the example for what it means to be a mother with unconditional love, and I'm grateful for it.

(And to Darlene, the mother I would steal for my own if I could, you are Sandra in every way down to the portability and undying love for your kids, and I love you to pieces. Chrissy, thank you for sharing your mom with me. I love you, too. Thanks for putting up with my incessant Doctrine Talk over the years.)

I'm so grateful for Carrie Pack and Tom Iacuzio for the beautiful cover that made my eyes fill with tears the moment I saw it. (And thank you to the models who depicted Adam and Brandon, Connor Apthorp and The Lee Artle. You're on a book cover, boys!) To Nicki, Choi, Annie and Candy: thank you for pushing me to make this book what it is. Nicki, you're still my favorite. Don't tell the others.

I originally wrote this ten years ago as a short story for a family member who needed it, but who I knew would never read it. I dedicated it to my dear friend who was at the time struggling with her faith as she came out, and who has been a champion of this story from the start.

I'm also grateful for the wisdom and unyielding support of the Mama Dragons, whose existence centers on keeping LGBT youth in the LDS church alive. The state of Utah as of this printing has a suicide rate among teens that is four times higher than the national average. Bless the Mama Dragons for breathing their fire and saying, "Enough. Love first." Please reach out to them on Facebook if you or a loved one needs support.

To anyone struggling as an LGBTQ person in the LDS faith: You're not alone, you're enough just as you are, and you're loved.

ABOUT THE AUTHOR

LAURA STONE, A DESCENDANT OF pioneer polygamists from the early days of the Mormon Church and a former Gospel Doctrine teacher, now keeps busy as a media blogger, ghostwriter and novelist when she's not raising her youngest child.

While the majority of her family still lives in Utah, she resides in Texas because it's where the good tamales are. Her first novel, *The Bones of You*, was published by Interlude Press in 2014 and was named a finalist for a *Foreword Reviews* IndieFab Book of the Year Award. Her second novel, *Bitter Springs*, was published by Interlude Press in 2015.

@interlude**press**

Twitter | Facebook | Instagram | Tumblr | Pinterest

*For a reader's guide to **And It Came to Pass** and book club prompts, please visit interludepress.com.*

interlude press
you may also like...

Bitter Springs by Laura Stone

In 1870s Texas, the youngest son of a large, traditional family has been sent to train with a freed slave and talented mesteñero so he can continue the family horse trade. Bitter Springs tells the story of a man coming into his own and realizing his destiny lies in the wild open spaces with a man who loves him, far from expectations of society.

ISBN (print) 978-1-941530-55-9 | (eBook) 978-1-941530-56-6

The Bones of You by Laura Stone

Oliver Andrews is focused on his final months at Cambridge University when his life is up-ended by a US morning show clip featuring his one-time love and newest Broadway star, Seth Larsen. Oliver faces choices that will either lead him back to love or break his heart. The Bones of You is full of laughter and tears, with a collection of irritable Hungarians, flirtatious Irishwomen, and Shakespeare-abusing actors that color their attempts at reconciliation.

ISBN (print) 978-1-941530-16-0 | (eBook) 978-1-941530-24-5

Flying Without a Net by E.M Ben Shaul

Dani Perez, a secular Israeli working as a software engineer, has never had trouble balancing his faith and his sexuality—until he meets Avi Levine, a gay Orthodox Jew and sign language interpreter. As they fall in love, they are challenged to reconcile religious ideology that conflicts with the life they are trying build together.

ISBN (print) 978-1-945053-11-5 | (eBook) 978-1-945053-12-2

CPSIA information can be obtained
at www.ICGtesting.com
Printed in the USA
FSOW02n1623030517
33850FS